OUTLAW'S PROPERTY

A BIKER REVERSE HAREM ROMANCE

PROPERTY OF OUTLAW SONS
BOOK ONE

STEPHANIE BROTHER

Copyright © 2024 by Stephanie Brother

All Rights Reserved. This book or any portion thereof may not be reproduced or used in any manner whatsoever without the express permission of the publisher except for the use of brief quotations in a book review.

This book is a work of fiction. Any resemblance to persons, living or dead, or places, events or locations is purely coincidental. The characters are all productions of the author's imagination.

Please note that this work is intended only for adults over the age of 18 and all characters represented as 18 or over.

OUTLAWS' PROPERTY

A BIKER REVERSE HAREM ROMANCE

1

JESSICA

The window pane is cold, its chill prickling my palm. Outside it, darkness hides the frigid waves crashing against the rocky shore at the end of the vast lawn, but only a few days ago, it was lit up by fireworks launched from a boat out on the water.

I stood in this same spot, my hand cooled by the same window, watching a party I wasn't invited to, and made the same New Year's resolution as I do every year.

Live.

We're barely into January, but Victor's people have already scrubbed away all signs of the holidays. No lights, no snow, no decorations. Dreaming of a white Christmas here is as useless as waiting for a knight in shining armor to come take me away. All we ever get is icy rain and cold damp weather that sinks into our bones. Just once I want to build a snowman and go sledding. I want what I've seen in the movies.

The joy that I remember from the foggy memories I have of holidays with my parents… before.

"Jessicaaa, I don't wanna do homework. I hate math." Anne gets up from her desk and flops on the bed. Her golden curls bounce as she lands.

I straighten my glasses with a sigh, shaking off the doom and gloom that isn't going to get me anywhere. I love her to death, but I swear she went to bed a lovable kid at eleven years old, and woke up a surly tween the day she turned twelve. "Come on, you just have one more section to go. Problem eight is just like the second one, see? If you take the denominator and—"

Anne lets out a groan that sounds like it was ripped from the bottom of her soul. "Maybe if I had something to help me concentrate." She twists upright, kneeling on the bed in her PJs. "Like coffee."

"Nice try, sneaky." I poke her in the side and get a little giggle. Good, the kid is still in there somewhere. "You're too young for coffee."

She pouts, with a sly glimmer in her eyes. "Okay, then how about sugar? I hid some cookies in a pot in the kitchen."

"You're a sneak! Are you trying to get me in trouble?" I keep my voice light, but Victor doesn't like it when we leave Anne's rooms at night and she knows how her father can be. Well, at least a little bit of how her father can be. She'd be shocked if she knew the whole truth.

I don't particularly want to do fractions either, but if her tutor reports that she's not getting her work done, I'm the one who will pay the price. The consequences can be brutal, so let's just say I'm motivated. Much more than Anne, who has more wealth and privilege at her fingertips than most people will see in a hundred lifetimes. It could turn her into a total brat, but she has a good heart, and she's still too sheltered to fully understand her situation.

Her eyes lose their sparkle. "No."

"Then let's make a deal. If you finish this up before nine, we can go check the kitchen and see if your hidden treasure is still there. Marissa never cooks so I bet they are." It's a risk, but a huge one.

"Yes!" She wrinkles her nose at the mention of her father's newest girlfriend, but sits down and dutifully goes back to work on the assignment she was given for the holiday break.

I pick up a brush and braid her hair while she works, nudging her in the right direction when she gets stuck. Times like this make me almost forget how fragile my own situation is, but I can't get complacent.

Does that sound dramatic? It isn't.

Victor Kane, this sweet girl's father, murdered my parents when I was a little younger than she is now.

Ten years later, I still don't know why. Why he killed them, or why he took me instead of letting me die on the boat with them. It definitely wasn't mercy. If you ask me, he gets a perverse thrill out of keeping me around like a trophy. When people make him mad, he can point at me and say: "Look. See what I'm capable of? I'll take everything you love."

He's a monster, and I have to look him in the eyes every single freaking day. That sounds like it would be the worst part, but it isn't. What really kills me is that I'm used to it.

I fought as well as a child could. I cried. I tried to run away. None of it worked. The only thing I earned for my trouble was nightmares, and in the end, working for Victor is the only life I know. I've helped take care of her since she was a toddler, and been her full time Nanny since I was sixteen. Nobody talks about her mother. The rumor is that she tried to get away after she had Anne, and Victor had her removed from the picture.

Permanently.

I believe it. Victor doesn't have family. He has possessions.

"Done!" Anne drops her pencil on her desk and is at the door in a shot. She takes her silk robe off the hook and slips it on over her pajamas. "Let's go."

There's no matching robe for me. I'm wearing plain gray sweats, the only real option I have aside from my regular uniform: a shapeless navy skirt that reaches my calves, with a matching cardigan for warmth over a frumpy white blouse. Sometimes I envy Anne's bottomless wardrobe, but where would I use it? Most of the time I'm glad to keep a low profile. Being ignored beats the heck out of catching the wrong kind of notice.

"Okay, come on. It's almost past your bedtime, but if we make this quick we can be back before nine. Quiet like a mouse, right?"

Anne nods with a grin. She puts her finger against her lips and we slip out into the silent hall.

The shortest path to the kitchen means cutting through the open area in the middle of the main house and going past the steaming pool. There's a shadow of a helicopter on the far wall, cast from the helipad on the roof. Having the building all around us cuts off the bitter January wind coming off the water, but it's still freezing cold. We dash across to the other side and slip through the open glass doors into the large living room. From there, the kitchen is just around the corner.

A solitary guard looks up as we pass. He catches my elbow and leans in so Anne doesn't hear. "Hurry up, Ratty. Better get back to your hole before the cat notices you're out."

I shiver and shake off his grip. Victor's men named me Rat Girl, saying I'm always scurrying around in the shadows. They think it's an insult, but I'll take it over the alternative. I learned my lesson early. I was fourteen when I was just starting to realize becoming a woman might hold a new kind of power. One of Victor's bodyguards was handsome and liked to flirt when nobody was watching. That was all it took to make me start dreaming of us falling in love, and maybe he would take me away from this, and...

Let's face it, I don't know what I thought was going to happen. I was young and stupid. Catherine—Anne's old Nanny who was also in charge of keeping an eye on me—caught wind and went straight to Victor.

The next day, my back was covered in bruises, and I never saw that guard again. I was hurt and heartbroken, but now I'm glad it scared me enough to keep me from making the same mistake again. Catherine might've been a nasty piece of work, but now that I'm older and understand what was happening better, she did me a favor.

Oblivious, Anne slips ahead, making a beeline for a particular cabinet as soon as we get to the kitchen. She pushes pots and pans aside, practically crawling inside to get to her hidden stash.

"Got it." She emerges with a bag in her hand, full of cookies stolen from the catering before they ended up in the garbage. "I saved enough to share. Let's go!"

The ceiling light turns on, making both of us wince and blink. "What the heck do you think you're doing?" Marissa's shrill voice breaks the quiet with all the gentleness of a dish thrown at the wall. "Are you stealing food?"

"Stealing? This is my house, not yours!" Anne snaps back. "I'm just getting a snack."

"For now," Marissa growls. "Listen here, you little snot. I don't care that I'm not your mother. I'm not going to let you embarrass us by getting *fat*."

Anne freezes, red splotches staining her cheeks. Her body is just starting to lose its childish lankiness, filling out in places that are new and a little scary to her. There's nothing wrong with her. Not one bit. She could eat a whole bag of cookies every night and still be perfect.

I step in front of her, blocking Marissa's poisonous glare. "Don't be ridiculous. It's just a few cookies."

Victor's girlfriends come and go like a revolving door. Marissa has made it nearly two years now, and she might think that means something, but I've seen better women than her get kicked to the curb. Standing up to her is going to come back and bite me, but I'm not going to stand here and let her fat shame a little girl for wanting a cookie.

"You shut the hell up," she seethes. "You're the *help*. Maybe you should do your job and watch Anne, not enable her. If you can't follow simple instructions and be a healthy role model, then it's time for Victor to finally listen to me and get rid of you. She should be in boarding school where she can learn some real manners."

I bite my tongue. I can't afford to make her too mad while she still has Victor's ear. Without Anne, I don't have a place here, and without a place, Victor might decide my usefulness is over. Anne makes a small unhappy noise. I put my hand behind my back and she slips her fingers into mine. I give them a small squeeze of support.

Anne raises her chin in defiance. "Why are you so mean to Jessica? I finished my homework. Here. If the cookies mean so much to you, you can have them. Maybe if you ate a few you wouldn't be such a witch."

It's all I can do not to burst out laughing at the shocked look on Marissa's face.

But her shock turns quickly to rage. She glares right at me and reaches out, grabbing Anne by the wrist and yanking her away from me. "You are a horrible influence on her. I don't know why he bothers keeping you around."

"Yeah, well I don't know why he bothers keeping you around either," I snap. "Let her go!"

"What the hell is all this yelling about?" Victor strides into the kitchen, his hard dress shoes echoing off the marble floor. The disaster is officially complete.

"Baby," Marissa croons. "I was taking care of it. Anne's nanny is useless. I think you need to seriously think about what I was saying. I—"

"Shut up." He doesn't even bother looking at her. "Jessica."

Just the one word, not even said very loud, but with complete conviction that he will be listened to. My stomach drops, twisted into a knot that threatens to unfurl so fast I'll puke. Victor is a man that's used to being obeyed without question. In another universe, he could use that power and charisma for good, but in this one, he's just a monster. His cold gaze is fixed on me. That's never good.

"Daddy, I'm sorry," Anne whispers. "It's my fault."

I wonder if he knows she only calls him that when she's afraid of him.

"Maybe I've been too lenient. You've forgotten your place." He glances towards Marissa before his hard gaze shifts to Anne. Her shoulders curl in, slumping under the weight of his gaze. "Keep my daughter out of the way. I need to have a word with *the nanny*."

Anne's chin wobbles. "I'm sorry. I just wanted a snack. I didn't think it was a big deal."

"Enough! You're old enough to learn a lesson about respect, and consequences." His eyes shift back to me. "I understand that you're fond of Jessica, but she's our servant, not your friend. Marissa, make sure Anne watches this. It's time she realizes that obedience comes at a cost." He peels off his suit jacket as he speaks, folding it neatly and placing it on the kitchen counter before rolling up his sleeves. "Jessica, come here."

My feet move on their own accord. I don't want to. I really, really don't want to, but running away will only make it worse. It's better to take whatever punishment he decides on and be done with it. "Please let her go back to her room," I whisper. "She doesn't need to see this." There's no point in groveling. I'll live, and he's always careful to not leave marks where they will show.

"What's happening?" Anne's question is so quiet, so unsure that it breaks my heart. We've grown up together in a lot of ways, but in two different worlds.

"Shh," says Marissa, grinning in ghoulish delight. She's hated me for a long time and the feeling is mutual. "This is what happens when you don't listen."

Victor grabs my ponytail and wraps it around his fist, pulling me to my toes. His other arm pulls back before punching me right in the stomach. No warning, no time for me to react. Anne screams as I buckle over in pain and shock, struggling to suck in air. Everything is numb for a moment, before the pain hits. I pinch my lips together and try to breathe through it so I don't throw up on his feet. I don't want to give him an excuse to do worse. Or traumatize Anne more than she already is.

"What do you have to say for yourself?" he asks calmly.

"I'm sorry. We were out after curfew. It's my fault."

Adrenaline has taken over, making my voice unsteady and my breathing quick.

"And she insulted me!" Marissa adds.

Victor yanks my head up. "Is that true?"

I open my mouth, wanting to deny it and try to save myself more pain, but maybe I'm better off admitting it because he'd never take my word over hers anyway.

"Answer me!" he growls, shaking me by the hair.

My glasses fall, hitting the floor and sliding across the tile. If they're scratched, who knows how long I'll have to live with it before he decides it makes him look bad. "Fine! Yes, I—"

And that's when the explosion rocks the whole building.

2

GHOST

A TWIST OF THE THROTTLE AND MY BIKE GROWLS, LIKE the rumbling purr of a monster eager to slip its chains. It's times like these that I really feel the connection to the metal beast underneath me. I itch to let loose and open it all the way, but this isn't a joyride. There will be other nights to feel the wind tear at my skin as the asphalt flies by under my wheels. Tonight I need to stay in formation. My brothers trust me to be where I'm supposed to be, and that trust is what binds us together.

Riot and Tex ride at my sides, exactly where they should be. All sworn and blooded members of the Outlaw Sons are my brothers, but the three of us have worked, lived, fought and partied together for years. There's no one I'd rather have at my back. We've been through some dark shit, and if fate is kind, tonight's business will be done in time to wash off the blood and find some warm, willing bodies to end the night with. Or fuck, it's been a while since we shared a woman. Maybe we should fix that.

Hellfire leads the pack. It's only been two years since he took over, but there isn't a man here who wouldn't take a bullet for him. He sits his saddle regally, leading us into battle with his long, black hair tied back and whipping behind him like a rallying banner. As an officer, I follow close, with my boys right behind, followed by a handpicked selection of members who have seen enough action to be ready for a target like Victor Kane.

He's a mean fucking snake, and weapon smuggling pays well enough to make him a tricky man to get to.

Which is why we've waited for him to be away from his primary estate, which might as well be a fortress. This would be easier if we could just blow the place to kingdom come and mop up what's left, but the man who hired us has a hard-on for doing the final deed himself.

The weight of my iron is a comfort at my side, sitting loose and ready. And tucked away where I can get to them in a pinch, all my knives are oiled and ready to go. Never leave home unprepared.

Riot raises a fist to get my attention and points. Up ahead, the wall around Kane's holiday estate grows as we get closer. The gate is firmly shut, with two guards in front of it. They're already moving by the time I can see them clearly. One has a phone in his hand, probably calling for backup. That's fine. We're not going for subtlety. We want all eyes on us while Savage and his team sit tight, ready to make a door.

I'm no fucking philosopher, but there's a golden moment just before the action starts that feels unreal. All possible futures hang in the balance. The plan might go perfectly, but let's be real. Something always goes to shit. We just don't know how yet. The trick is to roll with what fate throws at you and hope it doesn't hit any vital organs.

Kane isn't a soft target. He's a fucking arms dealer. We dabble in it ourselves, which is how we know just how important it is to hit him hard and fast before he can call in a fucking drone strike or some shit.

From off to our left, a launcher fires, and the missile streaks ahead with a piercing whine, straight for the main gate. The dense smoke trail makes it hard to see if the guards get out of the way in time, though they start scrambling the moment they hear the dull thump of the launch. The explosion when it hits is loud enough to make the air feel dense in my ears and sends a shockwave through the ground that I can feel through my bike.

We stay mounted, riding straight through the smoke until we get to the wreckage. The doors are blown clean off their hinges, only twisted metal showing where they were attached. There's a body pressed up against the wall by the power of the blast, so at least one of the guys is out of the equation already. The ground is littered with shit that could easily take a bike out of commission, and only hard earned practice lets us seamlessly spread out and avoid both it and each other as we blow through into the courtyard in front of Kane's mansion. Surprise is our main advantage, so it's important to get in fast before they fully mobilize. I leave my bike near the front entrance, slipping my piece out of my belt and into my hand.

Hellfire points at the front door. "Knock knock, boys."

Tex nods, raising his gun and punching a dozen holes in and around the lock. Riot flexes his massive shoulders and grins. He charges at it like a human battering ram, ripping the whole fucking thing off its hinges. He ducks low, rolling in as the forward team advances.

"Down," snaps Hellfire and I drop. His gun barks twice and a guard that just arrived around the corner screams and spins into the wall. A red streak is left behind as he sinks to the floor.

"Move in," commands Hellfire as he monitors the other teams who are spreading out to force Kane's defense to split their attention.

"On it." I slip past Tex, checking that the entry is clear before we advance. These moments are what I live for. When life and death are on the line, and the only things keeping me on the right side of it are my own skills and the support of my brothers. The adrenaline flowing through my veins is better than any high. I'm like a fucking junkie for it.

Our group leapfrogs our way through the building, two guys covering while one advances, working our way towards where we think Kane is most likely to be found. This is the part of the plan that can never be one hundred percent predicted. He might be in his office, or maybe he had the urge to take a late night swim. Fuck, he could be sitting on the can with his pants around his ankles for all we know. I'd fucking pay to see the look on his face if that's the case.

Glass shatters as one of Kane's men fires a machine gun through the windows from a pool area. We drop low as bullets tear holes in the wall behind where we were standing. Tex recovers quickly, zeroing in on the shooter and taking him out with a single crack that nails him in the chest. He stumbles backwards, gun still firing even as his eyes glaze over and his body hits the water.

"Everyone good?" I check the others.

They grunt yes, so we keep moving. The house is fucking crawling with guards now, but they're on the back foot, making it easy to take them on as they show up. Jackal, one of ours, takes a hit to the arm but it's more blood than damage. Otherwise, we're all sporting the right number of holes when a man who looks more like a butler than a guard pops out of a doorway and Riot grabs him by the front of his shirt and smashes him into the wall. The guy's head bounces with a crack.

"Where's Kane?" Riot growls.

The guy doesn't answer, probably still trying to remember his own name, at least until I shove the still warm barrel of my gun right up under the guy's chin, forcing him to look up. That improves his focus, fast.

"Tell us where your boss is, or we're spreading your brains all over the fucking ceiling, Jeeves," Tex drawls.

"I… I don't know. I swear I don't know." His face is pure panic, and the acrid stench of urine hits my nostrils. "Please. I'm just his chef. I really don't. I just—"

Riot gives him another little love tap, and he slides to the floor, boneless. After giving him a quick pat down Riot shrugs. "He's clear. Should be fine. Concussion maybe. I don't see him causing trouble."

I nod. Sometimes it's kill or be killed, but if we can help it, we avoid bringing civilians into it. "No argument. Let's go." I take the lead, out through the pool area, where the shooter that wasn't as smart about his career choices is floating in a slowly spreading cloud of red. Considering he was trying to do the same to us, it's not gonna keep me up at night.

The teams come together in the kitchen, where an open bag of broken, discarded cookies lies strewn across the floor. Odd. "Find anything?"

Savage shakes his head. He's another officer, the two of us serving unofficially as Hellfire's VPs while the club rebuilds after losing General. "First floor is clear. They must have headed up when we rang the bell."

Hellfire cracks his neck and sighs. "The upstairs is sealed off like a bunker. Solid steel. Going to have to make another hole."

I pat Riot on the shoulder. "Sorry, pal. I don't think even you can charge through that."

"On it!" Skyhigh, our best demolitions guy, comes running with a camo backpack. He and his backup work to place explosive charges around the barrier. "Step back, fuckers!"

We pull back, and then Skyhigh taps a button on his phone. A moment later, the charges go off. The door slams open with a crash that nobody in the house could possibly miss. We hold back for a second, waiting to see if there's a welcoming committee. It's eerily quiet.

"Alright, boys, in we go." Hellfire waves us forwards. "Let's find this asshole and collect our paycheck."

3

JESSICA

Anne and I huddle together on the floor of the safe room. I have an arm over her shoulder, and hers are wrapped around my chest, holding me tighter than she has in years. "I'm sorry. I'm so, so sorry," she whimpers.

"Shhhh, none of this is your fault." I'll never forget the look on her face when she saw her father punch me, the utter disbelief. She's used to him being strict and uncaring, but with her, the whips he wields are his words and his attention. Victor won't win father of the year, but he's usually careful to keep her shielded from the cruel, brutal side of his life. Guess that's changed.

Her grip is putting pressure on my bruised stomach, but I need the comfort as much as she does. This isn't the first time someone has attacked Victor, but this is the scariest. As soon as the explosion hit, his guards split us up, taking Victor and Marissa one way, and us another. Rocco, one of the guards, is standing watch at the door, focused on whatever information he's getting through his earpiece, and not on us.

"You're okay, right? We're going to be okay, aren't we?" Anne asks, her voice thin with fear.

"I don't know. We need to stay quiet and do what we're told. They probably aren't here looking for us." I try to keep my voice calm. I can freak out later.

Shouts and gunfire carry through from the first floor, moving from room to room. The only tears I'd shed if Victor ends up dead would be from joy, but I can't share that with his daughter, and right now my safety is tied to theirs. It would be ironic if Victor finally gets what he deserves, and instead of free, I end up dead in the crossfire.

"Why didn't we go with Dad?"

Rocco glances our way. "They're looking for Mr.

Kane. He's safer if we don't have to split our attention."

Safer for him, but what about us?

"Can they get in here?" I ask.

He shrugs.

Well that's reassuring.

Apparently my lack of confidence is obvious, because his lip curls like he just smelled something bad. "If you're not happy, then you're welcome to go out there and take your chances. I'm here to watch the girl, not you. What'll it be?"

"Don't leave me," Anne whispers into my neck.

"I would never."

Someone knocks on the door. Two quick raps and then three more slowly. Rocco nods like he's listening to someone, and opens the door. Two guards I don't know slip inside, one with red hair and the other with dark neck tattoos. Rocco leaves without saying a word.

I pull Anne even closer. She's practically sitting in my lap. "It's going to be okay. They're here to keep you safe, right? There's food and water, and I bet I can come up with some more math for you to work on if you get bored. Victor will deal with whatever is going on and then we can fly back to the city. You like flying in the helicopter."

She nods. "You think so?"

The guards look nervous, which doesn't feel like a good sign, but I paste a smile on my face. "Absolutely. This will all work out for the best, promise. Hey, how about we see if there are any snacks in here? What Marissa doesn't know won't hurt us." I untangle myself from Anne and pull her over to the small stash of shelf stable food.

There are bottles of water and a few cans of beer and soda. I consider it for a short moment, then grab cola. Anne's eyes light up when I give it to her. No cookies, but there are some granola bars, and I take two, handing one to her.

Anne takes a sip from her can and grins. "You didn't really mean it about the math, right?"

"No. You think I would do that to myself?" I stick out my tongue and she laughs.

The danger isn't forgotten, but the gunfire has died

down and for a second we relax. Right up until another, smaller, explosion shakes the building.

"What the fuck was that?" the redheaded guard asks his buddy.

The walls of the safe room might be intrusion proof, but they're definitely not sound proof. More cracks that have to be gunshots sound like they're coming closer. I don't know exactly what business Victor is in, but I know it's not legal. Even if every single other sign didn't point that way, he murdered my parents, after all. That's not the work of an investment banker. It shouldn't be surprising that it's finally catching up to him, but it is. If they succeed, what will happen to Anne? To me?

I can't decide if I'm excited or terrified. Both, I guess.

Anne nibbles on her granola bar. I'm not even sure she knows she's doing it. Her eyes are fixed on the door and she's snuggled right up against my side again.

Something is happening outside. There aren't any windows, but men are yelling to each other close enough that I can almost make out what they are saying. A moment later, there's another explosion, so close that my ears are ringing. Anne screams and drops her can, the soda leaking out and covering the floor.

The guard with the tattoo snarls. "Shut the fuck up. You trying to get us killed?"

"It's okay, Anne. It's okay." I put an arm around her and hold her tight. She's shaking like she has a fever. "We're going to be fine. I promise."

Gunshots, sounds of struggle, screams. The more we hear, the tighter my hold on Anne gets.

"I can't breathe," she gasps.

"Sorry." I force myself to let up.

Voices right outside the door. Both guards draw their weapons and get into ready positions at either side of it. "Get back," hisses the redhead. "Stay low. If things go to shit, run."

"Little pig, little pig, let me iiiin," a deep voice croons from the other side of the door. "We can hear you in there."

"Fuck it," says the one with the tattoos. "I'm not going down for that asshole or his brat."

"What the hell do you think you're doing?" The

other guard grabs him as a thundering roar blasts all four of us.

The door blasts inwards, smashing against the opposite wall and taking the coward with it. A thick cloud of smoke billows to fill the whole room, so I can't see a thing. Only Anne's tight grip on me lets me know she's still right next to me. It's not until the ringing fades that I realize we're both still screaming.

"Don't come any closer!" barks the redheaded guard. I don't know who he thinks he's fooling though. Even I can tell he's not the one in control.

A massive, undeniably male silhouette fills the doorway, so broad his shoulders almost touch the frame on both sides and tall enough that he has to duck a little to step inside.

"Keep back, or I'll—" The guard's shout is cut short as the big man wraps a massive fist around the guard's throat and slams him up against the wall. The man puts a gun right up underneath the guard's chin.

I pull Anne against me, pressing her face into my chest. "Don't look!"

"Or you'll what?" the big man growls.

"Riot! Wait! It's not Kane. There's fucking kids in here," another man shouts.

"Aw, fuck! Sorry." The man he called Riot grabs the surviving guard and pulls him out the door. A moment later, a gunshot echoes in the hall.

The guy in the door winces. "Fucking smooth, man."

He tucks his gun into his belt and holds up his hands like he's trying to convince us we aren't in danger. Yeah right. Everything about him screams deadly. His leather jacket hangs open, with a gray T-shirt underneath, stretched tight across his muscular chest. Dusty jeans cling to his muscular thighs, hanging over scuffed up black leather boots. Colorful tattoos crawl down both arms so elaborately that it looks like he's wearing a long sleeve underneath. He looks exactly like what he is, a killer.

I shield Anne as he takes a step closer and the light hits him. He has dark blond hair, shaved on the sides and tied back on top, with a tight, reddish-brown beard. When he locks his eyes with mine, they're pale gray, like clouds just starting to think about a storm, but hard like granite. I wet my lips, rooted to the spot and unable to look away.

A moment later, a third guy swaggers in like this is his home and we're the intruders. His eyebrows go up when he spots us. "What the fuck? I thought Kane's family was supposed to go back to town after that party." Deep hazel orbs, like a sun dappled forest floor widen as he takes us in. I try not to show anything, but it feels like I'm being *seen* for the first time in a long while, and I'm not sure how I feel about it.

Like the first two, he's dressed in jeans and leather boots, with a heavy leather jacket that has a yellow patch on it. It reads Tex, with a stitched outline of the state behind it. His hair is thick, brown and a little wild, and he has a five o'clock shadow that does nothing to hide the sharp jut of his chin. His nose is crooked like it's been broken. He smiles at me, tiny lines appearing at the corner of his eyes. There's something about him that makes me want to trust him, which is ridiculous because clearly these men are the farthest thing from safe.

"Pretty sure there's only one kid here, Ghost. Hey, darlin', what's a pretty girl like you doing in a place like this?" His low drawl is seductively smooth on top but with a deadly rasp under the surface that drags across my skin leaving goosebumps in its wake.

"Hiding from you," I blurt out. My glasses slip and I shove them back into place.

He stares at me for a second and then laughs. "Fair enough, you got me there."

The man he called Ghost gives me a second look, and it's just as piercing as the first. "We don't have time for this shit. That has to be Kane's kid, so who the fuck are you?" When I hesitate, he puts his hand on his gun in silent warning. "Now! I don't like repeating myself."

Anne flinches, sobbing softly. The instinct to protect her makes me braver than I feel. "Stop! You're scaring her. She's only twelve."

"So answer the question. Are you Kane's woman?" He cocks his head, eyeing me. "Don't look the type."

"His—No! I'm Jessica. I'm just Jessica," falls out of me. "I'm the nanny. Please don't hurt us. I'll do whatever you ask."

"Jesus Christ, you're making me feel like a fucking monster," Ghost snaps, just as Riot comes back in. I try not to imagine what he did to the red headed guard, but it's hard not to imagine his lifeless body just outside the door.

"Shhhh." I hush, stroking Anne's hair to comfort myself just as much as her. Luckily she's staying quiet. These aren't the kind of people we should push. They would murder the both of us and then go out for lunch without a second thought.

Riot's square face is framed by a thick, black beard, and his expressive brows knit together as he looks at us. Inside his jacket, I can see a black T-shirt with a skull logo on it that's doing its best to contain his massive chest, before narrowing into his dark jeans and heavy boots. Under the logo, the T-shirt reads Outlaw Sons MC. A motorcycle club?

His full lips quirk with amusement. "Well, shit. Who had their money on Mary Poppins here being a complication?"

4

JESSICA

"Have to say, I'm not a fucking fan of terrorizing kids," growls Riot, pacing back and forth. "I hate bad intel."

They've moved us out of the safe room and onto the second floor terrace. Anne and I are huddled together. Her eyes are closed and her head is resting on my shoulder, but I know she's not sleeping from the death grip she has on my fingers. The glass railing blocks some of the wind, but not nearly enough to make the cold January breeze off the ocean any easier to deal with. After everything that's happened, though, it's hard to tell where being cold stops, and shock from everything that's happened begins.

I did my best to block Anne's view of the dead as we were marched out here, but I'm sure she saw at least some of it. Some of the men were nameless faces, but others had been around for a while. None of Victor's guards were particularly nice to either of us, but just seeing people we talked to a few hours ago lying still on the ground is more than enough trauma for a lifetime.

"Here." Ghost walks over with a couple of blankets taken from the TV room, draping them over our shoulders.

"Tha—thanks."

His expression is dark and concentrated, keen eyes constantly scanning the estate. "Don't look so fucking surprised. You look cold and we aren't here to torture women and kids."

Of the three of them, he scares me the most. He's obviously in charge of the other two, and he's so steady you'd think this is just any other day for him, but he's not cruel. I know the difference. These men might kill with ease, but not because they enjoy it. Victor would let me freeze out here unless it caused him a problem or made him look weak. I lick my lips, considering if it would be best to try and cooperate, or just stay quiet and not piss them off, hoping they eventually let us go.

"It's true. I don't know who told you, but Anne and I were supposed to leave a couple days ago. Victor changed plans at the last minute," I offer.

The enemy of my enemy might not be my friend, but giving them a little harmless information feels like a peace offering.

Ghost nods. I can almost see his brain filing it away. One more piece of the puzzle solved. He slips a hand into his pocket and pulls out his phone, glancing at the screen. "Cooper's incoming. We have Kane isolated."

Tex is leaning against the wall, pressing one foot against it with the other on the floor. He grins crookedly. "All in all, this wasn't as big a fuck up as it coulda been. Hellfire said they caught the fucker trying to sneak out. Revenge is a hell of a thing if you ask me. We could be gone already if Cooper didn't want to do this personally."

A tear runs down Anne's cheek. She brushes it away quickly with the side of her fist.

"Could you guys be a little more sensitive? You're talking about her father."

"Aw, shit. Forgot about that." Tex actually looks a bit guilty. "It's nothing personal, kid. Your daddy's pissed off a lot of people. We just happened to be the only ones good enough to get to him. If it wasn't us, it would've been someone else eventually."

"I want to go home," Anne whispers.

"When this is over, I'm sure they'll let us go and I'll make sure you're safe," I promise. "Right?" I look back and forth between our captors. They don't meet my eyes.

Riot is the first to respond. He crouches down, getting on level with Anne. "Nothing is sure in this life, but so long as you and your nanny behave, I'll do my best to make sure you get out of this. Do you trust me?"

She starts to nod, then shakes her head. I half expect him to get mad, but he just chuckles.

"Smart kid."

Ghost motions to Riot. "Watch her for a second, will ya? I want to have a little chat with the nanny." He takes me by the arm and leads me away from Anne, who is watching us with wide, blue eyes.

"I'll be right back!" I hope.

Ghost boxes me in, putting his back to the others and getting close enough for a little privacy. I don't want to notice the rich scent of cologne clinging to his skin under the leather, dust and remnants of their fight, but I do. "Look, I'm going to be straight with you because pretending this is a fun little adventure is bullshit that won't help anyone. Her father is a walking corpse that hasn't gotten the message yet. I don't know how you feel about your boss, but it would be in your best interest to work with us until this is over. Keep his daughter calm and out of our hair, and I'll do my best to get you through this."

Hearing him say out loud that they're here to kill Victor nudges something deep inside me that feels an awful lot like hope. "I hate him."

"Excuse me?"

"You asked how I felt about Victor. I hate him. I—I won't help you hurt anyone, but don't worry. I'll take care of Anne. She's a good kid. Nothing like her father."

Ghost cocks his head and considers me for a long moment. "If you hate him so much, why do you work for him?"

"I… I'm here for Anne."

He reaches out and tilts my chin up, searching my face for the truth. "Fair enough. So long as whatever you aren't saying doesn't fuck with our goals, you don't owe me shit."

When his hand drops away, it's all I can do not to take a step towards him.

Ghost turns away. "The house is secure. Don't know about you guys, but I feel fucking exposed up here. Grab the girls and let's get them downstairs. I want to hear what's going on with Cooper and Kane."

Tex and Riot grunt in agreement, and before I know it, Riot slings me over his shoulder like I don't weigh a thing. I let out a surprised gasp, followed by an equally surprised squeak from Anne when Tex gives her the same treatment. I wiggle a little. My stomach aches where Victor punched me and this is putting pressure close to the bruise.

"I can walk, you know."

Riot pats my ass. "Why walk when you can ride?"

"I don't ride bikers." As soon as the words are out of my mouth I hear how it must sound. "I mean—"

"I get it. You're too good for assholes like us. It's your loss, Fran."

What? "My name is Jessica."

"Yeah, I know, but you're the nanny. Get it? The Nanny?"

Anne, bouncing on Tex's shoulder, looks over at me, confused. The whole situation is so bizarre that I almost laugh in spite of seeing a bloody handprint smeared down the wall behind her. The house looks like a warzone, my tormentor slash boss is probably going to end up dead, and one of the men responsible is cracking nanny jokes.

"I have no idea what you're talking about."

"Seriously? Fucking classic TV. It's going to be hard to explain some of my nanny fantasies if you haven't seen the show."

"You could always keep them to yourself," I grumble.

Riot sighs. "But you're the first actual nanny I've met. It seems like a shame to waste the opportunity."

"Riot…" Ghost says in warning.

"Fine."

Tex snorts.

Who the heck are these guys?

5

RIOT

"I don't like this," Hellfire snarls. "We're working on borrowed time." He tries to run his hand through his hair but it gets caught on what looks like dried blood.

Sgt. Terrence Cooper, the guy who hired us for this job, looks him dead in the eyes, not backing down an inch. "You don't have to like it. I'm paying you."

I start to laugh, but cover it up with a grunt when Hellfire glares at me. Cooper's got balls, I'll give him that. Thirty years ago, he might've made a decent prospect, but career Army or not, he's spent most of the past decade or so behind a desk and it shows. He's not in horrible shape for pushing sixty, but he's a long way from boot camp. I bet this is the first time in years that he's seen any real action.

"Then get in there and do what you have to do. We're here on your dime, but you can shove your money up your ass if you think I'm going to risk my men more than I have to just so you can play out your little revenge fantasy. If you weren't tight with General, we wouldn't even be standing here."

Cooper nods. "I know you think I'm being an old fool, but he would've understood."

I'm not sure that's true. Maybe the General he knew a lifetime ago would have gone along with his little revenge fantasy, but the man we swore to follow would've put the safety of the club above his personal need for blood. I wasn't there when Cooper hired us, but from what I've understood, he's retiring and wants to tie up one last loose end before he goes. Kane was responsible for the death of one of his best friends. After trying to take him down legally for over a decade, Cooper finally decided he'd rather go outside the law and see justice done than let him get away with murder.

That's where we came in.

I hope he gets what he wants, but in my experience, death doesn't solve as much as you might think it would. Even if you can spit on their grave, the pain doesn't fucking go away. Still, I'd rather drink and fuck my sorrows away knowing my enemies are six feet under instead of knowing they have a fucking beach house like Kane, so maybe I'm no better.

A door opens and Savage walks down the hall towards us, followed by Poe, one of the newer guys.

"Good to go?" Hellfire asks.

"We're clear. Kane is tied up like a fucking Christmas ham, and Poe got us into the security system. I can't guarantee someone didn't make a call before we took control, but there's no sign a distress signal went out."

"Good." Hellfire nods towards the door, while looking at Cooper. "You've got ten minutes. Clock starts now."

Cooper clears his throat. He looks a little green around the edges, like a kid who's been waiting in line for a roller coaster but now that it's his turn, he's not sure he's up for it. "Right."

"Cold feet?" I ask.

"Not a chance." Cooper narrows his eyes at me.

"He's got a kid, you know. We found her hiding in a bolt room with her nanny and a couple guards. Twelve years old." Why the fuck did I bring that up? I'm I trying to talk this guy out of killing a man who probably deserves it ten times over? I won't lose a minute of sleep over Victor Kane, but I'm not a fucking monster. Watching his daughter curl up into her cute little nanny while trying not to cry didn't exactly fill me with warm fuzzies.

Instead of making him rethink his plan, Cooper's expression hardens at the mention of Kane's daughter. "Ted's kid never got to be twelve. They made me the godfather, you know that? I was there for the baptism. I guess in a way, this is me seeing my duties through. I feel bad for the girl, but she's better off without a man like him raising her."

Cold. Do two wrongs make a right? I wonder what will happen to Kane's kid. I suppose Jessica can figure it out.

Cooper carefully pulls a gun out of the holster under his jacket. "This was Ted's. It's taken me a long while to get this far, but—"

"Tick tock, tick tock," Hellfire snaps. "You paid us to get you here, not listen to your fucking TED talk. You're down to seven minutes. I suggest you use them."

We walk him to the door of the room where we're holding Kane. Savage opens it, and through the doorway, I see Kane tied to a chair, his arms behind him, with a wad of cloth shoved in his mouth. Behind him are massive glass windows overlooking the roof terrace and the inky water of the coast. He tries to speak, but it just comes out a mumble.

"What was that? Are you worried we'll steal all your business once you're out of the picture?" I grin at the glare he gives me. "Don't worry, we'll take good care of your customers."

I'm just fucking with him. We might pick up a little business if Kane's out of the picture, but we aren't interested in playing in his league. We source gear mostly for other bike clubs, preppers, enthusiasts, even some mob families that aren't too fancy to associate with us. He's known for offering some of the most advanced shit on the market. High tech, expensive weaponry that appeals more to the international crowd. Doesn't surprise me that he clashed with the military.

"Get out. It's my turn." Cooper's voice is a low, focused growl.

Hellfire taps his wrist to remind Cooper he doesn't have all day, and nods. We close the door behind us. Whatever happens now is on his head.

"What are the chances of him being sensible and just putting a bullet between Kane's eyes?" I ask.

Savage runs his hands over his face, looking tired and annoyed. "Zero."

"Shit. If this was a spy movie, I'd be yelling at the screen for him to just get it the fuck done before something goes wrong."

He looks at me like I'm the problem here.

"What? We're all thinking it."

"Yeah, but you don't fucking say it out loud!" Hellfire snaps.

"That's the problem, isn't it? If he eats shit, how's he gonna pay?"

Voices carry through the door. He must've taken Kane's gag out, because they're shouting at each other. We exchange glances.

"It's fine. He's tied up so tight the only way he's getting loose is if Cooper cuts him free and that would be—"

Whatever Savage was about to say gets cut off by what sounds like all the windows exploding at once.

I hear the sound of boots running our way, and we all draw iron as Hellfire slams open the door. We stay out of line of sight for a moment in case someone is going to start shooting, then I cautiously look inside.

The windows are all blown out, and Kane is standing behind Cooper, with a knife blade pressed to his throat. Where the fuck did he even get a knife?

"He had nothing on him, I swear to fucking God," Savage snarls. "We both checked him."

Kane sneers. "Put the guns down and bring me the girls if you want this idiot to live."

6

JESSICA

"Are they going to kill my dad?" Anne asks softly.

We're being kept together, along with Marissa in one of Kane's meeting rooms downstairs. When they first threw Marissa in with us, she was sobbing so hard it felt like she was trying to win an Oscar, but when it didn't win her any attention, the tears dried up fast. Ghost and Tex are watching us, along with a guy named Jackal who has his jacket draped over one shoulder and a makeshift bandage tied around his arm.

"Of course not," Marissa snaps. "He's worth too much. I'm sure they just want money."

Ghost laughs, but it sounds more mocking than amused.

I stay quiet, not wanting to lie, but the truth isn't easy.

Anne looks down at her hands. "It's because he's a bad person, isn't it? I'm not stupid, you know. You can tell me."

"I know you aren't." I look around, helplessly.

Tex walks over and crouches down in front of us. "What do you know about your father, kid?"

"He does business with bad people. People who hurt people. He… he hurt Jessica."

Tex looks up. His rich hazel eyes take me in. "Why would he do that?"

I can't hold his gaze and look away, adjusting my glasses even though they don't need it.

"Oh my God. You can't really be falling for Jessica's pathetic little mouse act, can you?" Marissa whines. "Anne likes her because she's a pushover. Victor *has* to be strict. Otherwise she wouldn't get anything done at all."

"For fuck's sake, woman," Jackal snaps. "Your pussy must be magic if Kane puts up with you, but you're so fucking sour I'd be afraid my dick would fall off."

Anne's jaw drops before she slaps a hand over her mouth to muffle the gasp.

The door slams open and everyone jumps. The three men all reach for their guns, going from vaguely bored to full attention in the blink of an eye. They relax when they see it's one of their own at the door, a man with thick, unruly black hair and sharp features.

"Poe? What's going on?" Ghost asks.

"Kane's got Cooper. Bring the women up."

My blood runs cold. "No."

Poe nods. "He's threatening to kill Cooper unless we bring them to him."

Tex takes me, Ghost takes Anne, and Jackal leads Marissa up to the second floor where they were holding Victor. There's no teasing or joking this time. Every step feels like an eternity. I was so close to finally getting away from him, and now I might end up right back where I started, and after this, he'll be looking to find someone to beat on. Maybe he won't care about me. It's Anne and Marissa that are important, right?

"We'll be okay, right?" I ask, feeling like Anne when Tex's silence is my only answer.

We are marched into Victor's library upstairs. The wall of windows is nothing but sparkling rubble, with thousands of chunks of glass strewn around the floor and outside onto the terrace. Victor stands near the window, forcing a man's head up with his arm under the man's jaw and holding a knife to his throat. A trickle of blood is dripping lazily from the blade.

"Just shoot him!" Victor's hostage snaps. That must be Cooper.

But they don't. "Where you gonna go, Kane?" Ghost asks. "There's no way outta here."

"If you want this guy alive, leave the women here and back the fuck off! I'll send him back to you when I know I'm safe!"

"The helicopter," I whisper, but nobody is paying attention.

Cooper struggles, but it doesn't do him much good. "Shoot him!"

A biker with long black hair has his gun trained on Victor. He looks pissed. "You think we're stupid? Hand him over first and we'll think about it."

I've seen Victor angry plenty of times, but this is the first time I've ever seen him afraid. He slowly steps backwards through the destroyed window, forcing Cooper to stumble after him or slit his own throat by resisting.

Anne is crying. "Daddy?"

"You won't leave me with them, would you? Give them what they want, baby!" Marissa pleads.

I feel like I'm the only one that can see him for who he is, a horrible selfish monster that would sacrifice all of us if it saved his own skin. I stretch up on my toes to whisper to Tex without everyone else hearing. If things go wrong, I don't want to give Victor even more reasons to punish me later. "The helicopter! There are stairs behind him."

"He's going for the chopper!" Tex yells.

Everything happens at once. Victor swears and drags Cooper up the stairs as Tex and Ghost grab me and Anne, pulling us away from the fight and keeping us from running after him. Marissa actually manages to do something for once, and brings her hands down on Jackal's injury, distracting him just long enough for her to make a run for it.

"Daddy!" Anne screams.

"Does he know how to fly that thing?" Ghost asks.

I nod. "He doesn't usually fly it himself, but has his license."

"Fuck."

The unmistakable sound and force of the rotors engaging just above us floods the terrace. Glass and debris goes flying and anyone still outside has to duck for cover. I watch in horror as the helicopter starts to ascend, swinging back and forth dangerously.

"What the fuck is he doing?" Tex asks.

"Oh fuck," Ghost breathes out. He grabs Anne, who is hysterical at this point, and pulls her back into the house.

The helicopter is swinging because Marissa didn't make it fast enough. She's trying to climb in, but Victor won't wait. She's still hanging from one of the skids as it finally clears the roof.

But not for long.

"Don't watch." Tex curls me into his chest, blocking me from seeing her fall.

It doesn't block the sound of her scream as she loses her grip, or the sickly thud of her hitting the lawn.

7

JESSICA

"Where are you taking us?" I twist in Tex's arms as he marches me out of the house. I manage to land a good stomp on his boot, but I think it hurts me more than him. I wanted this to be my ticket out, but not if it means just being someone else's prisoner, and not if it puts Anne at risk.

"Easy, honey. You're coming with us one way or another, and this'll go a lot smoother if you stay quiet," he says with a deep chuckle that slides right through me. "Look at your little friend over there. She's watching you to see how to react. The more you fight me, the more scared she's gonna get. If you keep calm, she won't panic and that's safer for everyone."

"Is that a threat?"

He blows out a frustrated sigh. "It's reality. We can't let you go and we can't stay here. Thank her daddy for that. He's got our guy and we have you."

I shiver, partly from the cold but mostly from the thought of what's going to happen when Victor decides to cut his losses. Anne is his daughter, he'll save her even if it's just to save face, but how important am I to him really? Not very. He didn't even bother to try and help his own girlfriend.

No tears come when I think of Marissa lying cold on the lawn, but it leaves a sour taste in the back of my mouth. She was horrible, but she trusted him to care at least a little.

"Mount up! This place is dust in ten!" Hellfire yells. "You know your routes. Follow your team lead."

All the bikers seem to know what to do, breaking into smaller groups as they go to their motorcycles. Riot is holding Anne off to the side. Her wide, terrified eyes are locked on me.

"Jess? What's happening?" she shouts.

"Keep her calm," Tex whispers in my ear.

"Th—They're going to take us somewhere safe and um…"

"We'll contact Kane for the trade," he offers.

"And they'll talk to your dad about fixing all of this. It's going to be okay. I promise." More softly, I whisper to Tex, "Please don't make me a liar."

Ghost helps me awkwardly mount up behind Tex on his motorcycle. I give Anne a weak smile and wrap my arms around his waist. It leaves me no choice but to lean into his wide back and hold on tight. Riot holds Anne in front of him on his bike, cradling her to his chest. She looks so small, gripping his forearm for dear life.

When the engine starts, I let out a startled yelp. I'm not used to this kind of close contact, especially not with men like this, and the steady rumble of the motorcycle is… confusing. It feels good in a way I'm not sure I should feel good right now.

"What did he mean by 'this place is dust'?" I ask Tex.

He laughs. "You'll see."

We ride out of the ruined gate, and as soon as we are on the road, Tex floors it. Dark asphalt zooms by underneath, so fast and close it's scary. I'm used to being protected inside a car, and right now the only thing keeping me safe on the bike is my grip around Tex's chest, and my thighs clutching the outside of his. If I'm holding too tight, he's not giving any sign of it, and as the minutes pass, I relax in spite of myself.

At least until a massive blast cuts through the night, so powerful I can feel the gust of air as it blows by us, even this far away. I twist to look, my grip on Tex tightening again. Smoke billows up from the direction of Victor's beach house. A second explosion sends sparks and more smoke soaring over the trees.

Holy crap! I didn't think the dust thing was going to be literal.

As the miles pass, I finally resettle enough to observe a little. My life depends on keeping a clear head. The bikes flow along the road like a flock, moving and adjusting to each other in ways that are mysterious to me, but the riders seem to understand instinctively. Riot is off to our left side with Anne, and Ghost is ahead of us, the club logo clear on the back of his jacket, with Outlaw Sons in big letters underneath. It's almost like a pirate flag, with a masked skull and something that looks like maybe engine parts crossed behind it?

We ride under an overpass. The rumble of the bikes echoes and multiplies until it's almost a physical pressure. A growling wave that threatens to pull me under.

Am I riding to freedom? Or death?

Eventually we pull off the highway into a section of the city I've never seen. I was never allowed to drive or go out on my own, so all I really know are Victor's estates and a vague memory of the suburban neighborhood where I grew up. I can smell the salty tang of the ocean on the wind but I don't see the water.

We drive down a four lane street, lined with houses that look small and packed together, then past shabby looking strips of stores and businesses. I almost feel like I'm in a movie even though I know this is probably normal and I'm the one with the messed up version of what that means.

Up ahead, a street light turns red, but the group doesn't even slow down. It's late, and there aren't many other cars out. The few that are, wisely choose to wait for the bikers to pass through. To the right, spotlights illuminate a walled compound. On the side of the wall is a massive lit sign with their logo that says Outlaw Sons MC, and over the top of the wall I can see the roofs of several houses and what looks like…

Is that a church?

It seems impossible, but it is. A guarded double gate swings open into a courtyard in the center of the buildings, and sure enough, off to the side is an old brick church with a high tower. There are lights on inside, shining out through colorful stained glass windows. When we ride through the gate, it feels like entering a whole new world. A town within a town.

We ride right up to the front steps of a long, rectangular building. Offices maybe? No, a school. I can see windows evenly spaced down the side where classrooms probably used to be, but now a lot of them are covered up. Once I realize what I'm looking at, the layout makes more sense. I went to Catholic school a lifetime ago before Victor took me, and this reminds me of it. A church with a school, and houses for the priests and nuns. Strange to think that one day the bell rang for the last time, and the roar of motorcycles moved in.

We pull up behind Ghost, who swings his leg over his bike and before I even get a chance to wonder how I'm supposed to dismount, he eases my grip on Tex's chest, puts his big hands around my waist and lifts me right off, like I don't weigh a thing. My legs feel like rubber and I have to grab Ghost to keep from falling after he sets me down.

Tex laughs. "Welcome to the party." Like we're just dropping by for a visit.

Riot puts Anne down on the asphalt next to his bike, and she runs right to me. I hold her close. "Are you okay?"

She shrugs. "I guess? That's kinda a stupid question." Tweens.

"True. I suppose we're pretty far from okay, but we'll get there eventually." I hope I sound more confident than I feel. There are a lot of things I can imagine happening while being held hostage, and most of them aren't good.

"Church!" Hellfire bellows. "All hands on deck. Someone get Bonnie." He stalks across the courtyard and towards the church. A couple of bikers standing by the side door visibly straighten and get out of his way.

The door opens, and instead of song and prayer, heavy rock music comes out. Ghost, Riot and Tex surround me and Anne, leading us inside after Hellfire. The music echoes off the high ceilings, and the air smells like leather, beer and motor oil, not incense and candles.

"Wow," Anne whispers.

I agree. The inside is mostly gutted. Some of the old pews are pushed to the sides, but there are also plenty of tables, chairs and couches. The altar is bare and there's a bar behind it. There's a massive wooden chair that might have been left behind, and in place of a cross, there's another banner with the club logo hanging below a solitary leather vest. Others dot the wall to the sides, but whoever that vest belonged to, it clearly stands alone.

The inside is full of bikers. They make a path for Hellfire, and nod at Ghost and the others, watching us with something between confusion and suspicion. They're a scary bunch, big and broad-shouldered, and every single one looks capable of murder. I've never felt so small in my life. I squeeze Anne's hand, and she squeezes right back.

"Turn that shit off," Hellfire yells. "Ring the bell."

The music quiets immediately, and a few moments later, the deep toll of a church bell rings out.

Hellfire climbs up the steps to the altar, leans over the bar to pull out a beer, and then drops into the wooden chair with a tired grunt. He looks up at the vest on the back wall and raises his bottle. "Wish you were here, you old asshole. This job is a pain in my ass."

"Jess?" Anne whispers. "What's she doing?"

She?

Between the bikers lounging on one of the couches is a girl about my age. She's barely dressed, sitting in one of the guy's laps, and leaning down between the other's legs to... Oh my God.

I put myself between Anne and what's going on. "I'm not sure we should be in here," I hiss.

Riot looks around, not understanding.

Tex shoulders him and points. "Zip it the fuck up, Crank! There's ladies present!"

"And what are we then?" a feminine voice pipes up, laughing.

"Gone!" Ghost shouts.

There's some grumbling, but not much as the scene morphs from a grown up frat party into an organized meeting. Well, semi organized anyway. Bikers file in from both the side and the back of the church, slowly filling the room.

"What the hell's going on?" a new woman's voice cuts straight through the rumble of burly men, sharp like a chainsaw. "Where's Cooper? Don't tell me you lost that idiot. General'll be rolling in his fucking grave if you messed this up." Her voice is low and raspy, and she sounds like she's used to being listened to in a room full of men.

"I didn't lose shit!" Hellfire barks. "He lost his own damn self!"

The crowd parts to allow in a sturdy woman with steel gray hair, wearing a leather jacket that looks a lot like the men's. She's got a patch on the left side of her chest that says, "Bonnie." Underneath it, another patch is sewn on that says "Boss bitch." Her face is tan and freckled, lined but not wrinkled.

She takes one look at us and stops in her tracks. "Who the fuck are they?"

Ghost puts his hand on my shoulder. "Bonnie, meet

Jessica and Anne. Anne is Kane's daughter. They're our leverage to get Cooper back."

She looks me straight in the eyes, assessing, then shifts her gaze to Anne. Her face softens a little and she sighs. "So what? You just assume that since I'm a woman, I'm the one that's supposed to babysit? What's next? Need me to go into the kitchen and make you a sandwich?"

Scattered laughs sound through the church.

Hellfire stands and flings his bottle straight into the wall where it shatters. The place goes silent. "Take them back with you. Keep them safe and secure while we figure this dumpster fire out. That's a fucking order. Unless you want to be responsible for putting a damn twelve-year-old in one of the cells."

Bonnie's back straightens and she nods. "Understood." She waves to us. "Come on. You two look like you're about to fall over. Let's get away from all this testosterone." When we don't move right away, Ghost gives me a shove.

This time, Anne and I hurry after her.

8

TEX

I settle to the side next to Riot, and watch Jessica and Anne follow Bonnie out the side entrance. Jessica casts a glance over her shoulder at us, looking lost. I nod, and her lips twitch in just the barest hint of a smile.

This whole situation is fucked up. I'm not her man, but we were the ones that found them hiding during the raid, and I can't shake the feeling of responsibility. This is no place for an innocent girl and a kid.

Ghost and Savage step up onto the altar, sitting opposite Hellfire.

"Alright boys, get fucking comfortable, because this is a fucking story and a half." Hellfire sweeps his hand at the crowd.

He starts at the beginning, outlining what went right —most if it—and what went wrong—Terrence fucking Cooper. That jackass let his thirst for revenge stand in the way of actually getting it. The mood is grim as Hellfire details how Kane got away, taking our client with him. More than one guy looks fit to kill when they hear how Kane sacrificed both his daughter and his woman.

"He just let her fall? That's fucking cold, man."

There's a lot of nods. The boys don't even know the names of half the girls they screw, but that's just fun and games. If they claim a woman, they take responsibility for her. You don't turn your back on the people who rely on you.

"And he left his fucking kid behind without a fight," growls Riot. "Ratshit coward."

Crank raises a hand. "So we're in the hostage business now? What's the plan?"

"Looks like it." Hellfire nods. "I'm not fucking happy about it, but on top of not getting paid, it's not going to be good for business if it gets out that we lost our fucking client."

"If it's not his woman, then who's the other chick?" Junker asks.

I look his way. "The nanny. Just some poor girl who got dragged into our shit. Should we let her go?"

It would be a shame. She's cute in a mousy kind of way. Reminds me of the smart girls in high school who used to check me out during practice when they thought I wouldn't notice. The ones who would blush and get all shy, but were usually the freakiest if you managed to get them alone. Damn, I wouldn't mind seeing Jessica's hair out of that braid, and those pretty lips wrapped around my cock.

"Not yet. We keep both of them until we know more and figure out what the fuck the next step is," Hellfire adds. "Shitty for her, but having her around might help keep Kane's daughter calm."

I put my hand up. "Question. The whole mission was to give Cooper a clear shot at Kane. We did everything but put that fish in a fucking barrel, and he still fucked it up. Let's say we arrange a clean exchange. Do we just turn the girls over, collect our guy and go on our merry fucking way? You think Kane isn't going to turn around and take a shot at us as soon as it's over? No matter what happens, we just put a target on our heads."

Savage crosses his arms in front of his chest, nodding. "You're not wrong, but good options are fucking scarce. For now, we should play dumb and focus on getting Cooper back in one piece. Rich assholes like Kane are always happy to think we're too stupid to think ahead. It makes it easier to get the jump on them later."

"We could cut our losses," Ghost says with a careless shrug. "Sacrificing Cooper would be a small hit to our reputation, but we've built back from worse. Kane's a professional. He understands the difference between a personal hit and a job. Besides, as long as we have his kid, he's the one at a disadvantage."

"Just keep her around as insurance? I don't like it." Hellfire frowns.

"Neither do I, but it's an option. She's worth more to him than Cooper is to us. Cooper goes down, we're out some money. His little girl gets hurt, it makes him look weak." Ghost leans back like the cold mother fucker he is.

Everyone looks to Hellfire, who weighs Ghost's words before shaking his head. "Even if that's true, we're not doing it. That's not who I am, and that's not who we are. We took the job, we see it through."

Heads nod all around the room.

Outside these walls, where people like black and white answers that help them sleep at night, they call us the bad guys. But they don't know shit. We live in the gray zone between their white picket fences and the real evil. Clubs like the Outlaw Sons are a fucking life raft for men who fall through the cracks and might otherwise keep falling until they hit rock bottom.

Not that every MC draws their line in the same place. Some are nothing but law abiding, white-collar weekend warriors, and others wouldn't hesitate to put a bullet in that little girl's skull if it got them a paycheck.

General's cut, with his blood still staining the leather, hangs on the wall as a reminder that we paid a steep price to keep from going down that road.

"Man, if I didn't know Ghost as well as I do, I'd think he was a goddamn monster sometimes," Riot says softly.

I nod. "No shit. Glad he's on our side." Ghost learned early that you can't throw away options just because they're distasteful. He's a better leader for it, but if he hadn't managed to hang onto his own humanity, he'd be fucking scary.

Poe stands up from his spot towards the back. "Yeah, alright. So we all agree this hostage situation isn't a long term solution, but it's what we got. Kane has access to shit we could only dream of. For all we know he can take out the whole damn compound from fucking space. The only thing keeping him from doing that is his daughter. We probably have a couple days tops before he's recovered enough to hit back."

The members go back and forth, debating as Hellfire listens from the altar, sipping his beer and letting us throw our thoughts around. It would be easy to think he's too easy going to be president, but that would be a mistake. We'd follow him into hell *because* he respects our opinions and suggestions, and at the end of the day, every single man here trusts him to make the final call.

Finally, he shut us all up by coming down the steps and walking down the center of the church. "We keep the girls close and put the ball in Kane's court.

I'll make contact when we're done here. We need to keep all options open. Stay close to home, and don't go out alone. Anyone with a civilian family, if they can be traced back to the club, think about getting them behind the walls or sending them on a little vacation. We don't know what the fuck Kane will do, but we know he don't play nice."

"Jesus Christ, I hope we take this guy out by the time everything is over," Riot grumbles.

Hellfire grins. "And since Ghost and his team have already been dealing with the hostages, they can keep doing so."

Ghost snaps to attention. "What the fuck? You're putting us on babysitting duty? What about Bonnie?"

"She'll help, and she's a damn good shot, but they need more protection than even a tough old bitch like her can give. The girls already know you a little, and I trust you to keep them safe. Clear?"

I nod. "Crystal."

9

JESSICA

Anne and I follow Bonnie out of the church and over to the house next door. I bet it used to be where the priests lived, but now there's a staircase built onto the side that leads up to the second floor that she leads us up.

Bonnie's hair is long and full, a wavy mane pinned back in the center of her head. She's not particularly tall. A little bit shorter than me even, and I'm only five-five. But there's something about her that feels larger than life. Anne can't take her eyes off her.

She shoves open the door, which leads straight into a small kitchen full of mess and clutter. The walls are painted a warm coral color, and there isn't a spot that doesn't have some sort of knickknack or decoration. The walls are covered in posters and photographs. Most aren't framed, but there's one larger one of Bonnie with a biker that has to be about her age. He has long, gray-black hair and a thick handlebar mustache, and in the photo he has his arm slung over her shoulder and his fingers running through her hair.

"Bathroom's through there and to the right." She points into the next room. "Don't even think about running. It's a long ways down and you won't make it over the wall before someone spots you."

Anne looks up at me with pleading eyes. She's hardly said a word since we were taken, and it worries me.

"Thanks, we'll be right back." I walk Anne to the bathroom and wait outside. "Go on. I'll wait here, promise."

The toilet flushes after a few minutes, and I hear the water run for a good long time before Anne comes out. Her eyes are red rimmed and her face is wet. "I want to go home," she whispers, breaking my heart.

I wrap my arms around her and hold her close. "I know."

"Either of you hurt? Need sewing up?" Bonnie calls from the kitchen.

Anne's jaw drops and she actually lets out a small laugh. "Who are these people?"

"No, I think we're okay," I shout back.

We go back to the kitchen and find Bonnie rummaging through her small refrigerator. It looks to be mostly full of diet soda, energy drinks and pickles. She pulls out a couple of cans of something labeled 'Electric Blue 24 Hour Kick!' and puts them on the table. "Sorry, I wasn't exactly expecting company. I've got roasted peanuts and protein bars. You girls hungry?"

Anne takes one of the cans, gripping it like she's afraid someone is going to swoop in and rip it out of her hand. "I'd like a protein bar, please." Normally I would never say yes to her having an energy drink, but she more than deserves a break, and it's not like anyone is around to find out.

Bonnie nods, opening a cabinet door and pulling out a box that says Salted Caramel Chocolate. She tosses one to Anne and one to me. "What about you? You're too young to be her mother. Sister?"

Anne giggles. "Jessica's my nanny." She peels the bar open and nibbles on a corner before taking a huge bite and chewing in absolute bliss.

"Nanny, huh? Fancy. Bet you wish you were getting overtime for this." Bonnie grins.

Overtime would mean I was getting paid in the first place, but I smile back. I'm used to playing my part. "Something like that. Do you know what's going to happen to us? How long do you think we're going to be here?"

She sighs. "I wish I could say, honey. I'm not in the loop anymore, and even if I was, I get the feeling this job is so far off the rails that nobody has the answers you want. All I can tell you is that you could be in worse places. The Sons are a rough bunch of assholes, but this isn't the kinda club you need to worry about having a pretty girl like Anne around. They might teach her a whole new vocabulary, but they won't mess with her. You maybe, but only if you're up for it."

Anne washes down the last of the protein bar with a big gulp of sugar and caffeine. "What do you mean?"

Without even giving me time to think of a nice way of explaining, Bonnie answers. "I mean we don't put up with rapists and predators around here. Civilian law might not apply inside the walls, but some things are just being a decent fucking human being. General didn't let that shit float, and neither does Hellfire."

It might not just be the guys that are going to give Anne a new vocabulary.

"Oh!" Anne's eyes go wide. "That's good. Right?"

"Yeah… yeah that's good." I'm struggling to focus. Too much has happened in the past couple hours, and it feels like something out of a movie.

Bonnie seems to understand. She tosses Anne another protein bar and motions to me. "Come on. I've got a spare bed in my junk room. I don't know what Hellfire expected me to do with you two, but he gave you to me so it's my call now. Just because you're in a shitty situation doesn't mean it needs to be worse than it is."

She flips on the light in her living room. It's just like the kitchen, colorful and packed full of stuff, but warm and friendly. There's a well-worn couch with a crocheted blanket thrown over one end. A big screen TV with some sort of video game console underneath, and more pictures of bikers, many of them including that same man from the kitchen photo. On the wall is a frame with two patches inside. One reads "Property of" and underneath, "General."

I'm very tempted to ask about it, but it feels special. Personal. The kind of thing a friend would know, and I don't know Bonnie well enough to know if it would be rude, so I don't.

Her junk room is exactly that. It looks like everything she couldn't find room for anywhere else just gets thrown through the door and forgotten about. There's nothing gross or dirty about her apartment. It's all clean, just nothing like the empty, minimalist style that Victor prefers. Every inch of Bonnie's place feels like her. Warm, friendly, kind of a mess, but in a way that makes you feel like you could curl up on the couch and be at home. Tears spring to my eyes. I try to stop it, but once the first hiccup comes out, the sobs follow right after.

"Are you okay? Jess? What's wrong?" Anne freezes. For the first time, she looks like she might really panic. Up until now, I think she's been taking her cues from me. So long as I could hold it together, so could she.

Bonnie's in the middle of sorting a pile of clothes off the bed. She drops what she's doing and rushes over, putting her arm around me and helping me sit on the edge of the mattress. "She's fine, baby. It's just a lot. Sometimes it takes a while before the feelings kick in. Right, Jessica?"

"Y—yes," I stammer, trying and failing to keep from bawling.

"Anne, help me get this bed cleared off. Just the clothes in a pile. A night on the floor won't hurt anything. I think you both could use some sleep, or at least the chance to lie down and not have to be strong for a while."

I swipe away the tears, angry that I'm finally out of Victor's reach, and instead of celebrating, I'm crying. This woman looks tough as nails. She probably thinks I'm useless. "I'm fine. I'll help."

"Sit your ass down and take a breath for Christ's sake," Bonnie snaps. "You've seen who the hell knows what today and been taken hostage by a motorcycle club. Instead of going home and curling up in your own bed, you're stuck here with me. Cry if you need to fucking cry. You earned it. I'll make sure nothing else happens to either of you tonight."

10

JESSICA

I wake up in Bonnie's spare bed, still in the sweats I was wearing the night before. The curtains are mostly closed, but a shaft of bright sunlight slips in through the side. The clock on the wall says it's after three in the afternoon, which is completely impossible.

I've never slept that late in my life. Not that I remember anyway.

I actually watch the second hand count off two more minutes before I'm willing to believe it isn't just stopped at that time. Every morning my alarm goes off at six sharp. I have to get ready, put on my uniform and make sure everything is ready when Anne gets up at seven because her tutor comes at eight. Weekends are a little more lenient, but she's expected to eat breakfast at nine with her father and Marissa.

My heart skips a beat when I realize what's missing.

Anne.

I jump out of bed and rush into the living room.

Bonnie is on the couch holding a game controller, and Anne is sitting on the floor next to her with a controller just like it.

Anne leaps to her feet when she sees me and rushes over. "I had cereal with tiny marshmallows in it, and Bonnie let me try her coffee! We're playing Mayhem City Five! This is awesome!"

Oh my God.

I'm not sure if it makes me feel better or not that Anne is acting like she's on the best vacation ever. She's going to need a detox and therapy. So much therapy. We both are.

"That's… great," I squeeze out, trying to sound supportive.

"You slept *forever*."

"She needed it, kid," Bonnie says from the couch. "I hope you don't mind me keeping an eye on her. You were dead to the world in there."

"What are you wearing?"

Anne grins and spins in a circle. She has a pair of hot pink leggings and an oversized black sweatshirt with some kind of scary looking band logo on the front. Her long blonde hair is pulled back in a bouncy ponytail, and glittery bow earrings dangle from her ears.

"Bonnie has so much cool stuff. She said you can borrow clothes, too." She goes back to the TV and picks up her controller. "We're helping this cult, who are really the bad guys, but Bonnie says they've got shi—lots of cash."

"Um… okay. That sounds useful." I have no idea what she's talking about.

Bonnie stands up and pats Anne on the head as she walks by. "You keep that up. I'll go help Jessica. Shout if you need backup." She steers me into her bedroom.

The bedroom is the first place that doesn't feel entirely like Bonnie. The walls are deep blue, and the bedding is slate gray. There are splashes of color, and Bonnie obviously uses it, but it feels different.

"Do you live here on your own?" I ask softly.

She pauses as she rummages through her closet. "I do now. Used to live in the first floor apartment with my man, but he's gone. Aha! Found some stuff that's probably about your size. Those days are behind me, but as you can see, I'm not that great at decluttering." She pulls out a couple pairs of jeans and some shirts. "Here, take these and you can use my shower. It's through there. Towels are under the sink to the left."

Her bathroom is once again a shrine to all things Bonnie, aside from a solitary razor near the sink, and a bottle of cologne with dust on the top. I take out what's left of my braid and shower quickly, using the shampoo and conditioner she has standing on the side of the tub. It smells like watermelon candy. Slowly, the hot water sinks into my bones and I grin.

I'm free.

Okay, not *free* free, but as close as I've been in a long time.

These people aren't keeping me because they have a cruel master plan. Here I'm not rat girl, Victor's little punching bag. I can just be me, Jessica. Anne's nanny.

I barely recognize the girl looking back at me from the mirror when I'm done. I brush out my hair and actually leave it to dry loose around my shoulders in soft brown waves. Without my hair pulled back and slicked down, my glasses even look kinda cute.

I try on the first pair of jeans. They're tight, but with a little wiggling they fit just fine. The only problem is that they hug me like a second skin and there are horizontal slits cut all the way down the fronts of my thighs. I turn around and look over my shoulder, blushing at how sexy they are. No one's ever seen my butt that clearly.

Could I really be the kind of girl that wears these jeans? Maybe I need to find out before saying no too fast.

The first shirt is a pretty pink, but it's cropped so high I'm afraid my boobs are going to fall out. Nope. I can only handle so much so fast. I end up settling on a black sweater that isn't too short or too tight.

It's soft and fairly modest other than that the neck hole is huge and it keeps falling off my shoulder.

Seeing myself in the mirror gives me a little thrill. I don't know if this is who I want to be, but maybe it's one version of who I could've been if I'd gotten the chance to grow up normally instead of being kept under lock and key.

Nervous, I walk to the living room and clear my throat. They look up from their game. "How do I look?" I wet my lips nervously. Bonnie picked these out in the first place, but I still feel self-conscious. It's way more revealing than anything I've ever worn.

"You look amazing, Jess!" Anne yells eagerly. "Like Sandy!"

Bonnie chuckles. "Do kids still watch that movie?"

"Oh, definitely. At least girls with limited streaming options. Last summer was non-stop Greased Lightnin'." Nervously, I twirl.

"Gorgeous. You're going to have to watch out. If the sluts get a look at you they are going to think there's fresh blood to compete with."

"The *what?*" I ask in horror.

"The sluts. Club girls. Don't know if you noticed, but there aren't exactly a ton of women around here. Forget what you know about feminism when you go through the front gate. This is a boys club, and girls are only allowed if they have something to bring to the table. If you know what I mean."

"That's horrible! I thought you said they weren't like that."

She snorts. "I said they wouldn't hurt you or Anne, and that's the truth. I never said they weren't a bunch of Neanderthals. Around here you're really only going to find two types of women. Old ladies like me who have a man willing to put his name on the line for her, and the girls who are just here for a good time. Most just drift through for parties, but the ones the boys take a liking to and let stick around are called sluts. Not everyone makes the cut, so it's a badge of honor around the clubhouse. You don't have to like it, but they made their choice and they're fucking proud of it."

I look over to see Anne pretending not to listen, but her person on the TV is running aimlessly in circles, not aiming her gun anywhere. I give up. So long as she makes it out of this with all her fingers and toes I'll be happy.

"Now what'dya want for lunch?" Bonnie asks, slapping her hands on her thighs and standing up. "Someone will be up to check on you soon enough I think. Might as well have food in your stomach for it."

11

TEX

I rap my knuckles against the glass on Bonnie's front door. Not sure what I'm going to find on the other side. I know Ghost texted earlier to make sure everything was under control, but shit, they're not used to this kind of life. They might have locked themselves in her spare room for all I know. Bonnie has a good heart, but she's not exactly the softest woman in the world.

"Come in!" Bonnie yells from the other side.

I turn the knob and step inside, ready for a lot of things, but not what I find. "Holy fuck."

The girls are sitting in the kitchen together, and Bonnie has a small suitcase worth of makeup spread out on the table. She's giving Jessica a makeover as

Anne watches. In the background, Mick Jagger sings about Satisfaction.

Jessica turns my way and my world tilts and rearranges itself. Last night, scared with no makeup and dressed in shapeless clothes, she was cute, but it didn't prepare me for seeing her like this. Her golden brown hair is out of the braid and hanging loosely around her shoulders. Her *bare* shoulder. Her skin looks so silky smooth I'm almost afraid to touch her.

But I do, running my calloused fingers over her bare skin as I walk by to go lean against Bonnie's counter and admire the transformation. Jessica's breath catches at the touch.

She's fucking gorgeous. They did a good job dressing her up just enough to make it clear that she's no little church mouse, but nothing that takes away from her natural, innocent beauty.

Jessica licks her lips nervously, drawing my attention right to how full and pink they are. "Is everything okay?"

"More than okay, baby. You look amazing. I just didn't expect to see you looking so..." Fuckable. "Settled in."

She blushes and reaches for her glasses, slipping them back on. It doesn't make her any less pretty. If anything, it proves I have a thing for smart chicks.

"Bonnie has been really nice," Jessica says. "Considering the situation, we're doing pretty well I guess."

"Good, good… Last night was a fucking mess. I'm so damn sorry you have to deal with this, but we can't just let you go home. Either of you."

Anne looks up. "She lives with me."

A live-in nanny?

Jessica nods. "It's okay. I wouldn't want Anne to be here alone, anyway."

"Yeah, we're pretty much family," Anne adds.

Oh? That doesn't sound like it matches up with what Ghost said about her not being Victor's biggest fan. I want to trust her, but I'm not stupid. How much do we really know about this woman?

Jessica hesitates but she smiles at Anne. "I've worked for Mr. Kane for a long time. She's like my little sister."

How the fuck long could she have worked there? "How old are you?"

"Twenty-one."

I want to get her away from her sidekick. Both because she's fucking hot, and because I want to get her somewhere she can talk without a kid listening to her every word. If she isn't really what she seems, it's better to find out now.

"Hey Bonnie? You good with watching Anne for a while? I'm heading over to the Burnout to meet Ghost and Riot, and I think maybe Jessica could use a field trip."

"Sure, we're good here. We have a criminal empire to build, right kid?"

"Yep!"

"What do you think?" I ask Jessica. "It's not quite freedom, but it beats sitting around here all day."

"I don't know…"

I push off from the counter and get closer to Jessica. "Come on, you look too damn good to waste the day in here. You're officially off duty. We'll keep you safe."

She looks up at me with big brown eyes, framed by sexy round librarian glasses. "Promise?"

I twist a lock of her hair between my fingers and give it a tiny tug. "Cross my black fucking heart."

She smiles shyly and looks away. "Okay."

More than one brother takes a good long look as I lead Jessica down from Bonnie's place and over to where my bike is waiting. She loaned some leather boots and a jacket from Bonnie, and if I didn't know better, I would say she fits right in.

She doesn't have a fucking clue how it looks when I help guide her though getting onto the bike behind me. Last night was an emergency situation, but this feels different. All the boys know the score, but when she puts her arms around me and settles against my back, it feels like a fucking statement.

"Stay close and hold on. Do you remember last night? When I lean, you lean, got it?"

"Got it," she answers. I can feel the nod, and I can sure as fuck feel her hands slide around my chest and flatten over my abs.

If we weren't on high alert, I'd be tempted to take her down the coast for a ride so she can see that a motorcycle is more than just a way to get from point A to point B. It's a beast with as much temperament and personality as a horse, and as close to flying as we can get without leaving the ground.

Don't want to piss Hellfire off, though. Bringing her to the bar shouldn't be a problem since all three of us will be around to make sure nothing happens. The Burnout is practically club grounds, and right around the corner.

I doubt it's her sort of place. Barely above a complete dive bar, but that's just the way we like it. I take it easy on the drive and pull up out front alongside the long line of other bikes. The storefronts on either side are blacked out, but big neon letters proclaim The Burnout open, even if all the bikers milling around didn't give it away. Rock music rumbles out the front door, loud enough to feel the vibration in my chest.

I put my hands around Jessica's waist and lift her off my bike before she gets the chance to try and do it herself.

"I can do it," she grumbles.

"I'm sure, but then I wouldn't have the excuse to put my hands on you."

Her cheeks are already pink from the ride, but they go a shade darker. I rest a hand on the small of her back and guide her to the door.

The bouncer opens as soon as he sees my jacket. "Tex," he greets with a curt nod. "Your friends are at the bar." His gaze lingers a little too long on Jessica.

"Thanks." I switch my hold, putting my arm over her shoulder. She might only be around until this shit gets sorted, but she's ours for the moment and I don't want anyone to fucking doubt it.

12

JESSICA

I don't have a ton of experience with men, but the way Tex walks with me feels possessive. Like he's a big scary dog, growling every time someone else sniffs in my direction.

I kind of like it.

Especially because as soon as we're inside, if I didn't have him next to me, I would've run right back out. I've never been anywhere like the Burnout. It's smoky and dark, the air heavy with leather and beer on top of the musk of people crammed together.

I can hardly see a thing with all the tall, leather-clad bodies blocking the way. I have to rely on Tex pushing his way through like a plow. I stick close as he splits the crowd easily with his massive bulk.

Tex leans down so I can hear him. "Let's get you something to drink and grab a table."

I nod, feeling like a total fake. Looking around, I fit right in wearing Bonnie's old clothes, but I have no idea what I'm doing. The closest I've ever come to a bar is watching TV, and even then I've been limited to what I can watch with Anne.

Is it obvious? Lots of people seem to be looking my way. Maybe everyone can see it on my face that I don't belong here. Heart pounding, I play it cool and trust that Tex and the others will keep me safe.

Bonnie was right about this being a man's world. Guys outnumber girls by a large margin, and the women that are here are mostly on the arm of a man. A girl about my age, in a ripped tank top and a little skirt that barely hides anything, watches Tex pass with open interest even though she's in the lap of a big, bearded biker with her arms around his neck.

I narrow my eyes and glare at her. She grins and turns back to her man, nuzzling the side of his neck as he talks to another guy. Still deep in his conversation, the biker slides his hand up her shirt and she wiggles on his lap.

Watching feels wrong, but I seem to be the only one that feels that way. Is that… Is that the kind of thing they're going to expect from me? Would they even want it?

Do I want them to?

And now that I have that stuck in my head, it's hard to get rid of. I'm inexperienced, not naive. Growing up in Victor's house definitely stripped me of my innocence in everything but the literal sense.

I don't see Riot and Ghost until we are practically at the bar. Tex once again lifts me up onto the stool. It's funny how easy it is to get used to being moved around. It's kind of fun.

"What the hell?" Ghost asks. "You think it's a good idea to have her here?"

"Bonnie had everything under control. They were playing dress-up in her old clothes. Seemed a waste not to let Jessica show 'em off."

"I'll say," Riot runs a hand through his dark hair, pushing it out of his eyes. "You clean up nice, Mary Poppins. Want to know what else a spoonful of sugar helps go down?" He flicks his tongue against his top lip and winks.

"Some of us aren't so bitter we need the extra help," Tex says with an easy laugh.

Ghost snorts and raises his hand to get the bartender's attention. "What's your poison, Jess?"

"Um... a cola? I don't really drink." I examine the wallful of bottles behind the bar, not even knowing where to start.

The bartender comes over. He's totally bald and reminds me of Mr. Clean if Mr. Clean was a biker. A gold hoop hangs from one ear, and tattoos crawl out of the neck of his t-shirt and wind around his neck. "What'll it be?"

Tex orders his usual, whatever that is. Ghost and Riot both have short glasses with something golden brown in them, and they ask for a second round of the same. When it comes to me, Ghost cocks his head and considers. "Cherry Rum and Coke for the lady, make it sweet."

When the drinks show up, the guys grab them and we find a table off to the side. They each take their own, but Riot holds the last glass out of my reach.

"What? Isn't that mine?" I'm not even sure if I'll like it, but I definitely want to try. I don't know how long this freedom will last, so I'm not going to waste a minute of it.

"It comes with a cost." He winks. "One kiss."

I blink. I've never kissed anyone, but obviously he doesn't know that. They probably assume I'm a little shy and not the usual type to hang out in biker bars, but they probably also figure I've had all the usual relationships and experience for a normal girl in her twenties. Would that girl go along with his teasing?

If I'm going to have a first kiss with someone, I could do a lot worse. Hopefully in a few days I'll be free to finally get on with my life so it won't even matter if I'm a bad kisser. This is just practice.

Oh God, I'm going to do it.

"Okay." I lean forward, hoping I'm getting this right.

When Riot's lips touch mine, I freeze, with no idea what to do. It's so much warmer and softer than I imagined, and his beard tickles my chin. He cups the side of my face and strokes my cheek with his thumb. "Am I that scary? I'm not forcing you, honey. Just playing. It's meant to be fun."

"I'm just… nervous I guess."

He chuckles, angling my face so I'm looking right into his deep, brown eyes. They crinkle at the corners as he smiles. "Let's try again. Just open your mouth a little and go with it, okay?"

I nod, just a little, not wanting to shake free of his tingling touch on my skin. I part my lips, and this time, when he leans in, we fit together better. More intimately. His tongue teases over my lips, nudging my mouth even a little more open. I close my eyes, not believing that I'm doing this, but trying to follow his lead. When our tongues meet, I get goosebumps. The taste of him is intoxicating, making me hungry for more.

He pulls away, leaving me confused and breathing heavy. "That kiss was definitely worth a drink." He laughs, and sets the glass in front of me.

I grab the drink and take a gulp without thinking. I cough a little from the fizz of the Coke, but it goes down smooth. Sweet from the soda and the cherry, with a slight bitter undertone that keeps it from being too syrupy. There's a whole, artificially bright red cherry on top. It's good. I put the glass down half full, not noticing the spreading heat of the alcohol until after. Wow.

When I look up, I find all three of them watching me, Riot clearly pleased with himself, Tex looking amused, and Ghost impenetrable. They're so in character I let out a little giggle.

It's the drink, I know it is, but I'm enjoying it anyway. It's easy to forget that the only reason I'm here is because of violence. I take off Bonnie's jacket, adjusting my top so I'm not flashing anyone. But even if I do, who cares?

Freedom is so precious, so fleeting. I refuse to waste any of it. The Burnout isn't on any Michelin star guide, but it's perfect all the same. I finish my first drink, listening to Tex tell a story about how he got a particular scar on his arm, his drawl really coming out when he's storytelling.

"So I thought I'd counted the shots. I knew the type of gun he had, and how big the mags were, so I was too fucking cocky. But it was a raw chase, both of us running our bikes at the limit, dodging cars on the highway, and I guess math was never my strong suit. I thought he was out and opened the throttle all the way to catch up, and the fucker shot me. Nearly ended my biker days there and then." Tex shrugs off his jacket and pulls up the right sleeve on his T-shirt.

There's a bright white line that slices through his shoulder and the top of his arm. "Burned like a motherfucker, but I managed to ram him right over the barrier and into the median. Beat the crap outta him for shooting me, then collected the bounty."

"I'll drink to that!" says Riot and raises his glass. The others follow and that's when I realize my glass is empty.

"I'll get the next round," Tex offers. He pushes away from the table, and when he comes back, he holds out a glass with something pale and golden. I reach for it, and this time it's Tex holding my drink away. "Pretty sure there's an established price for this."

I blink, confused for a moment, before looking to see Riot's reaction. I kissed him first. Does that mean anything? He waves his hand at me and laughs. "I don't own you, honey. Pay for your drink."

Twice as much practice is a good thing, right? I have time to make up for.

Tex takes a sip from my glass, and when our lips meet, he tastes like honey and something more. His stubble is scratchy, not like Riot's softer beard, but his lips are like velvet against mine.

This time I have a better idea of what I'm doing. Tex's kiss is more demanding than Riot's. He slides his fingers into my hair so he's cupping the back of my head and holding me close as we kiss. His tongue moves against mine, sweet and hot. Maybe it's the drink, but I'm on fire all over, sparks arcing over my skin and threatening to burn me to ash right where I sit.

It feels so freaking good. I close my eyes and breathe him in, soaking up everything that's been denied me. By the time he pulls away, I've completely forgotten this is just a game. At least until he sets the glass on the table and pushes it in front of me.

"This is called a Bee's Knees. Go easy on it, they're stronger than they taste."

I take a sip, remembering this same flavor on his lips, but this time getting more than just sweetness. There's lemon and something bitter in there as well.

"What do you think?" Tex asks.

I'm not sure if he means the drinks or the kissing. "I like it."

As the drinks get low and the music goes up, I find myself fixated on if we're going to get a third round or not. And if we do, is Ghost going to demand the same payment as Riot and Tex? He's so different from the other two, not nearly as cold and scary as I thought at first, but he doesn't seem like the type to joke around.

Alcohol, it turns out, is a dangerous thing, because when I finish my glass, I lick my lips and brush my fingers over my bare shoulder. I want to tease him just to see what he does. "So what drink are you going to get me?"

It's like one of those record scratch moments in a movie, where everything stops and the narrator says, "You might wonder how I ended up like this..."

Riot and Tex freeze mid conversation and look back and forth between us, half incredulous, half curious, waiting to see how it pans out.

Ghost's eyes narrow, examining me like he's got me under a microscope. Like he's mentally flipping through my possible motivations. Did I make a mistake here? Poking my head into a cage expecting a housecat and finding a tiger. Maybe alcohol is more trouble than I realized.

But then the corner of his mouth quirks, just a little. "You want me to pick?" The way he asks is full of implication. A threat and a promise, both of which send chills down my back.

I look at him, down at my empty glass, then back up at him. "Please."

He slides off his stool with a languid movement that's reminiscent of a great hunting cat and stalks to the bar. When he comes back, he's carrying nothing but a tiny little glass. It looks like an itty bitty coffee with whipped cream on top.

"Come here and get it," he commands.

Hypnotized, I walk around to him. "Um, do you want me to…"

"After."

I reach for the glass, but he takes my hands and pulls them behind my back. "How am I supposed to do it without my hands?"

Riot laughs like I said something funny. "Traditionally, you only get to use your mouth."

"Are you guys teasing me?"

"Nah, he's right," Tex confirms.

Hm. I guess it's a pretty small glass. I take a breath and lean over. Fortunately it's a high table, so I don't have to bend down or anything. It's a stretch, but I get my mouth around the rim, tasting whipped cream. I feel silly as I stand up and tip my head back. I'm expecting a coffee flavor, but it's just sweet and creamy. Ghost is there the whole time, right behind me. He takes the glass as soon as I've swallowed, a tiny bit spilling out onto my lips and chin.

He buries his fingers in my hair, but instead of cupping my head like Tex did, he makes a fist so he can control where I'm looking. His other hand slides along my thigh, over my hip and then settles on my butt. He makes me look up at him with a tug on my hair, and then yanks me close, right up against him, with my face tipped up.

Ghost doesn't give me a kiss. He takes it.

I melt against him as he plunders my mouth. There's an intensity about him, like I'm the only other person in the universe. Our kiss is only a single moment in time, both infinite and over far too soon.

It ends as suddenly as it started, and he eases me back so it's easier for us to look at each other. Someone nearby actually whistles.

"What was that?" I whisper.

He slides his index finger over my chin and pops the tip into his mouth. "Blow job shot."

13

GHOST

Jesus Christ. It's a good thing I'm going slow and the club is nearby. I'm riding one-handed, with the other holding Jessica's wrists so she doesn't forget to hang on. It'd be really fucking embarrassing if she fell off the back of my damn bike. I'm finding her a fucking helmet if she can't hold her drinks better than this.

Is she... is she *singing*? It's hard to tell over the wind, but I'm pretty sure she is.

That kiss was fucking worth it, though.

Usually, I stay way the fuck away from the innocent, shy types. Not that we get many of those around the club, but occasionally a girl gets an itch for something her usual boy scouts can't scratch. Some of the guys get off on that shit, but I can't be fucking bothered to play that game.

But there's something about Jessica that doesn't quite fit. My gut's telling me she's not lying, but there's more to her story. She's got a solid fucking backbone under all that sweetness. I like it.

Maybe it's just been too long. It's been two years since we cleaned house in the club, and I haven't had time for anything but rebuilding. Aside from the shit with Kane, it finally feels like we can breathe again. There's even a few prospects that'll probably be sworn in soon. In spite of the rumors, I'm not actually a fucking robot.

It would be nice to have something soft to sink into at the end of the day. Something that isn't just about getting off.

We roll through the gates into the compound and park in front. As our bikes shut off, it's obvious that she is, in fact, singing. No idea what, because the words make no sense and it sounds like one or two lines stuck on repeat, but it's fucking cute.

"She alright?" asks Tex, as he gets off his bike.

"Yeah, just hammered. Wanna grab her?"

Riot gets there first, supporting her as he helps her off the bike. "Easy does it."

Jessica blinks, a little unsteady, but then she pulls herself together. Somewhat. "Anne. I gotta check on Anne." She takes a step towards the main house and groans. "So many stairs."

"We'll get you there," Riot assures her.

"Do you think they're still awake?" Her eyes widen so much at her sudden realization that it's fucking comical. "I don't want to wake them up. Bonnie's been so nice to us. She's really, really nice."

Tex laughs. "So long as you don't piss her off, yeah, she is. But if you don't wanna make too much noise, you can crash in my room."

She smiles. "That's nice of you."

"Plenty of room at my place too," says Riot with a grin. "Bigger bed."

"Back off. Neither of you fuckers are taking her into the dorms, alright? If she stays anywhere, it's with me in the side house."

Tex rolls his eyes. "Give us some fucking credit, huh? I like my girls saying yes, yes, fucking yes, and to be sober enough to know whose name to be screaming."

"Yeah, mine," Riot says with a shit eating grin.

"Go to bed." I make it clear it's not a fucking request. "I'm taking her back to my quarters. It's more secure and fewer people have access. No matter how much fun she is, she's still a hostage. We can't forget that."

Jessica leans against Riot, eyes closed. I'm not sure she's paying any attention.

"You think she'd run?" Riot strokes a hand down her hair, letting it continue down to the curve above her ass. She makes a happy little noise.

"Nah. But we take no chances." I ease her away from Riot and pick her up, settling her in my arms with hers around my neck. "Kane's supposedly back in that fortress he calls home, so there's a good chance we'll make contact tomorrow."

"I don't feel great about handing her over to him. Or the kid," Tex says with a frown. "I know we need to negotiate for Cooper, but we all know Kane's days are still numbered."

"Yeah, I getcha, but we have to keep following the

script for now. Besides, a girl like her isn't gonna want to stick around here long term anyway."

We split up, with Riot and Tex heading to the old school building we turned into quarters for the members. I cross the small lawn between there and the side house. Back in the day, it was where the nuns lived, but we divided it into four separate units for officers or other ranking members that needed more space. Right now it's just me and Savage in there.

"Not going back," Jessica mumbles. "I hate him."

"Relax. You're not going anywhere tonight, baby."

I set her down on the couch after letting myself in. My place isn't huge. None of ours are, but there's a separate bedroom, and I have a decent sized living room with an open kitchen. Nothing fancy, but more than the hotplate, microwave and mini fridge most of the guys have.

I grab a bottle of water out of the fridge and hand it to her. "Trust me. Drink something before you pass out. It'll make the morning a lot less painful."

Jessica yawns, but as soon as the cold bottle is in her hand, she seems to wake up a little and look around.

"This is nice. I like those." She points to the black and white motorcycle pictures I have on the wall.

"I took them."

"Really?" She does a double take.

"Yeah, don't look so surprised. Never been any good at painting or shit like that, but cameras are cool." When did I last have anyone new in here? I don't even remember.

She leans over, snuggling into the couch. "I'll just sleep here."

"Like fuck you are. Come on." I pull her to her feet before she passes out and walk her to my bedroom. "You can shower or whatever you need to do in the morning. Bathroom's through there if you need it." I flick the light on as we walk by, in case she needs to find it fast in the dark.

"I don't have a nightgown or anything."

Funnily enough, I don't fucking have any either, but I grab a T-shirt out of my dresser. "Here, you can wear this. It'll be big on you. Get changed and keep drinking that water. I'll be back in a sec."

"Oh. Thanks." She flips the shirt around, looking for the right hole. Great.

I get ready for sleep in the bathroom, not wanting to make her uncomfortable by having to change with me right there. I thought I gave her plenty of fucking time, but even so, when I open the door, I get an amazing view of her from behind as she pulls my shirt over her head.

Fuuuuuck.

She looks hot as shit, with long, curvy legs, a nice round ass, and a graceful back with cute dimples right at the base. It's a shame to cover it up, but then again, I like seeing her in my clothes.

I clear my throat before coming in, love seeing her jump. "You take that side. It's a clear line to the bathroom if you need it."

She blinks. "Um, okay. Are you… Are you sleeping on the other side?"

I pull off my shirt and jeans, tossing them on my laundry pile. "Is that a problem?"

"N—no. Of course not." She might be sobering up, but I have a feeling that if she wasn't still a little tipsy, she wouldn't be so fucking obvious about staring at me like that.

Especially when her eyes drop to the bulge under my boxer briefs. I sigh. "Baby? You need to get in bed and go to sleep right fucking now, because if you keep looking where you're looking, there's just gonna be more to look at, and I don't think you're up for that. Read what I'm saying?"

Her cheeks flush bright pink and she crawls under the covers really fucking fast. "Sorry."

I can't help but laugh. "Nothing to be sorry about. I wouldn't mind giving you a show, but I'm trying to be a fucking gentleman here."

Jessica looks at me, her lips gently parted and an expression on her face that makes me wonder if she'd rather I didn't try too hard.

"Go to sleep," I growl, turning off the light before I do something she'd regret.

14

JESSICA

WHERE AM I?

My eyes pop open, showing me an unfamiliar wall.

Last night comes back to me in fragments. Bar, rock music, drinking... kisses. Oh my God, the kisses. I kissed all of them. Tex, Riot and Ghost. And I liked it. A lot. I think I even did pretty well, not that I have anything to compare it to, but they didn't have any complaints and I'm pretty sure guys like them know the difference between a good kiss and a bad one.

I just can't believe I actually did it.

The bed shifts, and someone makes a low, sleepy noise. I slap a hand over my mouth, holding in the squeak of surprise. I turn as carefully as possible to see who I'm sharing a bed with, because I'm very sure it isn't Anne.

Ghost is asleep beside me. He's kicked off the blanket, and his head is turned the other way, with one arm slung over his eyes. I want to reach out and touch him, but it might break the spell.

His hair is undone and loose on his pillow. It's shaved close on the sides, but long enough down the center to let him bind it back most of the time. Red glints in his short beard, and his lips are slightly parted. My eyes trail down his body, taking in the light dusting of hair on his chest that thickens as it approaches his boxers. His torso is covered in scars, signs of a dangerous life lived. Really dangerous, from the looks of it. And where there aren't scars, there are colorful tattoos, just like up and down his arms. At least there aren't any girlfriend names that I can see. Then my eyes drop lower.

My mouth goes dry, and it has nothing to do with not drinking enough water before I fell asleep.

Wow, from the look of the bulge under those shorts, he's big everywhere.

What if I... No, I can't. But he's so still, so deeply asleep.

Slowly, ever so slowly, I inch my fingers closer to his leg. The moment my skin brushes his, he stirs. I quickly pull my hand back, biting my lip as he shifts in bed and sighs. The moment he settles back into sleep, I can't help it. My hand slides down again, and I trace my fingers lightly across his thigh. I feel him stir, and then, all at once he jackknifes in bed and has me pinned beneath him before I can react, a knife at my throat that came out of nowhere.

I stay completely still, heart pounding like a rabbit caught in a snare. The most terrifying part is that I don't even think he knew he was doing it, because I'm inches from his face and I can see as comprehension fills his eyes and the tension in his body slowly fades. The hand holding the knife relaxes, but the blade stays in his grip. He looks like a feral creature, still ready to strike.

"Fuck!" he snarls, tossing the knife. "God damn, motherfucker! What the hell were you thinking?"

I'm shaking. It was a split-second reaction, but I can't forget the feel of that cold steel pressed against my jugular. "I'm sorry!"

Ghost lets out a long, shaky breath, and his shoulders sag. "Not you. Me. Did I hurt you?"

I shake my head, and then I realize that the heat pressing against me isn't just the weight of him holding me down. He's hard, and that length of his body is pushing into me. The whole thing was terrifying, and I don't understand how it could be so frightening but feel so… good? The sensation of him sliding against me as he moves away draws out a gasp.

He swings his legs off the bed and swallows. "You can't do that. Ever, you hear me? I thought—doesn't fucking matter. This won't happen again, I'll make sure of it. I'd never fucking hurt you on purpose, but if I'm not awake, I'm not myself. Understand?"

"Okay." It comes out as a whisper. The silence feels heavy. "Can I ask you a question?"

He hesitates. "Yeah. Sure."

"What were you going to say?" I inch a little closer, tugging down the edge of the t-shirt he loaned me so I don't give him a show.

"You said you thought something?"

Ghost rubs a hand over the back of his head, his shoulders stiff. "It's been a long time since I had someone stay overnight. I thought I was safe, but I guess fucking not." He gets to his feet and goes to the kitchen, filling a glass with water and draining it in one go.

My eyes go wide. He's hard, and not shy about it. We didn't... No. I'd know, right? This is so awkward. I remember kissing him, and coming back to the club, but the details are fuzzy. "Last night... did we—"

"Am I that fucking forgettable?"

I flush, getting out of bed and tugging at the bottom of the shirt, which only comes to my mid thighs. "No! It's just that everything is a bit of a blur, and—"

Ghost smirks. He puts down the glass and comes close again. His fingers tangle in my hair and he kisses me like I'd imagine a lover might. Deep, but soft and gentle in a way that's totally at odds with what happened just a few minutes ago.

I close my eyes and drink him in, reveling in his demanding touch and the heat of his powerful chest pressed against me. I hold onto his bicep, feeling it flex under my fingers. Suddenly, I'm perfectly willing to believe that I might've done anything he wanted to last night. Because I'm ready for him to do it all over again.

When we part, his forehead touches mine. "We didn't, because you were fucking hammered and I'm not going to fuck a girl while she barely knows who the fuck she is, especially not when she's a virgin."

"I—I'm not!" Even as I deny it, I'm not sure why. I guess it's just that they all seem so cool and sexy and… everything I'm not.

He laughs. "Baby, you'd know if I fucked you last night. You'd still feel me between those pretty thighs." His tongue touches his bottom lip. "And I wouldn't be looking at you standing there in my shirt and thinking about how long until I can jerk off, dreaming of flipping you over and fucking you in my bed."

"Oh." My breath catches, and I squeeze my thighs together at his crude language. It does something funny to me, pulling on a deep heat in my core that I haven't ever felt so keenly before.

"Are you thinking about it?" he asks. "Are we both going to be thinking about it later when we have a little privacy? I fucking will, and I'll be imagining your head thrown back and your fingers busy between those soft thighs as you touch yourself."

My knees are going to buckle. He must see it on me.

"Or maybe you could show me right now. Would you like that?" Ghost steadies me with one arm, and with the other he cups my hand in his and moves it to between my legs, pushing up his long shirt just enough for me to reach. I'm touching myself, but he's the one directing me. "You can do it now, if you want. I know you're wet for me."

Right here? With him watching?

I swallow and take a shaky breath. My fingers curl, putting a little more pressure on my clit, and I sigh, leaning into the feeling. I would never do something like this anywhere else, but it's like I'm in a whole different world here. Where rules don't exist and no one will ever know.

"That's right, baby. Just like that. Show me how you get yourself off. Do it nice and slow for me."

Ghost kisses me, his hand releasing mine, and then his fingertips trail up my legs, raising goosebumps. I keep touching myself, almost hypnotized by him. He's right, I'm soaking wet. I let out a moan, not able to stop the needy sound as I rub a shy circle over the swollen bud. I'm not the only one affected. He's breathing harder.

His big hand slides over the curve of my hip and up my side, pulling the shirt with it, until his thumb is stroking the sensitive side of my breast.

"Ghost," I whisper, not quite believing I'm doing this, but not able to stop now that we've started.

He kisses my jaw, my ear. The tip of his tongue slides along the curve. "Show me," he repeats, his voice low and rough. "Get off on those fingers. Show me how much you need it."

I bite back another moan, but not the small sounds escaping my mouth as my fingers start to work in earnest, sliding over my pussy and playing with my clit. The way he watches me, the feel of his body and his hands on me, and the way he keeps whispering encouragement and filth in my ear... I can feel myself building fast.

I've never come like this before, never touched myself like this with someone else watching and listening and wanting me like he does. He moves behind me, cupping my breasts with his strong hands and I arch into the feeling, my hips grinding against him. He groans and thrusts back, his thickness pressing into me with only his boxer briefs to separate his skin from mine.

"Oh God, Ghost. Please..."

He bites down on the place where my neck joins my shoulder and I explode in a wash of heat, coming hard enough that I nearly scream as he holds me upright against him.

"If I didn't have to go report to Hellfire, I'd be happy to show you how good it can be with more than just fingers," he growls.

As soon as he mentions Hellfire, reality snaps back. I pull away, gasping and trying to make sense of my feelings. Oh God. Anne! She's been alone with Bonnie all night. She's probably so scared without me there.

My voice is as unsteady as I was last night. This is happening too fast. "I need to go. I should check on Anne." I pull away, straightening the t-shirt, and feeling more than a little foolish now that it's over.

Ghost's lips tighten into a thin line. "You okay?"

"Fine. I'm fine. I just want to get back to Bonnie's so I can shower and make sure Anne is alright." I'm still shaking, but I can't quite tell if I'm upset about what just happened, or excited. I don't even know how to describe it. It felt incredible.

It felt… dangerous.

15

JESSICA

I close Bonnie's front door and lean against it.

One day. I've been away from Victor's clutches for one day and I'm already a mess. Pull it together, girl.

As friendly as Ghost, Riot and Tex are, I'm still a hostage here. If I doubted that after what happened at the bar and then just now with Ghost, it was made clear when he walked me straight to her door and waited for me to go inside before leaving.

But to be fair to the Outlaw Sons, I'm still treated better here than I ever was with Victor. If I could choose between being their prisoner or Victor's, it would be an easy call, but will I get to choose? If Hellfire negotiates with Victor and I'm part of the deal, it'd be naive of me to think he'd refuse just because some of his guys might be fond of me.

So far, I've let them keep assuming I'm just an employee because I'm scared that if I tell the truth, they'll think I'm more important than I am. The truth is ugly and complicated, but I can't believe that just having me to kick around is worth it to Victor on top of everything else that's happened.

Maybe he'll finally just forget about me. I'll miss Anne, but pretty soon she won't need me anymore anyway.

"Are you just going to stand there all day, or are you coming in?" Bonnie yells from the couch. Anne's curled up next to her, watching her play some sort of story game on the TV while she offers commentary and suggestions. On the table in front of them are empty fast food bags, and Anne's drinking from a cup with a logo that looks a lot like—

"Is that coffee?"

Anne starts drinking faster like I'm going to rip it away from her.

"Mostly whipped cream, really," Bonnie says. "She'll

be fine. There's a sausage, egg and cheese bagel on the table for you."

I shake my head, but grab the bag. "You guys haven't been playing the whole time since I left, have you?" They're not exactly making it easy to be a responsible nanny here.

"Don't be ridiculous. We made tomato soup and grilled cheese sandwiches last night—"

"With real butter, and the bread didn't even have seeds in it!" Anne crows.

"—I made sure she brushed her teeth and got a full night of sleep—"

"Which was easy since you never came back so I had the whole bed to myself!" There's a hint of an accusation there, but Anne's also grinning like she knows something funny. It makes me wonder how much Bonnie has told her. Or if she's treating this like all of the young adult books she's read with over the top romantic drama.

"—and then I had Poe and Crank head out to get us breakfast." Bonnie shrugs. "Anne has been the perfect guest. It's nice to have a gaming buddy again. General and I used to... well, it's nice." She hands the controller to Anne. "Here, why don't you play for a bit, and I'll be right back. I wanna talk to Jessica."

"Okay!" Anne's still acting like she's on the best vacation ever.

It worries me.

As much as I hate Victor, Anne's innocent in this whole mess. If he really had her mother killed, then she's almost as much a victim as I am. He treats her like a show pony. A pretty possession to trot out when he wants to play the part, and then lock away when it's not convenient.

Maybe we aren't that different. Anne's only twelve, so she's playing video games and eating all the junk food she can. Finally given some freedom, I immediately started drinking, kissing bikers and doing... whatever that was with Ghost.

I take a bite of the bagel and nearly have my second orgasm of the day. "Oh my God. This is so good," I moan.

"Want me to put on a pot of coffee?" Bonnie asks as she closes the door between the kitchen and the living room, isolating us from Anne, who's absorbed in the game.

I don't even drink that much coffee, but with everything else that's going on, why not? I didn't use to drink alcohol or sleep in strange men's beds either, but here I am. "Yes, please."

"Of course." Bonnie smiles. She sets the machine going and pulls out a couple of mugs. "You alright? I got a text from Ghost last night that you were staying with him. I hope he wasn't too hard on you. He's a good man, but not always the easiest."

I can't quite meet her eyes. He was quite hard, but maybe not how she meant it. Though, from what little I know about Bonnie, maybe it is. "It was fine. We just got back late and I'd had a few drinks so we didn't want to bother you."

She laughs at that. "Hah, it takes a lot more than a tipsy nanny to bother me. I bet they just wanted to keep you for themselves. You don't strike me as the four-way on a first-date type, though."

"A what? Four-way?" Holy crap, I've been feeling guilty for a few kisses and some touching and she was wondering if I was... "No! Nothing like that. They took me to the Burnout and bought me drinks. That's it!"

She raises her well styled eyebrows in silence.

"Okay, there was some kissing, but that's it."

More silence.

"Honest! I slept at Ghost's, but I didn't sleep *with* Ghost. Not like that."

Of course, now my mind is spinning ideas about what a foursome might be like even though I can barely imagine what a one-on-one would be like. I've always had an active imagination, though.

Bonnie nods. "I believe you. If you'd said Riot or Tex, I'd be offering to find you a pregnancy test, but Ghost is too responsible for that. I'm mostly surprised he let you stay with him. He's usually very private."

Thinking about the photographs on his walls, and the way he reacted when he woke up, that makes sense. I want to ask her questions about him, but I don't. It feels like a betrayal. I was given a little glimpse into his life, and maybe I'm being silly, but I don't want to shine a light on it to other people.

There's finally enough coffee in the pot, and Bonnie pours me a mug before warming her own. "Milk? Sugar?"

I nod. There is something I'm curious about, and in this case, Bonnie is the right one to ask. "Tell me about General. If it's okay, I mean. You've mentioned him a few times, and he's the one in some of the pictures, right?"

She nods, a wistful look on her face. "He used to be president of the Outlaw Sons. Hellfire was his second in command. Three, four years ago, we took in some new members who weren't happy with how things were being run. At first it was pretty civil, but they were dragging us in a bad direction. General was never gonna go along with it. When they figured that out, they tried to start a war with the Screaming Eagles as an excuse to take over from the inside." She snorts. "That's your first clue they weren't fit to run anything. They didn't have the guts to build from the ground up and thought we'd be easy pickings. They shot General and tried to blame it on the other club. It nearly got us all killed, but in the end Hellfire put himself on the line and the Eagles helped us cut out the cancer. I executed the man responsible for General's death myself." Her expression turns rock hard, then softens again and she sighs. "Killed him with my old man's gun. Didn't bring him back. Felt good, though."

The idea of funny, friendly, caring Bonnie blowing some guy's brains out seems so far-fetched that I don't feel like I should believe her, but I've seen a lot in the past couple days and I believe her. There's no denying the anger and sadness mixed in her eyes.

"I'm sorry. I shouldn't have—"

She waves it off. "It's reality. I'm a grown woman. I can take care of myself. Part of being an old lady is knowing we take on a certain risk loving the men we do. I knew that going into it, but... Oh, he was my dream man. Still is, even if he's not here anymore. I've thought about leaving the club. Most would, and by all rights, Hellfire could boot me out whenever he wants, but this place is my life, and it's my only connection to the man I love. I might not be wearing my property patch anymore, but it's always there, and when my time comes and I join him, it'll go into the ground with me."

"And your game controllers?" I tease, wanting to see her smile.

Her lips quirk upwards. "Maybe those, too. Like Ghost, General was a tough man, but he was good where it counted, right down to his bones. I'll never get him back, but I'll always have those memories."

"No kids?"

She shakes her head. "Nah, it never happened, and then we got old enough that we didn't want to go down that route. In some ways I regret it now, but in a way all these men are my kids." She looks meaningfully at the living room. "I know it's fucked up and won't last, but taking care of Anne has been the most fun I've had since General died."

I finish my bagel and lick the grease off my fingers even though there's a napkin right in front of me. I'm just as bad as Anne. "I really appreciate you taking such good care of her. She's having a blast. God, when I woke up today, I felt so bad, but I don't think she even noticed I was gone."

"Trust me, she did. Sometimes she goes quiet, and I know she's dealing with what's happened, but she's a good kid. Anyway, finish your coffee. I dug out a bunch more stuff that should fit you. They'll come for you later and I bet you'd love a shower and a change of clothes before that happens."

"God, yes. I smell like a bar."

Bonnie snorts, then opens the door to the living room. I take a moment to give Anne a hug while she's playing. "Everything okay?"

"Aah! Watch the arm, I'm almost winning this!" A score pops up on the screen, and there seems to be some sort of pause, because she puts her controller down and hugs me back. "I'm okay. It's a little scary, but Bonnie is so nice to me. I know you're doing what you can to make this better."

Am I? Or am I doing everything I can to help myself, and just hoping she'll be okay? I'm not sure what the right thing to do is. "I'm doing my best. Okay, I'm going to shower."

She wrinkles her nose as she pulls back and grins at me. "Good, you stink."

I gasp in outrage. "No you stink!"

"Don't care. I have coffee," she snaps back then takes a deep sip from her cup, daring me to stop her.

Bonnie's shower has really nice pressure and a detachable shower head. I scrub myself clean, enjoying some time to myself, and only myself. I've got a lot to think about. At least I think I do, but no matter what I try to focus on, it's Ghost, Riot and Tex that keep floating through my head.

The drinks. The kisses. The rumble of riding behind

them on their motorcycles. Ghost touching me this morning, making me touch myself.

And of course Bonnie had to suggest a four-way. How would that even work? The idea of the three of them around me, naked and pressing against me, trading kisses back and forth...

I take her shower head off the hook and rinse off, the thrum of the water beating against my skin lower and lower. I capture my lower lip between my teeth, close my eyes and take it where I want it, teasing myself with bursts of intense pressure and then slow movement along the edge. I brace one hand on the wall and groan, thinking about them and wondering if Ghost is doing the same back in his room like he said. Hot water streams over my tingling nub. I let it build and build and build until I throw my head back with a silent scream of release.

16

RIOT

"Bring them in," Hellfire orders.

Tex nods, going out into the church where Ghost is waiting with Jessica and Anne.

We're using Hellfire's office in the old sacristy to contact Kane. He kept the old wooden cabinets that the priests used to store all their robes and shit, but otherwise it's pretty well gutted, a new desk, and a pinup calendar of topless girls on motorcycles on the wall with a private bar underneath. It's not all fun and games, though. There's all the usual shit you need to run a business, like computers, a printer, and even a fucking ergonomic chair.

"You think he'll answer?"

Hellfire looks ready to tear someone a new hole. "If he knows what's good for him, he will. Right now we're willing to deal, but he's been avoiding us on the usual channels and the clock is ticking. Pretty soon we'll have to assume he killed Cooper and is stalling for time. If that's the case, the gloves come off. We can't sit around while he's preparing to mount a counter attack."

Tex and Ghost return with the girls between them. Anne is wearing sweatpants that are rolled up at the ankles, and a hoodie that's three sizes too big. Her cheeks are pale, and she looks very nervous and young. This isn't a fucking place for a kid.

Pisses me off that we're doing this. That it's our fault, but what's done is done. We can't undo taking Cooper's job.

Jessica is a completely different woman from last night. Her expression is frozen into a neutral mask, with her hair back in a braid like we first found her. Bonnie's clothes again, but just plain jeans and a black hoodie. She takes Anne's hand.

Hellfire nods at the girls. "I'm sorry to put you through this, but it has to be done. You said this is his private number?"

"Yes. As far as I know, the two of us, and..." Jessica flinches. "Marissa, his girlfriend, are the only ones that have it. It was only supposed to be for emergencies."

"Nobody say a fucking thing until I give the word." Hellfire puts one of our burner phones on his desk and dials the number Jessica provided. He puts it on speaker as soon as it starts to ring.

Once.

Twice.

The third one barely starts before there's a click. "Who is this? Anne? Jessica? Speak to me." It's Kane's voice alright.

Jessica draws her breath to answer but stops herself. She looks like it takes physical effort to force down the reflex, and she doesn't look happy about it. I don't know what kind of hold he's got on her, but there's gotta be something.

Taking care of his daughter. Living in his house. That's not a part time job at the mall you stick with just to pay the bills. She's been there for fucking *years*, and she's only twenty-one.

"Kane," says Hellfire, his voice full of false smiles. "So glad you could talk. You've been a hard man to track down."

"Do you have a normal name you can give me, or are you going to force me to call you by some ridiculous biker name? I don't know how anyone is supposed to take you idiots seriously when you're all walking around sounding like cartoon villains."

Hellfire laughs, not rising to the bait. "You took us seriously enough when you were running with your tail between your legs and piss in your shoes. The name's Hellfire, but you can call me whatever the fuck you want. Unless you want to call me Daddy. Gonna have to pay extra for that."

"Classy as expected. My daughter and the nanny, both alive?"

"Of course. Unlike you, we take care of our women."

Kane literally growls. "Prove it. They're the only ones that could've given you this number, but a little torture would be easy for animals like you, wouldn't it? Proof of life before you get one more word."

Jessica visibly flinches. She pulls Anne closer, and turns to Ghost for support. He puts a hand on her back, and it makes me feel… jealous isn't quite right, but it ain't wrong, either. I don't know what happened between them after he took her back to his room, but feels like there's something building there.

Hellfire nods to Jessica.

She nods back. Her hands are shaking enough that Anne is starting to look scared. "I'm here. So is Anne. We're both safe. They haven't hurt us." She nudges Anne.

"I'm here, Daddy." Anne's chin wobbles, but she's a tough kid. I guess growing up with Kane as a father would make you that way.

"Anne was your responsibility, Jessica. If anything happens to her, I'm holding you personally accountable."

"I'm sorry, sir. I'm doing my best." Jessica doesn't even look surprised. She flinches like a fucking dog that's used to getting swatted.

I didn't like the guy before, and he's not exactly winning me over now. What the fuck did he expect her to do? Ghost frowns, and Tex looks pissed.

"Jessica's taking good care of me," Anne blurts out.

"Not good enough."

Hellfire holds up a hand, signaling for everyone to shut up, and pointing to Jessica and then the door. Ghost nods, leading them back out of the office. "There you go. Maybe not happy, but safe and sound. Your turn. Put Cooper on. I want to know where we stand before we go any further."

"He's on his way. I haven't kept him in my office just in case you'd call," Kane sneers. "Besides, all the bitching and crying gets old. Blah blah blah. Maybe I let the wrong idiot fall."

"He's not the only one that keeps bitching. Just get him on the fucking line." Hellfire's tone is even. Unbothered. There's a reason Hellfire was General's second in command.

A minute, maybe two, pass while we wait. No one says anything, but each passing second raises the tension in the room. Give me a fight any day over sitting around waiting. If I could reach through the phone and choke the life outta Kane, I would.

"Hellfire? It's me. I—I'm fine."

Hellfire has to let out a little sigh. "You okay?"

"A little worse for wear, but all ten fingers and toes. Service and food could be better, though." He's trying to keep a light tone, but there's a note of embarrassment that's easy to pick out, even for me. I don't blame him. I'd feel like a dumbshit, too.

"Take him back," Kane snaps to someone on the other side. "There, are you happy? You showed me yours so I showed you mine. Now tell me how you see this going."

"Easy. Cooper for your little girl."

"And Jessica."

"We'll let the nanny go as soon as your kid is out of our hands. I'm sure she's dying to get back to her life."

Kane chuckles darkly. "No deal. I'd be trading you a man who wants me dead and has proven he's willing to pay for it. The girls are a package deal. I want them both. That's non-negotiable."

"Why does the fucking nanny matter?" I ask out loud before catching myself. That does get me an annoyed glare from Hellfire, but I already opened my big mouth. "What? I can't be the only one wondering."

"Because she's *mine*, that's why," he snarls. "But I have a counter-proposal for you."

"Alright," Hellfire says. "Let's hear it."

"Whatever Cooper's paying you, I'll double it if you'll work for me." The fucker sounds so smug it makes me wanna rearrange his face.

What the fuck?

Hellfire raises his eyebrow, genuinely surprised. "Why the fuck should we work for you?"

"Same reason you took this job. Money. Forget Cooper. He's an old idiot with a grudge. You can't seriously care what happens to him. You bring Anne and Jessica to me, and we'll draw up a contract. You've shown that in spite of everything, you have promise. I'll let you keep your little club, but you work for me. Think about it. How much time do you waste doing odd jobs for whoever's paying? I have access to some of the best gear in the business." There's a creak in the background. Chair maybe? I picture him leaning back and rubbing his hands like the villain he thinks we are. "Even if we manage to avoid killing each other long enough to do the hostage exchange, neither of us could afford to stop looking over our shoulders. You know it as well as I do. But if you worked for me, well… then we would know where we all stand."

Hellfire is quiet. Too quiet if you ask me. "Interesting suggestion."

I look at Tex, who's looking right back at me, neither of us happy.

Hellfire gives us a glance, then continues, "That's not the kind of thing I can say yes to right away. Give me a day or two, and your word that Cooper is safe while we negotiate."

"Done, as long as the same goes for Anne and Jessica. Hurt either of them, and the deal's off. I want regular updates. Think hard, Hellfire. You could stand to make a lot of money here. I make a dangerous enemy, but a generous employer."

Bull-fucking-shit.

"I'll call you back in two days," Hellfire says.

"Forty-eight hours. Not a minute more. I'm not going to let Jessica and Anne just sit and rot in that dump. And I swear, if they're not returned to me in the same condition they were in when you took them, I'm not going to be merciful. You know I have the means."

Hellfire cuts the call.

"You can't be fucking serious about listening to him. He—"

"Give me a little fucking credit." He cuts me off sharply. "Cooper's an idiot and a liability, but we took the job. That fucker is treating us like we're the same as him, no loyalty. He doesn't understand shit, but this gives us a little time."

I blow out a sigh of relief.

"But you asked a good question." Hellfire's fingers drum on his desk as he thinks. "Why does he give a shit about the nanny? You said she hates the fucker, right?"

Tex nods. "That's what she says, and I don't get the feeling she's lying. But…"

"But what?

"He's got a hold on her, and it's not just because he's her boss."

Hellfire takes the phone off the table and slips it into his pocket. "I don't like unknowns. I know she looks all cute and innocent, but that doesn't mean it's true. Find out what her deal is."

17

TEX

"Did Victor say something? What's going on?" Jessica asks. Her eyes dart between us, looking for reassurance.

As much as I want to tell her that everything will be alright, I can't. If she's been holding back something that could get our men hurt or fuck up the plan, her stay is about to get less comfortable. "We just have a few questions, and we know you can't speak freely in front of Anne. We're using one of our meeting rooms."

I really fucking hope my gut is right. We all do.

Ghost leads the way into the dorms. The whole building is a mishmash of whatever we need at the time. Most of the old classrooms have been converted to private rooms for the brothers, but the old cafeteria is still used for eating and hanging out, and the old gym has been stocked with workout equipment on one side, leaving the other free for shooting hoops.

You can hardly even see the blood stains from the executions anymore.

Other rooms, like the old teachers' offices are mostly used for storage, or meetings or interrogations. Which is exactly where we're taking Jessica.

Her steps slow and she hangs back. "I'm not on his side. You know that, right?"

I nudge her forward, rubbing her upper back as she walks into the room. "Relax. We're not trying to freak you out. We just need to clear up a few things. Nobody's going to hurt you."

It's an old break room, with a round table in the center and some chairs. Riot pulls one out for Jessica. She takes it, but she's looking real skeptical. Don't blame her.

Riot and I take either side of her, with Ghost across the table. He's being real fucking quiet, which a lot of people might not see as unusual, but

I know him better. He's no happier about this than we are.

Jessica's thigh brushes against mine, soft and inviting. I put a hand on her leg, trying to give her a little connection. I know what it's like to feel like everyone is against you.

Jessica lets out a shaky breath. "Okay. What do you want to know?"

"Before we start, there's cameras in this room. I can't turn them off, but I don't want you to think we're trying to trick you into anything." Ghost points to two spots in the room where tiny lenses are watching, hidden where they aren't obvious. "Tell us your full name and how you came to work for Victor Kane."

She shifts in her chair, uneasy. "Um... Jessica, Jessica Ainsley, and... it's complicated."

Shit. Not what we wanted to hear. Complicated usually means a whole lot of bullshit. "We got time, honey. Start at the beginning."

"It's not—" Jessica's face crumples. She takes off her glasses and stares down at them, her soft brown eyes sad. "I don't really work for him. Not exactly. Ugh.

That's not true. I do work for him, but it's not by choice."

Ghost leans forward, his expression dark. "Did he traffic you?"

"What the fuck?" Riot jerks back, shocked.

My eyes are locked on Jessica, taking in her reaction. She was surprised by the question, but she's doing a good fucking job at schooling her emotions. Just like she has been this whole time. Ice fills my gut. We thought we were the worst thing that's happened to her, but what if that's not true? I'd bet my life that her fear has been real. If she's some kind of special op ninja bodyguard for Anne, I'll eat my fucking boots.

Ghost keeps going. "Listen, we aren't the bad guys, not today anyway. We're not out to hurt you, and nothing you say gets back to Kane, I fucking promise you that. No matter what it is, you're safe with us."

"Not trafficked in the way you're thinking," she finally answers. "Or maybe it is. I don't know. I was eleven when he took me in."

"Were you on the streets?" I ask. "No shame in it, I've been there myself." Ever since I could get away from my asshole family. Just glad I found the Sons before the streets did me in or put me in prison.

She shakes her head. "No. I had a totally normal life until he killed my parents."

Even Ghost looks surprised at that little revelation. "He fucking what?"

Riot growls low in his chest, like a warning rumble. If Kane was here now, he'd be a dead man already, no further explanation needed. "You're gonna have to clarify that a little."

"I hate him so much. He's a monster, and I'm not going back." Jessica's shaking with anger. She doesn't look like a shy little mouse anymore, there's fire in her and it's finally blazing. "I don't care what it messes up. I'm not. Going. Back. You think you hate him? Try being me. I've spent ten years getting kicked around. Anne is the only good thing in my life. You want to know how long I've worked for him?" Her head snaps up. "He started me easy. Cleaning when I stopped trying to run away or hurt myself. Then helping Anne's old nanny when I was too tired to fight anymore. I was fourteen then. By the time I was sixteen he got rid of her, because what was the point of paying someone else when he had me?"

"Whoa, honey, you gotta slow down." I put my arm around her, trying to pull her closer. She shakes me off.

"Slow down? I don't even know why he had my parents killed. They must have done something to make him mad, but I wasn't part of it. I was a kid!" Tears run down her cheeks. "Would you do to Anne what he did to me?"

"Of course not. What kinda animals do you fucking take us for?" Ghost snaps.

Riot inches closer, like he's trying not to startle a wild animal. "Does he... did he... touch you?"

She laughs, but it's an angry, bitter sound. "It's not about sex. He's never even looked at me like that. But he's real fond of letting me know it every time I mess up. Never where you can see the bruises. That wouldn't fit the aesthetic, and Anne might ask questions."

I want to fucking kill him. I already did, but now it's personal. "Did he let you go to school?"

"No, but I had a tutor, same as Anne. After I got my GED, he made me take some online courses so I could better help her with her work. He made me into what he wanted me to be. I read the books Anne reads. Watch the movies and shows that she likes." Jessica looks around, eyes rimmed with red. "I'm not looking for pity. I lived in his house and ate his food. I go on luxury vacations and my best friend is a twelve year old girl who deserves the world. She's so much better than him, and I'm scared that if I'm not there, he's going to turn her into a monster just like him."

"Think back, baby. What do you know about your parents? Tell us anything, even if you don't think it's important," Ghost says.

"Um... Mom worked with computers, I think. Dad was in the military?" She shakes her head, unsure. "I think he was an officer, but I'm sorry, I don't remember. We lived in the suburbs. Had a pool. Mom and I were trying to convince Dad to let us get a dog."

"Do you remember their names?"

"Chester, Chester and Becca. We used to tease Dad because Chester is such an old guy name. Why? Do you think it matters? Victor has hurt so many people. Anne and I don't usually hear the details, but it's hard to miss that he isn't exactly a law abiding citizen, even if I didn't know from personal experience."

"Chester Ainsley. Tell me why that sounds familiar." It's tickling my brain.

Riot's fist hits the table. "No shit! Cooper!"

She looks confused. "What do you mean?"

Ghost leans back, head cocked to the side in thought. "You're supposed to be dead."

18

JESSICA

Bonnie opens her door and hands me a mug. "Here's your coffee. Brrr, I don't know why you're sitting out here. It's colder than a witch's tit."

"I'll come back in soon. I just wanted to watch the sunrise."

She nods. "Suit yourself."

Steam rises from the top of the mug. I blow on it, watching the swirls drift away. I feel…

Free.

Light.

For the first time in as long as I can remember, I'm not carrying anything alone. Oh, I'm still a hostage, officially anyway. I can't leave the compound any more than I could leave Victor's tender care, but it's not the same. Not at all. I'd been holding onto the burden of my past for so long that I didn't even understand the full weight anymore.

Even as I hoped to be free, I didn't dare open my mouth in case I found myself right back where I started. Victor beat rebellion out of me young, and if he was willing to do that to a child, I don't want to think about what he would do to me if he thought I had to learn my lesson all over again now. His little corrections were bad enough.

Seeing the looks on Riot, Ghost and Tex's faces as I told them my story healed something inside me. They might be violent, criminal, impulsive, crude, and a hundred other things that make them unfit for Victor's fancy society, but they were horrified.

And instead of getting me in trouble, confessing has bought me a little more freedom.

The freedom to sit outside when it's really too cold, and drink coffee made with too much sugar while watching the sun rise over the sliver of ocean I can see from the top step of Bonnie's apartment.

The sky is a swirl of orange and yellows. It's beautiful. If I make it out of this, I want a tattoo of exactly this. The sun coming up over the ocean, and promising a brand new start. The guys have inspired me with all their ink.

Is it crazy that I actually like it here? Because of my position—*former* position—I got to experience some of the luxuries of living with Victor, but I'd happily trade them all for coffee on the stairs and cereal with marshmallows.

Or maybe it's the company I like.

The dreams I had last night about Tex, Riot, and Ghost were pretty vivid. My subconscious has turned out to be wilder and kinkier than I could've ever imagined.

"Hey!"

I look down at the sound. There's a biker standing at the far corner of the church, trying to get my attention. I don't recognize him, but that's not unusual. Aside from my guys, I really only know a half dozen of them on sight. My guys. I grin at the thought. They aren't actually mine, but it kinda feels like it.

He motions me closer.

I'm only wearing socks, but I take my mug and tiptoe down the steps so we don't have to yell back and forth. "What?"

"I was sent to get you," he grumbles. "They want to talk to you more about Kane."

"Who? Hellfire? Ghost? Let me go get my shoes."

"There's no time. Come on." He looks annoyed, and I get a bad feeling about this whole situation.

"Let me just go tell Bonnie where I'm going. I don't want to worry her."

"Stop being so fucking difficult! I was sent to get you, and I'm going to do that," he hisses, voice low and pissed off.

"I'm not even wearing shoes!" I hiss back, stepping off the final step and onto the cement paving stones below. "Why are we being so quiet?"

He moves fast, grabbing me before I can run. My coffee mug drops to the ground, shattering and spilling its contents out in a steaming puddle. I try to scream, but he clamps a gloved hand over my mouth and holds me tight as he drags me into one of the deep nooks in the side of the old church where we'll be out of sight unless someone walks directly in front of us.

"Easy there, ratty," he whispers into my ear. "Wouldn't want to draw too much attention now would we?" His voice drips acid, and I finally place it. Troy, one of Victor's men. Just needed him to start calling me names first. "We need to have a little chat."

I struggle, but he's too strong. I try to cry out, but his grip covers my mouth so completely I'm struggling just to breathe. Troy was always one of the guards I avoided at all costs. Most of them were nasty, but just doing their jobs. Troy enjoys being nasty just a little too much.

I rear my head back, managing to smack him in the face. Not hard enough to make him let go, but enough that he draws a sharp breath between his clenched teeth.

"You little bitch. You're going to fucking pay for that. Victor wants you back, but he never specified in how many pieces. We could leave some fingers behind for your new boyfriends to find if you don't quiet down. Fucking slut, you looked pretty comfortable up there. I bet you're down on your knees already for these animals, eager to please. It was always bullshit that we weren't allowed to fuck you." He pulls out a vicious looking knife that looks deadly sharp. I stop immediately, totally believing he's willing to cut my fingers off. "That's better," he growls in my ear.

I wait, shivering against him and terrified for whatever's coming next. My chest draws so tight I'm surprised my heart is still able to beat. What is he doing here?

"I like the new clothes." He runs a hand over my tight jeans, cupping my ass. "You know, if you dressed like this back home, maybe you wouldn't be so alone all the time. Maybe that's why he keeps you in that old lady nanny uniform. I bet Mr. Kane is waiting to have you all to himself once the kid is shipped off and doesn't want our sloppy seconds."

Voices carry on the cool air as a couple of Sons come closer. I don't recognize them right away, but I have to get the attention of someone—anyone—if I'm going to get out of this.

Too bad Troy isn't too dumb to understand what I want to do, though. With one hand still firmly over my mouth, he tips my head back and runs his knife up the front of my shirt. "Easy now, we don't need any heroes, do we? I'm supposed to bring both of you back, but if you somehow don't make it in the confusion, I'm sure Mr. Kane will understand."

Does he really think he's getting out of here? The Outlaw Sons can't be more than twenty feet away as they come up the walk and pass by the old rectory, on their way to the garage, but I don't dare risk it. I've fought too hard to survive this long just to let this asshole be the end of me right before I finally get to live my life.

"What the fuck? Bonnie could use a little decluttering, but I don't think smashing her shit on the ground is the way to go. Not very mindful," notes one of them, his voice curious.

"Mindful?" the other one says with a laugh. "What the fuck are you talking about?"

"You're so fucking uncultured. I was watching this documentary about organizing, and…" Their voices trail off as they keep going, the sound of their boots fading along with my hope of a rescue.

"Is Anne up there? Where you were sitting?" Troy growls softly. "If you're helpful, I'll not only let you keep all your fingers, I'll even show you how to use them when we get back."

That's definitely a threat rather than a promise. If he thinks that's going to make me help him, maybe he really is that dumb. I pretend to try and speak, muffled by his glove.

"Are you going to behave?" He presses the knife against my throat. There's a slight sting, followed by a trickle of wetness. "Shit," he mutters.

Ghost would absolutely destroy him. Even half asleep, he had more control than Troy. But that doesn't help if Ghost isn't here.

I don't even want to nod, in case it drives the blade deeper, but I do just barely, and make a noise that I hope sounds affirmative. Finally, he takes his hand off my mouth. I draw a deep breath, feeling like I can breathe for the first time since he grabbed me.

"The school," I whisper, hoping to send him to the place that has the best chance of being filled with bikers at this hour. It might kill me, but I'm not repaying Bonnie's kindness by sending him her way, or putting Anne in danger.

"She's in the school? Fuck. Where?" He relaxes his knife hand.

I slam my heel backwards, catching Troy on the inside of the thigh and not quite on his balls as I'd intended. There's a sharp pain across the side of my neck, but either I'm dying or I'm not. Worrying about it will just waste time. "Help! Someone, help me! Please!"

"You little bitch," Troy roars. "I'm going to—"

"Going to what?" snarls Riot's gravelly voice.

Troy's head snaps to look in Riot's direction, giving me time to pull even farther away. I run straight past Riot, making a bee line for the steps and not stopping until I'm out of their reach. After a quick glance to make sure I'm clear, Riot aims his deadly gaze on my attacker.

Troy holds up the knife trying to defend himself, but Riot only pauses long enough to get into a ready position as they start to circle each other.

"Who the fuck are you?" Riot growls, promising some pretty horrible things with the furious tone alone. "And why was her NECK BLEEDING?"

"Fuck off," snaps Troy. "I'm not telling you shit."

Riot chuckles, sending a chill down my spine. He's usually so easy going. This isn't a side of him I've seen yet. "You gonna stick me with that toothpick? I'm gonna make you fucking eat it unless you drop it right now."

It's not a threat, just a fact. Like this is already predetermined. Troy doesn't have even a little bit of a chance, but he doesn't know it yet. I'm not sure I should watch, but I can't look away.

Troy jumps forward, swinging the knife at Riot. Not fast enough. Riot sidesteps, grabs Troy's arm and uses his momentum against him, throwing him forwards until he crashes into the wall with a loud grunt. Riot rolls his shoulders to loosen them as he advances.

Troy whirls to face him, holding his knife up but not looking so confident anymore. Riot shakes his head. "Want to try again? I dare ya."

Troy lunges, but this time Riot doesn't send him anywhere. Instead, he grabs Troy's wrist and twists him around into a grapple. There's an audible crack followed by Troy's high-pitched scream.

They spin around and I wince when I see the front half of Troy's lower arm sticking out at a weird angle, his shirt sleeve soaked dark with blood.

"You should never have fucking touched her!" Riot roars. The noise is drawing a crowd. Yelling and footsteps, but Riot's only focused on Troy. And now he's the one holding the knife.

Troy must know it's over, but he charges, screaming. Riot jams the blade right into his mouth and through Troy's throat. His eyes go wide, his scream turns into a gurgle, and then Riot twists his head sharply to one side with a sickening crunch of bone and cartilage. When he lets go, Troy drops to the ground, limp and lifeless.

"Told ya I'd fucking make you eat that knife."

I turn away so I can throw up.

19

JESSICA

"Jesus, Riot. We were planning on questioning him," Savage says.

He showed up right after Riot killed Troy, along with someone they called Sinner. Instead of an Outlaw Sons patch on his vest, Sinner's says *prospect*.

"We were tracking him on the cameras. Wanted to give him enough rope to hang himself, and when I saw he went straight for Jessica, I thought it would be a good idea to see how she reacted. We were already on our way when you hulked out on him."

Riot's furious expression nearly sends me running and it's not even me it's aimed at. I'm amazed that Savage doesn't seem phased. "Look at her fucking throat and tell me that you had it all under control!"

"Look at how you're acting and tell me you're not biased!" Savage snaps right back. "But it went further than it should've. I'll give you that."

"Does Hellfire know? Or were you acting on your own?"

"He'll know soon enough. I'm not hiding anything."

I'm still wiping the taste of puke out of my mouth when Savage comes over. He crouches down and puts a hand on my back. "I'm sorry we didn't act faster. We weren't sure it had anything to do with you until he'd already made his move."

"Did I pass the test?" I look him in the eyes and he takes my anger with a nod, no excuses.

"That fucker deserved what he got," Riot declares over his shoulder at Savage. "I fucking dare you to tell me otherwise."

"Nah, it was an honest kill. Just would've preferred you disabled him. How's her throat?"

Riot tips my chin up and examines the cut. It stings when the skin stretches. "It'll hurt, but not too deep. Doesn't need stitches."

"You knew who he was. Right, Jessica?" Savage asks.

"Not at first, but yeah. His name was Troy. He's worked for Victor for a while. I don't know exactly how long, but a few years at least."

"What did he want?"

"He didn't say a lot, mostly just threats, but he wanted me to tell him where Anne was. I—I tried to send him towards the school, but then Riot showed up."

"Is that enough? If you were watching you should know she wasn't in on it. I'm going to go get her cleaned up unless you got a fucking objection," Riot growls. "She's not even wearing shoes."

Savage nods. "Go on. I'll report to Hellfire and Ghost. Our timer isn't up with Kane, so I'm sure he'll have something to say about it. This is clearly a breach of the deal."

Riot scoops me up. I expect him to bring me back to Bonnie and Anne, but he takes me into the school where they questioned me yesterday. We don't go in the same direction though, he carries me up to the second floor and stops in front of a door with a plaque that says Riot. He shoves the door open and kicks it shut behind us.

I look around. His room isn't bad for a converted classroom. The ceiling is high, and there are windows all down the side opposite the door. In one corner, they've built out a small box room that could be a large closet, but is probably a small bathroom. Along that same wall is some basic kitchen stuff. A counter with a sink, a microwave and a small fridge.

There's a shabby, round table with a couple of chairs, but most of the room is the bed.

Riot opens the door into the little room, confirming that it's a bathroom. He returns with some first aid supplies and a wet cloth. He kneels in front of me while I fix my eyes on the ceiling so he can examine my neck.

I draw a sharp breath when he starts cleaning the blood. "It stings."

"Could be a lot fucking worse. You're still breathing. He didn't get you too bad." Riot pulls out a large, rectangular bandage that he applies like a patch. I'd be surprised, but I guess with the life they live they're prepared for anything.

"He wasn't supposed to kill me." And that's when the enormity of it all hits. I almost just died. Victor would have been mad, but Troy seemed willing to take that chance. A sob wells up inside me, and I can't hold it back. And then I'm ugly crying, all the tension draining as I fully realize exactly how badly that could've gone.

Riot pulls me close so I can bury my face into his neck. "Hey... You're gonna be okay. I promise. Things are gonna work out."

I look up, my lips quivering as I try to stop my tears. "Are they? God, you guys broke me! I never used to cry. Crying just gets you in more trouble."

He laughs and hooks a finger under my chin, careful with my bandage. "Honey, even I know that's fucked up. You aren't alone anymore. Let it out once in a while. It's okay. You're not broken, you're healing."

Riot leans in, and then his soft lips are against me, his thick, soft beard brushing my face. Stunned at his words as much as the kiss, it takes me a second before I kiss him back, but it doesn't take long before he teases my mouth open and our tongues are dueling. Kissing and crying, all at once. God, I'm such a mess.

When he pulls back gently, a horrible realization comes to me. "Oh God, I must taste like puke! I'm so sorry!"

He laughs. "Relax, Maria. I knew what I was getting into. I think I got a spare toothbrush, if you give me a sec. Or do you want a shower? Your shirt is…"

I look down, where blood has dripped all over my clothes. "Yeah, that sounds good. Who's Maria?"

"Sound of Music?"

I blink in confusion.

"Add it to the viewing list, nanny." Riot pulls a shirt out of a dresser next to his bed and throws it my way. "Come on, let's get you cleaned up."

I follow him into the small bathroom.

He grabs a towel off a hook and gives it a sniff. "It's clean, I swear. I just wasn't expecting company. Are you good? Do you need anything?"

"No, but…"

"What?"

"It's embarrassing. Could you leave the door open? I

know I'm safe in your room, but I thought I was safe out there, too."

Riot's expression shifts, his eyes darkening and a playful smile tugging his lips. "You want me to keep you company, baby girl?"

He stalks forward, forcing me backwards until I bump against his bathroom wall. He cages me there, hands on either side of my shoulders. He's so close that I can feel the heat of him, but we aren't touching anywhere else.

Not yet.

My breaths come fast as he lowers his lips, stopping just short of kissing me. "Can you? I don't know if I want to do… anything, but…"

"Not gonna do anything you don't want." He undoes the button on his pants, pushing them down and revealing his boxers.

"Wait!"

"What's wrong?"

I have to tell him what happened with Ghost, right? What if it means something? I don't know what I'm doing and they're obviously friends. I don't want to cause trouble. "The other morning, when I woke up with Ghost, we... fooled around."

Riot smirks. "That old dog. Tell me more."

"We didn't have sex, but he made me... I guess technically I made myself, but only because he told me to!" Ugh, that explanation is about as solid as Swiss cheese.

"You played with yourself for him? Did he watch you come?" Riot doesn't look mad, he looks really freakin' turned on.

"Yes," I whisper.

"Damn, sure wish I was there to see it."

"He's not going to get mad, is he? That I'm in here with you?"

"You're worried about our feelings?"

"Well, yeah. Of course I am."

"Baby, no one's made any commitments here. I can't speak for everyone, but me, Tex and Ghost, we understand and respect each other. So long as you keep your little playtime explorations to us, you're fine. We're having fun. If things start getting serious, we'll talk about it and you'll know. Fair?"

I nod, relieved. I might not understand biker culture, but it's pretty clear they play by their own rules. I pull my shirt over my head.

The room is small, and it's awkward to undress in front of each other, but it's kind of fun, too. He's built like a Greek statue, but I'm no goddess. Nobody has ever seen me like this before.

Riot looks me over, then whistles softly. "Fuck, you're gorgeous. Let's get you clean before we get dirty." He pushes back the shower door and leans in to start the water.

I'm naked. With a naked man. And we're going to shower together. If I hadn't had my encounter with Ghost, I'm not sure I'd be this daring, but now I want to see what Riot will do, and how it'll make me feel.

The water's just shy of scalding, exactly how I like it. I try not to think about how much he's seeing as he helps me tip back my head and let the water run through my hair without getting too much on the bandage.

"Hold still," he says, and gives the shower head a nudge so my hair is out of it, before he starts rubbing in shampoo. His strong fingers massage it into my scalp in a way that makes my knees weak. I put my hands against the tiled shower wall for support and close my eyes. It's easy to forget we're completely naked when he's making me feel this good.

He rinses, keeping the water off my face with his hand, then reattaches the shower head. I try to move back into the stream, but he stops me. "Wait." Riot takes a cloth and squirts some body wash on it. The rough texture feels good on my back, and even better as he moves downwards over my hips and down my legs.

"That feels nice," I whisper.

"Good." His voice is deep and raspy, more than usual.

I try not to think too hard about how he's got to be looking right at my butt when he's down low like that. The washcloth comes up the insides of my legs, but it's not until he passes my knees that I start getting nervous for real. Nervous, excited, tingly. Hot, not just from the shower, but from deep inside as well.

"Um…"

"Easy, girl, easy."

Swallowing hard, I step a little wider to give him room. He passes my knees and glides over the insides of my thighs. I close my eyes again, leaning into the wall so I don't fall. Just as I think he's going to touch me between my legs, he veers back instead, sudsing up my butt. Part of me wishes desperately he continued all the way up instead of taking a detour, the other part of me relieved.

"You're being very thorough."

He's been rubbing my butt a lot more than it needs, I'm pretty sure. And it has an effect on me. I don't mean to push back against him, but I do anyway.

"This ass deserves a lot of attention," he says with a little laugh, and then he stands. He steps close, right up against me. Something thick and hard presses against the small of my back, and it takes a brief moment before I realize what it is. "You're poking me," I whisper.

He slides the washcloth up to right underneath my breasts. "With you in front of me, it's impossible not to. Is that too much?"

I deserve to live a little, don't I? Heck, I deserve to live a lot. While I'm here, shouldn't I take everything I can get while I can?

"No. You're fine." I shake my head for emphasis. "Don't stop. Please."

"I fucking love it when you're being good for me, but how about we see if being bad is even better?"

20

JESSICA

"I'm still wet!" I squeal as he drops me onto the bed.

He leans in with a grin. "Good."

We were naked together in the shower, but it was so cramped in there that I didn't feel very exposed, and I barely even got a glimpse of him. But this is different. I'm embarrassed for a second, and clasp my arms over my breasts, but then I get a good look at him and forget about myself.

Wow.

Riot is all muscles. Big, broad shoulders, powerful arms and a wide chest that tapers into narrow hips. Muscle shifts in his thighs when he moves, and between them... I was not ready to see all those inches of flesh pointing right at me as he stands at the end of the bed, taking me in. It looks so swollen it must be painful, and every inch of him is glistening right out of the shower.

Something in my memory of biology must be lacking, because I'm having a hard time believing that anything that big is actually intended to go where I was taught. "I... I'm not sure I'm ready for—"

"Relax. There's plenty we can do without going there today."

"Like what?"

He grins and kneels at the end of the bed. "You look good enough to eat."

"You want to do *that*? Really?"

"Fuck yeah, I do." He climbs onto the bed like a leopard stalking its prey, and grabs my ankles, pulling me closer before pushing my thighs back so I'm completely open to him.

God, no one's ever gotten so close to me. Not like this.

"Ooooh!" I let out a shuddering moan as his broad tongue swipes through my sensitive folds. My back arches, pushing off the mattress. Oh, holy cannoli. That's very different from my own fingers.

I close my eyes and focus on breathing as he does it again, sparks blazing down from my swollen nub to the tips of my toes. I'm going to explode if he keeps this up, but if I do, I won't have died in vain.

He hums against me, his lips and tongue working together until my legs are trembling and my hands are fisted into the sheets. It's too much, I can't hold on. I'm either going to fly to bits or scream loud enough that the whole club knows what's happening, and I'm not sure I care.

"You okay?" he asks, looking up at me from between my thighs. His face glistens, and I realize that's from me, but it feels too good to mind. "Too much? Want me to stop?"

Is he crazy? With both hands, I thread my fingers into his thick dark hair and pull him against me. "Never stop," I breathe hoarsely. "Please, never stop."

Riot chuckles and gets back to it. He flicks his tongue against the sensitive bud at the apex of my sex. A wave of pleasure rips through me.

The more he works his strong tongue against me, into me, flicking it over the top of me, the more I can settle in and really luxuriate in all the different sensations, including the soft tickle of his thick beard against my thighs.

My fingers run through the thick strands of Riot's hair as he starts to get aggressive. His lips and beard are wet from my body. A molten pool opens deep within me, threatening to overflow. My toes curl and my pulse races as I close my eyes and moan. "Oh, God. Riot!"

He growls right up against me at the sound of his name on my lips. He slides a thick finger inside me, and it's just what I need to go over. The wave of my orgasm crashes down, and I buck up against his face. He doesn't stop, driving me on until I'm limp and panting in front of him.

I didn't know it was possible to feel like that.

Feeling like jelly, exhausted and overwhelmed. I force my breathing to slow, hoping maybe my racing heart will do the same. Every so often, a little aftershock courses through me, a pleasurable twitch, a little carnal reminder of what he just did to me. And when I finally open my eyes, he's right there, lying next to me, propped up on an elbow and looking back

I reach out and touch his face, running my fingers over his features. Those bottomless brown eyes couldn't possibly belong to a brutal killer, but I've seen him in action.

"Welcome back," he says behind a very confident grin. "I was starting to worry I'd lost you."

I shake my head slowly. "No... just floating. Is it always like that?"

"Good question. Guess we won't know until we do some research."

"Oh God, not yet. I don't think I could take it." I roll into him, pressing my forehead against his powerful chest as he puts a strong arm around me. His cock, seeming even bigger and harder than before, is right there between us. I slide my hand down, not sure what to do, but wanting to try. "Show me what to do."

"Not everything has to be an even trade, baby. If you don't want—"

"But I do." I wrap my fingers around him, shocked at the heat, and how velvety his skin is. He draws a sharp hiss when I do, so I let go again. "Was that wrong? Show me."

"Fuck. No, definitely not wrong. Don't stop." He covers my hand with his and moves it over his rigid length, showing me how to stroke him. Slick drops of clear liquid come out of the tip and coat my hand, making it easy to slide up and down his length. "You can hold a little harder. Don't be afraid of it," he says huskily. "Fuck, yeah, just like that."

His breathing comes faster, and I pick up the stroking, trying to keep up. He lets go of my hand and grabs my thigh hard, like he needs me to hold on to. I follow my instincts, building a fast, twisting rhythm until even with my inexperience, it's obvious he's balancing on the edge.

Wetness leaks onto my fingers, his whole length slick as my hand spreads it out. He moans, a heavy grinding noise deep in his chest. His hips move, pumping into my hand, small, insistent thrusts.

His fingers dig into my thigh, so hard it almost hurts. "Jesus, I'm close."

"Show me," I whisper. This is all new. So exciting. I need to see.

"Fuck," he hisses and then he swells against my palm as he thrusts one last time.

His cum burns hot stripes on my skin, some of it going so far that it hits my breasts, then my belly and my thighs. I never imagined how much there would be or how far it would spurt. By the time the last of it slides down the side of his dick, coating my fingers in slick fluid, I feel like I'm covered in it. "Holy crap. I might need another shower."

"Sure. In a minute," he whispers, sounding pleased and lazy. He smiles. "Fuck, you look sexy."

"I'm a mess."

"A sexy mess." His smile widens, intimate and teasing.

"You're sure this won't be a problem with the others?" I kinda want to do it again, and I'm curious to know if it's the same with every man, or if things would be different with Ghost.

Or even Tex. So far we've only had the one kiss at the bar, but what a kiss. I feel connected to him, just like I do Ghost and Riot. Hopefully that isn't one sided.

He shakes his head. "Nah, but I'll have a talk with them. No one owns you. Hell, we'd take real good care of you together. Promise."

Together? Bonnie's teasing about a four-some comes back to me. It seemed impossible at the time, but maybe… no. No. That would be too greedy, wouldn't it?

On the other hand… I dip my fingers in the sticky liquid spattered over my chest, trying to imagine how that would work. Life keeps showing me that nobody knows how much time they have. It would be a shame to waste it.

21

GHOST

Hellfire's phone rings only minutes after our boys confirm that they delivered our present. We were even generous and gave the knife back. Still stuck in his throat.

There's no fucking way we're letting a scumbag like Kane think he can dictate the negotiations, and then fuck around inside our own damn property. If that's what he thinks, then he needs a lesson in how this fucking works. Knowing what he did to Jessica, I'd be happy to teach him.

"Stop growling. He'll think I have a fucking dog in here," Hellfire snaps. Holding the phone up, he taps the answer button and puts it down on the table between him, me and Savage.

Jessica and Anne are also here, with Tex and Riot keeping an eye on them. We need proof Cooper is still alive, because there's no trusting that fucker, and we assume he's gonna ask for the same.

"North Pole, Santa speaking," Hellfire says with a nasty grin. "Sorry we missed Christmas, there was a little confusion. Someone put you on the naughty list."

"What did you barbaric fuckers do to my man?" snarls Kane so loud the phone speaker crackles.

I glance at the girls. Maybe we shoulda had them wait outside the office, but they are as much a part of this as we are. Keeping them in the dark won't do them any favors in the long run.

"The real question is what the fuck was your man doing inside our walls, Kane? We had a deal and you went and fucked it up." Hellfire doesn't give a fuck about there being ladies or minors present. He shifts in his chair and leans back. "I'd like to know exactly what you were thinking when you decided to pull this shit."

Kane snorts. "As if I'd trust you with Jessica and my daughter's safety. Anyone with a brain between their ears would want their own reassurance. You'd do the same."

"Maybe we have. Are you sure you can trust all your men?" I cut in.

I want him running scared. Anything we can do to make this fucker uncomfortable.

"Stop fucking around." There's a hint of a stress in Kane's voice, and I fucking love that we're getting to him.

"Seems to me," Hellfire says casually, "that the one fucking around is you. We've stuck to the deal, kept your girls safe. In fact, the biggest threat to them so far has been your man putting his knife to your nanny's throat."

Kane snarls. "So you say."

"Yeah, so I fucking say," Hellfire says with the kind of ice that means some fucker's gonna get murdered if he doesn't watch his step. I know it well. Often I'm the one doing the honors. "Look, we went into this in good faith. We've kept both your girls safe, and you repaid that by double crossing us. That has to have a price, Kane. You've fucked up once, which means one of the hostages is off the table. Fuck up again and all bets are off. Is that clear?"

"I can destroy your whole fucking club, you know that, right? I'll blow you off the fucking map. Your compound will be the newest beachfront property."

Savage makes a 'blah blah blah' motion with his hand, mimicking a mouth talking.

I stifle a laugh and lean in so he hears me clearly. "We've decided that since your man didn't seem to care if Jessica made it out, that she must not be very important to you. We're not total assholes, so you'll get your daughter back, but the nanny's ours for now."

Anne twists in her seat, looking at Jessica with wide, desperate eyes. Jessica puts her finger against her lips and mouths 'shhhhh'.

I wonder what the girl is more afraid of. Us? Or going home to her monster of a daddy alone. I didn't get the impression that he's been knocking his little girl around, but can't imagine he's much of a father either. He left her behind to save his own sorry skin, if nothing else.

"Out of the question," Kane snaps. "Both girls, and if we're reduced to making stupid threats, then this negotiation is over. We'll exchange the hostages tomorrow."

"And if we don't?" Riot asks with a deadly growl. Ever since he found Jessica in that dead guy's grip, he's been a little blood thirsty.

"Then this is war. And in war there are casualties."

I doubt he's actually seen action. Not the kind he's alluding to, but I have. Enough that I won't lose a second of sleep over his death. And he will die. There are a lot of souls on my conscience, and many that I'd undo if I could.

His won't be one of them.

Hellfire takes over. "Don't be a melodramatic idiot. We can both keep waving our dicks around, or you'll get your daughter back when we get Cooper. The nanny goes wherever she wants once all this is done. If she doesn't go back to you, then maybe you need to look into a better benefits package for your employees. That's not my fucking fault. Now get Cooper on the line. I wanna hear that he's alive. I don't trust a fucking word you say anymore."

"Say hello, Cooper," snaps Kane, obviously annoyed as fuck.

"Hello, Cooper," Cooper jokes, voice shaky. "The food sucks, but they've been keeping their hands off me. Christmas party 2004 was worse."

"There you go. Now let Anne and Jessica speak so I know you animals haven't ruined them."

"I'm fine, Daddy," Anne responds. "But I want my own bed again. My pillows are way better. Has anyone watered my—"

"Where's Jessica?" Kane interrupts, not even letting her finish.

"I'm here. And I quit. I'll take care of Anne until this is over, but I'm done. Do you hear me? *Done.*"

Anne gasps. "Jessica! No!"

"You don't get to choose, Jessica," Kane says, menacingly. "And to prove it, you said I could only have one of them. Give me her. Jessica for Cooper, and then when it's over, you give me Anne. I don't think even you people would hurt a child."

The fuck? "You want Jessica before your own daughter?"

Anne looks like someone has physically hit her. We've all assumed that his daughter is going to be the most important to him, but now we know more about Jessica's background, sure, we get that she's not just the nanny? But wanting her before Anne is fucking psychotic.

"What the fuck are you playing at, Kane?" Riot growls deep inside his throat.

More to the point," interjects Hellfire. "While Jessica is here, there's someone to keep track of Anne. We're not gonna send her to you, and then play babysitters for a twelve-year-old. What the hell is wrong with you?"

"Dad!" Anne yells, her voice cracking. "I do everything you tell me. What are you doing?"

"It's just business, Anne. One day you'll understand."

"I will *never* understand," she growls, sounding like an angry kitten compared to when one of us does it. "Never."

Jessica tries to pull Anne in for a hug, but Anne pushes her away.

"Here's the fucking deal." Hellfire holds up his hand in a signal for the rest of us to shut up. "I'm running outta patience. You fucked with the wrong club, so you're gonna have to do some thinking. Accept the trade as we've proposed or we're fucking coming for you. I'll let you think about that for a bit. Let's start that forty-eight hour timer again, but this time the ball's in your half of the court. If you don't have anything for us by then, we're coming for you." And with that, Hellfire taps to end the call. "Take the girls outta here."

Tex nods, guiding them out the door. For once, Anne isn't even looking at Jessica. I don't know that I blame her. I'd be pissed if my father chose the nanny over me, too. Not that I know who my father even is, but if I did, I'd probably feel the same.

"What's the next step?" I've known Hellfire for a long time, but if there's anything I've learned about him, it's that you never know what he's gonna do until he does it.

"I will not have my whole damn club held hostage by some fuck that was born with a silver spoon up his ass. We'll let him stew in it, and hope he realizes that he's on the losing end in this deal. Meanwhile, we start prepping gear, call in any brothers that are out on jobs and start strategizing on how we'll burn his whole estate down with him in it." He waves at the door. "Now get the fuck outta my office. I need some time to think. Days like this I wonder why I fought so hard to be in this fucking chair."

22

TEX

I get back to the church after dropping the girls off with Bonnie, to find Riot and Ghost on one of the couches drinking beer. They look like they're in the middle of something. "It's been a long fucking day. Any left for me?"

Riot reaches down to where there's already a bottle waiting by his side. He throws it my way. "We've been talking."

"I've been gone five fucking minutes. How much talking is there to do?"

Riot doesn't bother beating around the bunch. "Jessica."

"What about her?"

"I want her, and I don't want it to be a problem with you guys."

Ghost swings his bottle from the tips of his fingers. "He got a little taste this afternoon and wants to go back for the main course."

"You wanna claim her? I like her too, but you've known her like three fucking days."

Riot shakes his head, but he looks conflicted. "No! I mean, not yet. I like her, but none of us know where she'll be in a week. If she's smart, she'll get the hell out of town and not look back. And don't put it all on me. I'm not the only one. She and Ghost fucked around the morning after we went to the Burnout. She confessed to me today because she was feeling guilty about messing with both of us. It was fucking adorable."

"Well, shit. I didn't know I had to take a number if I was interested." I haven't known her any longer than they have, but if I'm being honest with myself, I've been waiting to shoot my shot too, and it sounds like I might already be too late. "What did you tell her?"

Riot takes a long drag from his beer. "That she's free to do what she wants, but that if she wants to keep things simple, stick to the three of us. I could be wrong, but she seemed pretty happy with the suggestion, and I told her I'd make sure we were all in agreement. She didn't want us pissed at each other."

"Three?" My cock perks up along with my ears. Maybe the door isn't closed yet.

Ghost nods. "Yeah, but slow down, cowboy. She's a virgin. Or at least she still was when she left my room."

"Same." Riot confirms.

"We've shared before." I've learned to trust my gut over the years, and it's saying to not pass this up. "Unlike you guys, I haven't had her in my bed, but if no one's objecting and she's game, I'd sure love to get to know her better. All of her."

Riot looks to Ghost and then to me. "So we make this good for her, right? No objections?"

"And what if someone starts feeling a little possessive?" I ask. Hasn't happened yet, but we wouldn't be having this conversation if Jessica was like the usual girls we get around here. From the moment I met her, I liked her. She's got backbone, and fire. It takes a lot of both to make it through what she has without crumbling.

"Then we deal with it like fucking adults," Ghost answers. "This club is my home and you two are my brothers. I won't get in your way if you've got something you want to pursue."

I shake my head at him, laughing. "Are you that sure you're not the one that'll want to put a patch on her?"

"It's not... I'm not safe for her," he admits. "She's dealt with enough shit in her life, she doesn't need mine on top of it."

"Still having nightmares?" Riot asks softly.

Ghost stares down at his bottle. "No, not for a while. That's why I thought it was safe, but I nearly took her out when she woke up before me."

"But you didn't."

"No, but that's not a risk I'm willing to take."

"I fucking like her," slips outta me before I fully think about it. There's something about her that makes me want to keep her safe from any more bullshit like she's already been going through. Is it her? Or just a fucking savior complex? I don't know. But I want to explore it, and her.

Riot nods, oddly serious for him. "We're in agreement then? No matter what happens in the future, we give her a taste to remember us by?" He holds his bottle out, bottom first.

"Agreed." I clink it with my own.

Ghost does the same. "I'm in. There's a party tonight. Let's bring her."

23

JESSICA

THE INSIDE OF THE CHURCH HAS A TOTALLY DIFFERENT vibe when there's a party going on. The lights are low, and the whole place is flickering with candles while heavy music fills the air. Tex grabs a plastic cup off the bar and fills it from a keg before handing it to me with a flirty smile. "Gotta make sure you start the evening right."

I take it, feeling a little extra blasphemous in spite of not being religious. Since the whole church is a motorcycle club now, I suppose parties in the church are par for the course. Up front, the baptismal font is filled with ice, and has bottles sticking out of it.

I take a sip. It's beer. Not my favorite, but right now Anne is mad at me and even though I don't blame her, I'm in the mood to forget about it for a few hours. Besides, she has Bonnie, her new best friend.

Okay, maybe she isn't the only one feeling a little replaced.

"Where are Ghost and Riot?" I ask.

"Don't worry, they'll be here a little later."

Slow, groovy hard rock fills the old church, seductive and grindy. There are even more people here tonight than there were the night Anne and I were brought in. In some ways it reminds me of the Burnout, except here, the only patches are Outlaw Sons. No other bikers are invited to this party, though there's plenty of girls hanging off their arms.

And other places. I take a big gulp of my beer.

"Can I ask you a question?" I lean in so Tex can hear me.

"Shoot."

"Bonnie said the girls who hang out here are called sluts. Is that true? Or is she just messing with me?"

He laughs. "It's true, club sluts is what we call them, but in other places they might be patch bunnies, sweetbutts or a bunch of other things. Some nicer than others. It all boils down to the same thing. They're here because they want a taste of danger and a rugged biker to make them lose their minds, even if it's just for the night."

"Does that make me one? Is there an approved list somewhere? Do I have to put my name on it?" I giggle, more from nerves than the beer.

"Do you want to be?" Tex's hand moves to the small of my back. "Is that why you're dressed up to party tonight?"

"Maybe I do. Do you like it?"

Bonnie loaned me a short skirt and a shirt that's long and flowy but nearly see through, and open on the sides. You can pretty much see my entire bra. She helped me style my hair in big waves, and my makeup is nearly as heavy as the other girls I see in the church. I even have a bright red silk scarf around my neck to hide the bandage.

Suddenly the crowd parts, exposing a circle of cheering men who are watching another two guys wrestle each other right in the middle of things. The men slam into each other a few times before one of them gets a good grip and flips the other one to the ground, though he gets dragged along so they crash together. I squeeze closer to Tex, eager to not get caught in whatever this is. He pulls me in, pressing me against his side protectively.

"Fuck, fine, I give!" the man at the bottom yells, but he's laughing through his thick blond beard.

"Yeah?" The guy over him has gotten one foot on the floor, grabbed the bearded guy's collar and looks ready to drive his fist into the other guy's face. And they're laughing?

"Yeah. Jesus. You go first. I'll grab a beer and catch up later." Bearded guy rolls his eyes and holds up his hand. With a grin, the other one helps him up just as a woman, probably a couple of years older than me, wearing itty bitty cut-offs, a black tank top and motorcycle boots, breaks free from the crowd, only to be pulled right into the free arm of the winner of the fight. She laughs as he holds her against him, his big hand very obviously cupping her breast.

"Were they just fighting over a girl?"

He laughs. "Pretty sure it was just about who gets to go first. That's the kind of thing you can expect if you want to be a slut. You'd be available for whatever member wanted you. Still interested?"

I shake my head. "What would I be if I just wanted that with a few guys?"

Tex grins down at me. "Do I know them?"

"You might."

There's a football game on the TV, but no one's watching. Groups of bikers are talking, and across from us... oh. A guy and one of the sluts are very, very busy making out, and he's got his hand down the back of her shorts, which appear to have popped open in front to make it easier for him. At least she's not between his legs doing what that other girl was doing the first time we came in. I avert my eyes, not wanting to be too obvious.

Tex sits down on one of the couches and pulls me into his lap, facing out. His hand sneaks into the front of my shirt, not groping me, just lightly resting on my stomach. "Go ahead, look all you want. If they wanted privacy, they wouldn't be doing it out here."

I try to look away, but my gaze keeps going back. It looks so raw, so wild, and it's doing things to me.

Tex's other hand rests on my thigh, sliding up until his thumb is under my skirt and just a couple inches from my panties. "You like watching them?"

I swallow and try to pretend it's not making my body heat up, but I'm sure Tex can feel me trembling "I guess. Is that weird?"

"Nah. Watching can be fun." He leans in close, his breath tickling the back of my ear as his hand strokes the inside of my thigh. "Look over there."

Dancing on the actual altar are two women, a brunette and a dyed redhead, wiggling their hips and shaking their asses for the enjoyment of the cheering bikers around them. They're not shy about winding sexily around each other, either. I definitely don't lean in that direction, but anyone can see that they're beautiful, and the way they move, you'd have to be dead not to think it was sexy. I wish I had that kind of confidence.

The brunette pops the bra off the redhead, and after a moment of teasing both her friend and the crowd, she pulls it away and tosses it into the mass of watching men. The redhead has amazing boobs, and she touches them teasingly as they grind together.

Okay, maybe I'm a little jealous. And getting a little horny.

"I can feel you breathing faster, baby. What would happen if I pushed my hand a little higher right now? I bet you're soaked. If you were a club slut, I could take out my cock and slide right in. Do you think you'd make a sound?"

I'm pretty sure that if Tex slid into me, the whole club would be able to hear me.

"I could fuck you right here," he says directly into my ear where only I can hear. The hand on my stomach pulls me close until I can feel the hard outline of his cock between my legs, and his thumb slides just that last little distance to the crease where my legs meet my pelvis.

"Would you like that?" he asks.

I take a deep, shaky breath and shift in his lap. He groans and his hips lift, thrusting under me. Oh God, I think I would.

"I bet you're fucking tight." His voice is rough and raspy. The brunette is on her knees, with the redhead right in front of her. They're kissing, but I lose sight of them when the crowd shifts. Tex's thumb moves higher. "I can't wait to feel you around me, squeezing the life out of me until I can't help but come."

His fingers brush over the thin fabric of my panties, just lightly, but I'm so ready for it and Tex knows it. He knows what he's doing, and I'm starting to realize that he's not just teasing me, but teasing himself, too.

My nipples are so tight and hard, it hurts. "Please."

"I don't think so."

I almost fall off his lap when I spin to look at his smug face. "What?"

"I was talking to Ghost and Riot earlier."

"Oh?"

"About you, and us," Tex draws out slowly. "And about how we all want to show you a real good time. I have a confession to make. They aren't coming to the party unless I send a message."

"I don't understand."

Tex's clever fingers are playing around my belly button. "They're waiting in Riot's room. And if you're down for it, we can go join them. If not, I'll let them know and they'll meet us here. No pressure."

"All three of you? Together?" I can barely get the question out, I'm breathing so fast.

"Mmmhmmm," he hums, nuzzling my neck and dragging the tip of his nose over my skin. He nips my earlobe, then sucks the sting away. "So what'll it be? I know what I want. What about you?"

24

JESSICA

I swallow hard. For a moment the only thing that exists is me and Tex, right up until I hear the girl on the couch across from us moan out loud, "Fuck. Deeper. Cum in me, baby."

"Um… Let's go," I say breathlessly. No judgment, but I think I'm going to stick to the fantasy of public sex for a while, not the reality.

Tex never lets me out of his lap, he just scoops me up and carries me through the church, right past the two strippers—who now only have a single pair of panties between them—and out the door.

He carries me right into the school building, stopping to push me against the wall and kiss me until I forget what we're even doing. We break apart laughing when someone whistles and hoots at us. Then again, when we're at Riot's door, he kicks it with his boot instead of knocking so he doesn't have to lose his grip as he slants his lips over mine and sucks my tongue into his mouth.

The door opens and I fall right into Riot. "Looks like you got started early," he says with a chuckle. "Does this mean you're up for a more private party?"

I nod, tangled in the both of them and not minding one bit.

Out of the corner of my eye, I see Ghost stand up from Riot's kitchen table and throw down a hand of cards. "Damn, I wish we'd been there to watch. Looks like a good time."

"Harmony and Paris were on fire tonight," Tex explains. "Our little innocent here likes to watch."

Ghost looks intrigued. "Is that right?"

"Apparently so," I whisper.

I'm still not sure how this will work, but just like our first kisses, I trust them to show me. My shirt is the first to go, quickly tossed aside, followed by my bra.

Instinctively, I cross my arms over my chest, covering up.

"Honey, no," Tex says roughly. He takes my wrists and pries my arms away. "You're fucking beautiful. Never hide yourself, and especially not from us. We're never gonna hurt you. We'd keep you naked all day if we could."

Riot runs his hands over my hips. "I love your body. Didn't you get that earlier? He moves his hands up to cup my breasts, trapping my sensitive nipples between his fingers and making me draw a sharp breath in surprise. "If not, then I did something wrong, because I want to worship every square inch of your skin." Riot pushes my hair aside to kiss the back of my neck, just as Tex leans in to kiss my breasts. One big biker is nice, but being trapped between two of them is delightfully sinful.

Ghost peels his shirt up over his head as he watches Riot and Tex work me over. He throws it aside, revealing the patchwork of white scars and colorful tattoos that decorates his powerful torso and make sleeves on his arms.

"Stand up," Riot orders, his voice husky in my ear.

With his big hands cradling my ribs, he lifts, helping me.

Tex unbuttons my mini skirt and I wiggle my way out of it, along with my underwear. Then he places a kiss on my belly and starts working his way down, his lips hot against my skin. "We've got a lot of things to show you."

Riot steps back to peel off his shirt and unbutton his jeans, watching as Ghost moves in.

Ghost slides one hand into my hair and another cups my breast. His calloused fingers are rough and possessive, demanding rather than asking for my pleasure. He makes a fist in my hair, tugging it until I have to look his way so he can kiss me.

And when he does, Tex spreads me open down below and flicks his tongue over my clit. I have to steady myself, bracing against Tex's head and Ghost's chest as tantalizing sparks light my nerves on fire. Cool on the outside, Ghost's heart beats fast under my palm, as excited as I am.

"Come here." Riot takes control again, pulling me away from them and onto the bed.

He pushes me down to the mattress, leaving me on my back, looking up at him in all his naked glory. His thick length bobs above me hard and tempting. I smile nervously up at him as I wrap my fingers around it. His pulse races under my fingers. I start to stroke, like he showed me, eager to make him feel good again. His low groan is its own reward.

Ghost climbs onto the bed on my other side, now naked, and every bit as thick and hard as Riot. Tex joins the party, pushing between my legs and pressing my knees towards my chest to get himself full access with his tongue.

I don't really know how to handle one man, never mind three. I don't want to disappoint them. "Y— you guys need to tell me if I'm doing something wrong, okay?"

"It's the other way around tonight, baby. We're going to make you feel so fucking good, so if something isn't working for you, you need to tell us," Ghost growls. He takes my hand and wraps it around him, so that now I have one on each side. "Trust me, watching you enjoy yourself is half the fun. Just stroke real slow while Tex makes you feel good and we'll make sure it all works out."

I nod, and Tex buries his long tongue in my needy pussy, swiping greedily through my folds. I'm so slick with excitement that I can hear it. God, my fantasies were so tame compared to reality. "But I want to learn. Teach me something. How can I make you feel like Tex is making me feel?"

Riot grins and grabs a pillow. "Sit up a little, baby girl." I raise my head and shoulders off the mattress, which gives me a good view of Tex feasting between my legs. Mesmerized, I spread my legs wider to give him room while Riot slides the pillow under my shoulders. "Okay, ease back. Yeah, like that. Fucking perfect."

With the thick pillow under me, my head hangs back a little off the edge. It feels weird until Riot gets into position behind my head and guides his slick cock to my lips.

Oh. Now I get it.

He waits, letting me decide.

"Tell me if I do it wrong, okay?" I open my mouth for him.

"Watch your teeth. Other than that, I don't think you

could do this wrong if you fucking tried," he groans, nudging the thick head between my lips.

I touch my tongue to him, tentatively. Exploring. He mostly tastes like skin, maybe a little salty. A drop of slick wetness touches my tongue as I swipe it over the tip, and I spread it around, exploring the shape and feel of him. He groans, letting me know I'm on the right track.

I love the way they make me feel, but it's also fun to see how I can do the same to them.

I use Tex's techniques as inspiration for my own trials around Riot's cock. It's obviously not the same, but exploring with my tongue, and using different speeds and intensity to see how he reacts as I explore. It's not long before his hips are moving, thrusting gently into my mouth. He must be eager to go deeper, but it's a little scary.

"Put your hand around my base," Riot suggests. "It feels good for me, and that way you can control how deep I go."

I lose my grip on Ghost as he moves to straddle my chest. I can't see him in this position, but I try to reach for him with my free hand, to find his length again so I can make it feel good.

He brushes my hand away, and stops me with his commanding voice, "No, baby. Concentrate on the cock in your mouth and the feel of us touching your body. You've got everything I need right here." There's a little plastic pop, before something cool and slippery drips onto my chest. Did he finish already? No, too cool. He grabs both of my breasts and squeezes them together, wrapped tight around his cock. When he thrusts, he moves easily in the slickness he put there.

I gasp around Riot. It feels strange, but not in a bad way. My breasts are sensitive, and it's a very intense feeling to have Ghost sliding against me, so close by.

Being surrounded by three naked men is deliciously sinful. After being so starved for touch, this is like finding an oasis in a desert. A week ago, I was afraid I'd die without ever experiencing life, and now I'm being worshiped by three hard, dangerous, drop dead sexy bikers.

It makes me feel safe. Seen.

Loved?

It's too early for that. I'm not sure what my future will be, and right now I can't imagine having to choose between them. Tex, Riot and

Ghost are all mixed up together in my head and in my heart. If it came down to it, I think I'd rather leave and have this memory than be forced to settle down with just one and see the others move on.

Jealousy I haven't earned stabs me right in the heart. I shove it away and clear my mind. I refuse to spoil this moment by worrying about the future.

I grab Ghost's thigh, my nails digging into his skin as Tex's tonguing gets more intense. My back arches. If Ghost wasn't keeping me pressed down to the bed, I think I'd fly away. I close my eyes and hold on, remembering how it was with Riot, and feeling that same surge just out of my grasp, but even more intense.

After all, last time I only had one man pleasing me.

Now I have three.

I'm getting spoiled already. Maybe the biker sluts are onto something. If more women knew what they were missing, there wouldn't be enough men to go around.

Ghost slides off my chest, disengaging my claws and leaving me to dig my fingers into the sheets instead, but he makes up for it by leaning in and capturing my nipple in his mouth. His short beard tickles as his tongue swirls around my nipple. He nips lightly, making my core clench. And then Riot eases away from my head, sliding the pillow away and sucking my other nipple into his mouth.

I'm not going to last long. There's no way with all of this.

Pressure builds inside me, like a volcano preparing to erupt. My breathing comes faster and faster. There isn't enough air. My climax is… right… there.

"Oh Fuck! God!" I scream as my thighs squeeze tight around Tex's head and I come apart in a thousand pieces.

I'm drowning. I'm flying. I'm falling.

There are no words to fully describe that fleeting feeling of momentarily being one with everything in creation and flying among the stars, but it's addictive. With the way they touch me, kiss me, lick me…

I'm going to crave this high every day for the rest of my life.

With a gasp, I collapse onto the bed, my thighs releasing Tex instead of trying to rip his head off. Do

I pass out? I'm not sure, but when I open my eyes, they're all looking at me.

"There you are, honey." Tex's grin is wide. He's looking real happy with himself. And he has every reason to be.

"You're amazing," I breathe.

"And we're only getting started," Riot says, taking himself in hand and stroking as his hungry gaze rakes over my naked body.

But it's Ghost who moves between my legs. Instead of putting his mouth there, it's his cock. Not in me, just resting it on the outside, on the mound, but his intention is obvious. His gaze is lust-darkened, gray bordering on black. A nervous shiver races through me.

"Ready to learn something new?" he rumbles.

It's a big step, and I want it. I really do, but I'm scared too.

Apparently my reluctance is obvious. He strokes the outside of my thigh gently. Sparks trail his fingertips wherever he touches me, so I have to focus to listen. "Not gonna force you, baby girl." Ghost's voice is calm, soothing. Comforting. And underneath it all, there's a need aching to break out. "Nobody gets to control you anymore. Not even us. Not without your permission."

Freedom.

The idea is so unfamiliar to me, I almost have a hard time making my mouth form the word. But I want this. I really want this. "Show me."

He smiles, wide and genuine, without holding any of himself back. His fingers on my thigh spread wide, then he bends down and kisses my breasts, first one, then the other. His cock nudges the inside of my thigh as he moves, making me draw a soft gasp.

Riot tosses something that Ghost catches and opens with the tearing of plastic, before he covers himself. God, I'm so naive. I didn't even think about protection. No wonder Bonnie made that comment when I first got here. These men are dangerous in more ways than one.

Tex lies down next to me, taking my hand in his and wrapping it around his cock as he leans in to kiss me on the neck. "Hold on tight, honey," he says with a chuckle.

Riot drops on the other side, capturing my breast in his big hand. His thumb flicks over my nipple. "You look so fucking hot right now."

I reach for his steel hard dick, giving it a squeeze before dragging my nails lightly over that soft skin. He hisses with pleasure.

Ghost takes himself in hand. He slides the thick head of his cock slowly up and down through my folds, spreading my slickness all around and over himself. The anticipation is killing me. I squeeze Riot and Tex. How many other girls have emotional support cocks to keep them busy while they wait for their first time? I struggle to keep a straight face, because I don't want any of the guys thinking that I'm laughing at them.

And then Ghost moves, and I forget all about it.

He goes slow, his hips moving in a sinuous wave as the pressure turns to an ache and I feel myself opening for him and around him. I'm so wet, and beyond ready, but it's still a tight fit. Not pain, but an odd discomfort. The sensation of my body readjusting itself as it learns what I'm capable of.

Riot kisses my breast, then up my chest, over my collarbone, laying down a trail up into my neck. At the same time, Tex starts right behind my ear, then kisses his way in the opposite direction, towards the other breast. And all the while, Ghost works his thick length into me, inch by inch, letting me feel the stretch, and then pulling back before going a little farther. Each time I'm sure I've taken all I can, and each time he proves me wrong.

And then he's in. All the way.

"God yes," I moan, which turns into a little gasp as Riot nibbles my ear. "Don't stop." It's like he's made for me, like a lock and key. It's so tight that I can feel the blood pulsing through his length in a steady thrum as he just holds himself deep inside.

"Fuck, you feel amazing," he groans. "I'm gonna start moving now. Yeah?"

I nod eagerly. "Definitely yeah."

I thought I knew what to expect, but once he actually starts moving, it's a whole new world. The push and pull is so good that tears spring to my eyes. When he's all the way in, I feel stretched so good, and when he's out, I want him back. And as he settles into a steady rhythm, my hips move to meet him all on their own. I was worried I wouldn't have any idea of what to do, but instinct has that covered.

His thrusts grow harder, making my breasts wobble, but Tex and Riot are there to secure me with their talented mouths, and pretty quickly I fall into the rhythm. Stroking them while Ghost fucks me feels like a natural extension of our making love. I'm not sure I'm doing such a great job, but I get no complaints, and they do most of the work, setting their own speed as they thrust into my fists.

The four of us move as a unit, speeding together towards a finish line only we can see. Ghost's thrusts turn short and ragged, the sound of his hips against mine loud in the bedroom. Riot reaches down, and when his fingers find my aching clit, it's all over for me.

I come hard around Ghost's thick cock, moaning and squeezing my eyes tight as my orgasm hits. Fireworks burst behind my eyelids, a rainbow of color in the blackness. And then Ghost groans from deep in his throat and pushes all the way in one last time, coming so hard I can feel the pulse down his full length. It's so hot to think about his cock doing what I watched Riot's do, but inside me. A tiny, and really stupid part of my brain wishes he wasn't wearing the condom so I could feel it, all of it, but this is amazing enough in itself.

I melt into the bed, my stomach muscles actually a little achy after coming twice so close to each other. It's like I've been doing crunches. In a way, I guess I have. I giggle.

"You better not be laughing at me, girl," Ghost growls. It only makes me laugh more, which makes my core tighten around him, and he definitely feels it. "Oh, Jesus fuck." He pulls out, making me let out a soft moan as his thickness leaves me. I miss it already.

"So…" Tex runs a finger down along my side, tracing my shape, leaving goosebumps in its wake. He's still hard as steel. "You worn out then?"

Reaching out, I slide my fingers gently over his swollen tip. He hisses as I trace a line around the pronounced ridge. "Maybe not quite," I tease. Feeling a little more confident now that I know how good it feels.

He laughs as he shifts to get between my legs. "Damn fucking straight." As soon as he's wrapped, he pours a little lube into his hand and gets himself extra slick before gently pushing in. I'm more ready this time, and Tex doesn't have to start as slow as Ghost. He buries himself to the hilt in one long, slow thrust, watching me closely the whole time.

I close my eyes and moan his name as his hips hit mine. It's similar but not, his shape not quite the same, filling me slightly differently than Ghost. Still breathtaking, just different. I'm amazed I can tell the difference.

"Fuck, that's good," he moans, as he starts to move. "You were fucking made for us."

I reach for Ghost and find his muscular thigh, digging my fingers into it. He brushes my hair out of my face and leans in for more of those soul-touching kisses of his. My other hand finds Riot's washboard abs, and I move south until his eager hardness is in my palm. I stroke him in time with Tex's thrusts. As natural as breathing, we're moving together again.

I move my hips in time with Tex, drawing in all of him that I can, wanting him deeper, harder... just more. Maybe I'm greedy, but it feels so good. For the third time tonight, I feel the flames building. It's different now. My nerves are raw and it almost feels like I'm going to come in spite of myself. Every thick inch of him is stroking me from the inside. He's right there with me, braced on his strong, tattooed arms, panting and groaning.

"You're too fucking much, honey," he growls, driving deep and hard until his dick pulses inside me.

I imagine him pumping it all out, filling me until I'm an absolute mess. That's almost enough to tip me all the way over, but not quite. Tex lowers himself in a slow pushup that makes the coiled muscles in his arms and across his chest tense. He kisses between my breasts, over my collarbone, along my neck and down my jaw, right up until he reaches my lips and presses close. God, he tastes good. When he pulls away, I run my tongue along my lips, wanting to keep tasting him that way.

Just him pulling out is almost enough to set me off, so when Riot takes his place, I grab him by the hips and practically force him inside me. He laughs. "Eager, baby? I can work with that."

Riot pushes deep, and I'm glad Ghost and Tex got me warmed up. He's definitely the thickest. He's the broadest, too, so maybe there's a connection. It aches, kind of, but in a sexy way.

He hovers over me, his powerful arms penning me in with his hands pressed into the bed at either side of my head. Rolling my hips against him, I know he's going to take me that last bit, bring me to that final plunge, like going over a waterfall in a little barrel. I grip his strong arms and we lock eyes, as he drives me into the bed, over and over, with the powerful thrust and grind of his hips. Wrapping my legs around him, I hang on for dear life as he fucks the life out of me. He's the roughest by far, but right now, that's perfect. Exactly what I need as the grand finale.

"Almost there, baby girl," he says in a hoarse whisper. "Are you with me?"

"Yesssss," I hiss.

The pleasure spreads from my core through all of me, right up to where even my fingers and toes are tingling. I press up against him, seeking the last little push I need, and then we come together, him groaning as I scream out an orgasm that feels pulled from the bottom of my soul.

I go tight, every muscle clenching around his thickness. He throbs inside me, filling me up as I squeeze him dry. My fingernails dig into his back as he drives me through my orgasm, dragging it out longer than I could ever imagine. It's not until I lose my grip and drop to the bed, completely exhausted, that he eases up and lets himself relax.

"You three are going to kill me," I groan as I sprawl out on the bed, sweaty, satisfied, and not caring one bit what I look like. "But what a way to go."

25

RIOT

JESSICA BREATHES SOFTLY AGAINST MY CHEST, HER ARM thrown over me. Tex is on the other side, but Ghost went home at some point in the night. Fuck, who knew sharing Jessica would be so damn good? That it would feel so fucking right?

But am I being selfish?

She's just learning how to be her own person. I don't want to stand in her way of exploring the world, and getting involved in the Outlaw Sons isn't like joining a fucking tennis club. People would judge her for associating with a bunch of dirty bastards like us.

But when I see her sleeping in my bed, with the fading marks of our fingers on her skin, vulnerable and bare, there's nothing I want more than to make sure she stays here.

I glance at my phone. Six AM.

I've always been an early riser. It's the perfect time to go for a run along the water when the weather is good, or hit the gym while it's still empty.

Both our phones ding at once.

"What the fuck?" Tex mumbles, rolling over and reaching blindly for his cell.

Jessica grumbles sleepily when I push her arm away and sit up. Normally I'd let it wait, but both of us at the exact same time? It's probably important.

It's a text from Hellfire. "*My office ASAP. Bring Jessica.*"

Tex and I lock gazes. "Hellfire?"

"Yeah."

Jessica sits up, the blanket falling down around her waist and revealing a perfect set of tits. "What's going on?"

"Message from Hellfire. He wants you there, too." I run my hand over Jessica's knee, loving the smooth texture of her soft skin. I can already feel myself responding, wishing we had time for another round.

She flushes pretty pink, likely thinking the same.

We split up, Tex going back to his room to change. I throw on clean clothes and walk Jessica back to Bonnie's so she can do the same. I wait outside the apartment, and when Jessica comes out, she doesn't look happy.

"Anne's still upset."

"Don't blame her. She had to sit there and listen to her father talk about her like a fucking game piece. And then he picked you instead of her. I'd be pissed, too." I say as we head down the stairs and back to the church.

"I know. Victor's never been much of a father. He leaves it to me and his girlfriend of the month to handle Jessica, but she always gets the best of everything because she's his daughter. Anything less would make him look bad."

"That sucks. I've always been close to my folks. They never really understood me, and there was never enough money or time to go around, but I always knew they loved me. Honestly, I was such a fucking pain the ass that if they didn't, I'd probably have been out on the street as soon as I was old enough to get a job, like Tex."

Jessica nods. "I don't remember much about my parents, but I remember we were happy. My mom worked a lot, but sometimes when she was up late, we'd bake cookies together in the middle of the night and talk about everything."

"All of us though, here in the club, we're our own family. Ghost and Tex are my brothers in everything but blood. There's nothing I wouldn't do for them, and there's nothing they wouldn't do for me. Nothing we wouldn't share."

She smiles at that. "Like me?"

That gets a rumble outta me. "Yeah. Like you. Now let's see what's got Hellfire's panties in a bunch." I open the door and we step inside.

Tex beat us here, not surprisingly, and Ghost and Savage are waiting, too. They look up as we enter, their expressions grim.

"What's going on?" I let Jessica take the last chair and prop myself up against the wall, crossing my arms over my chest.

Hellfire turns his laptop around so we can all see the screen. "This just appeared when I opened up the computer this morning. No fucking idea how they did it, or how deep they got their fingers in our network, but it was here waiting for me."

"Kane?"

He shakes his head. "Maybe, maybe not. Read it."

On the screen is a big square of text.

I'm taking a risk reaching out to you, but I have too much to lose not to. When Victor's people trace this message, I'm dead. Don't let it be in vain.

Victor is just stalling for time. If you let him, Sgt. Cooper will never make it off the estate alive, and your whole club will be destroyed. I can help, but on one condition: Jessica goes free.

My reach is limited. You can't contact me directly, but I've hacked several networks around the city. I want you to go to Sparkie's Megastore on 5th and Long. 2AM tonight. Bring Jessica and I'll reveal more.

PS, your security sucks, get a real IT person

"What the fuck? Who's this from?" I look at Hellfire, then at Jessica, like she should have the answer.

"That's what I'd like to fucking know," Hellfire growls, his eyebrows knit tight over his piercing eyes. He aims them at Jessica. "Is there anything else you're keeping from us?"

"What? Nothing! I swear!" She looks as confused as we are. "I honestly don't know. You know my history. He's never given me any reason to think I'm anything but a sick trophy to him, and it's not like I have friends there other than Anne."

"Occam's razor. The simplest reason is probably the correct one. It's Kane, trying to lure us out. We already know he's strangely obsessed with Jessica," Ghost suggests.

Hellfire considers it and nods. "You're probably right, but this doesn't feel like him and the fastest way to find out is to follow the instructions."

"And be ready for a trap," I add.

"I don't like it," Hellfire says. "But we can't ignore the possibility that it's someone on the inside that has a grudge against their boss. We need to find out what the fuck's going on."

"And I want to go," Jessica says, her face a mask of determination. "I've been Victor's prisoner for ten years. Why is everyone suddenly so interested in me?"

Me, Ghost and Tex exchange hard glances, then nod. If we're gonna do this, we're gonna keep her safe. And if any motherfucker gets in our way, we're gonna fucking bury them.

26

JESSICA

Bonnie's in the kitchen with an energy drink and a sudoku magazine when I come in. She looks up. "Just the girl we needed to see."

Get in line, I guess. I never thought I'd miss being nobody. "Is something going on?"

"Nothing involving anything but digital weapons, but I think you might want to have a sit-down with Anne. The honeymoon's over. Her daddy might be a psycho asshole, but she's missing her own room and her usual routine."

"Thanks. I was thinking the same thing earlier. I'll go in and talk to her."

"Want a shot first?" she asks.

I laugh, but she doesn't look like she's joking. "Nah, I'm good. Maybe later."

"Suit yourself." Bonnie chews absently on the end of her pencil as she goes back to her puzzle.

I find Anne curled up on the couch with a book. For once the TV is off. I can't tell if she's so engrossed that she doesn't notice me or if I'm being actively ignored. It's not until I sit down next to her that she finally looks up to acknowledge my presence.

"Hey. Whatcha reading?"

She wrinkles her nose at me, then looks back down at the pages. "Not like you care."

"Of course I care." I put a hand on her shin, but she pulls it away, tucking it in under herself.

"You say that, but it's not like you're ever here. You're too busy running off with your *boyfriends*." She glances up accusingly, then looks back at the book.

I get it. It's been the two of us against the world for a long time. I was just a kid when I was handed the responsibility of taking care of her, and even though sixteen must have seemed ancient when she was seven, I wasn't like her old nanny. This life hasn't been fair to either of us, but here we are.

Messed up step-sisters. Sorta.

"You didn't seem like you cared if I was around or not. You've had Bonnie to play games with, and she lets you do whatever you want. I shouldn't have stayed out all night, though, I'm sorry about that."

"Nights. With an *s*. You got hurt, and Dad was so mean. It's scary without you. I had a nightmare last night."

"Bonnie's been here. She's good, right?"

Anne looks harder at her book, like she can stare holes right through it. She's not reading anything, unless she's learned to do it without moving her eyes. "Yeah. She's nice I guess. But she's not you."

"Listen. I'm doing the best I can, okay? I don't know what I'm doing here."

"But you said you quit! I don't want to go back without you! You've made new friends and you're going to leave me. Nobody really wants me around. Dad doesn't even care."

"What? No!" I can't give up my chance at freedom because she's mad. Is it so bad that I grab the opportunity to live a little too? I know she's only twelve and has a lot of reasons to be scared and angry right now, but I feel a trickle of annoyance seeping in anyway. "Listen, I'll try to be around more, okay? No one else, just us. And Bonnie, if that's okay with you."

"Whatever." She's not going to forgive me quite yet, but she lets me put my hand on her leg and squeeze her ankle.

Except I'm going with them to follow the instructions for the note later. "But I have to go out tonight and do something for the club. I won't be out all night though, it's not a date or a party. I promise."

She snatches her leg away again. "Yeah, right."

I don't think I'm cut out for this. "Sometimes I have to do things that don't involve you. I know you're not used to it, but I'm not *just* your nanny anymore."

Wrong thing to say. "It's all about you, isn't it?" she snaps angrily. Her voice rises with every word. "Dad wants you, those guys want you. Nobody gives a shit about me, not even my own father!"

"Come on, Anne, that's not fair. Of course I care about you, but there's more on the line here than a midnight snack. Or finishing your math homework. You aren't a little kid anymore, and you've seen everything that's happened lately. I'm struggling, too. Give me a break."

She buries her face in the book, eyes tightly shut. Looking like she's trying not to cry. "Just go out with your boyfriends. I don't care anyway."

"They're not my boyfriends." Is that true? Or a lie? I'm not sure right now, and there are bigger problems to deal with. "I'm coming back, okay? We're going to figure this out. I promise."

"You better." She takes the book, gets up and stomps to our room, slamming the door behind her.

Perfect. Just perfect.

Throwing my head back on the couch, I let out an exasperated sigh. How am I supposed to fix this? I love her, but I can't fix this, and we aren't in her father's carefully constructed world anymore. It was easy to give her all my attention when that was all I had to do, but as much as I want to make her happy, I can't go back to that. It would kill me.

"It's not easy at that age," Bonnie says from the doorway. "She's hurt. She's feeling alone, and she's jam packed with hormones that her body has no idea what to do with. This is a pretty rough situation for any twelve-year-old to deal with."

"You're right. I know you are. I just don't know if I'm doing the right thing."

"The right answer is never the one that makes you be less than your full self. If you give up everything that makes you you in order to make her happy, it isn't real." Bonnie sighs, her gaze going to one of General's pictures. "My mother and I were at each other's throats constantly. I grew up in what felt like a war zone and every decision I made was based on what would piss her off the most. Meeting General actually helped level me out if you'd believe it. I was on a fast trip to nowhere, and he took one look at me and knew we were meant for each other. It took me a little longer, but not much. He felt like home. As soon as I stopped fighting that little voice, everything clicked into place. Anne is angry at the world right now and you are the only person she knows she can yell at and still be loved. It's a fucked up kinda trust, but it's real. Be her safe space, but don't give in. She'll come around eventually."

I surprise us both by giving her a hug. It takes her a second, but she puts her arms around me and hugs me back. "I'm glad you're here. I think we both need you."

She pats my back. "You be careful out there. Got it? Don't get sappy or anything, but I'm kinda getting used to having you two around."

27

TEX

Jessica walks into my room, looking around curiously. Ghost's right behind her. My room is about the same layout as Riot's place, except I didn't bother with a kitchen table so I'd have room for a small couch and a TV. That and I'm on a corner, so I have windows on two sides.

"I like what you've done with the place. It's very... you." She takes my Stetson hat off the hook next to the door and puts it on before dropping into my leather couch.

She looks cute as fuck in it. And when I get a look at the shirt she's wearing under Bonnie's leather jacket, my job drops. It's not cropped, but it's tight all over, making those amazing tits scream for my attention. I fucking love how comfortable she's getting in her own skin.

"Just 'cause I painted the walls and hung a few things up? Easy."

There's a calendar with topless girls on motorcycles hanging on my fridge. January is especially gifted. She points at it. "Not sure about that, though. She looks cold."

Ghost laughs. "Would you rather we take pictures of you and have one specially made?"

"What? Is that a thing? No way. I could never…" She trails off with a considering look on her face. "No. Right?"

"I'd fucking love it. So long as we only made three editions." I pull aside my coffee table so I can sit in front of her. Putting my hands on her knees, I push them open and close the distance. "How would we start, though? Maybe all your clothes on for January, then slowly strip you down? Get you naked by July to celebrate summer? Then dirtier and dirtier until December, where you're sweaty and panting and covered in cum? Fuck, that'd be hot."

"I should've brought my camera," Ghost says with a laugh. "I suppose this will do." He pulls out his phone and takes a quick snap. "I like the idea. Fully dressed, but looking like you're counting down the minutes to when one of us will be buried between your thighs."

She holds her hands up, covering her face, but she's laughing. "You guys are bad. I'd die if anyone ever saw that."

"Just us, honey. Just us." I can't take my eyes off that amazing rack trapped in her tight shirt. I wrap my hands around her waist and start pulling it up to reveal more of her.

She stops my hands with hers, but her smile is a little naughty. There's nobody hornier than a virgin who just discovered sex and I'm more than happy to help her scratch whatever itch she wants. "Just you and whoever might visit your room." She tips her head towards the fridge.

Ghost sits next to her, brushing her hair to the side and twisting it between his fingers. "We share with each other, but you're fucking crazy if you think we'd leave shit like that around for anyone to see."

I can literally feel the shiver that goes through her. I'm starting to think she doesn't mind the idea nearly as much as she's acting. "We've got a few hours to kill…"

"You want to teach me something new?" She licks her lips and grins.

I don't waste a fucking second to get her shirt up her sides, loving the smooth inches of skin I'm revealing. I wanna see all of her, but I'll fucking happily start here.

"Arms up, honey," I order.

Even in the bra, her tits bounce enough when they're exposed to make my dick thicken up. I peel the tight shirt up past her head and off her arms, then toss it aside, before burying my face right into that deep cleavage between those sexy orbs of soft flesh. Working my way around the edge of her bra cup, I kiss and nibble at her tender skin while letting my hands explore her. She feels so fucking good in my hands.

Ghost watches, relaxed with his hand over his dick as I undo her bra and it goes slack.

I tug it out of the way without ever taking my mouth off her luscious tits, sliding down so I can suck one of her hard nipples into my mouth. She closes her eyes and lets out a soft moan as she tips her head back onto the couch, reveling in the sensations while her chest rises and falls quickly in time with her racing heart.

"Is there something in the water here? Why can't I get enough of you?" she complains and starts unbuttoning her jeans. Fuck, I love an eager girl.

"Let me help." As soon as her zipper's down, I yank them down to her ankles.

While I get back to her breasts, she slips her fingers into her panties. Jesus, she's fucking playing with herself. If I wasn't ready to fucking bust outta my jeans already, I sure as fuck am now. One of the sexiest sights I know.

When her fingers come back out, they glisten, soaked in her dewy juices. I lean in quick and suck them into my mouth, getting a taste of her sweetness. She gasps in surprise, then follows up with a little moan as I twirl my tongue. As soon as I let her hand go, she digs her wet fingers into my hair and urges me to look up at her. Fuck, I could lose myself in those pretty brown eyes. She looks like a librarian porn star, all naked on my couch except for her panties and glasses.

She wets her lips and swallows hard, like she's building courage. "I want to taste you."

I stand to loosen my pants and grin. "Your wish is my command."

28

JESSICA

Ghost wastes no time, stripping down and taking over Tex's position on the floor. He smiles as he pulls my panties down and yanks them off my ankles, putting all three of us on equal, totally naked, ground. Then he pushes my thighs up and buries his tongue between my legs as I stretch out on the couch. His technique is different. It's amazing how they all do the same basic things but in their own specific ways.

That's not a complaint.

Ghost uses more steady pressure with his tongue than small flicks, and he brings his hand into the mix, teasing the wet seam between my legs with the tip of his finger. Tex climbs up on the couch, putting one hand on my chest and pushing me back as he straddles my chest, pointing himself right at my lips. His cock is steel hard, with a big drop of precum right at the tip that looks ready to drop any moment.

I lean forward and swipe my tongue over it. Yum.

"Fuck," he hisses, watching eagerly. I wrap my lips around the whole head and give it a suck. "Jesus. Now that's a picture I'd love on my calendar."

I rest my teeth on his delicate skin.

"Fuck, I got it, no pictures," he laughs, then nudges his hips forwards, pushing more of himself inside.

I grip his powerful thighs for support, loving the way his muscles coil under his skin and flex against my palms. I swirl my tongue around his length, exploring the feel of it, the texture of the skin, finding the bumps where veins pump hot blood through his length in time with his pulse. And then he pulls back, before coming back in, slowly fucking my mouth while I do my best to make it feel good for him.

Ghost slips a thick finger into me while he licks higher up. I'm so slippery for him that he slides it all the way in with ease. It's not as nice as a thick cock in there, but it's nice. Really nice, especially together with that talented tongue. Sinful tingles are spreading from my greedy pussy, raising goose-bumps on my skin that tingle up my chest and down my arms. I grip Tex harder and try to focus on making him feel good with my mouth.

Each thrust goes a little deeper, testing how much of him I can take. The full thickness in my mouth presses my tongue down and stretches my jaw. I try to keep my teeth from scraping his skin, but it's hard. He watches, his multicolored hazels fixed on me as he slides back and forth between my lips. I feel small and vulnerable with him looming over me, and with Ghost controlling my lower half, I'm trapped between them. They could make me do anything. You'd think it would scare me, but I trust them to stop if I get scared or uncomfortable.

And knowing that makes me brave enough to do whatever they want.

Ghost slips a second finger into me, alongside the first. At first I thought it might be his cock, but it's just that his hands are so big. So strong. And his fingers are so thick. They slide in, stretching me open with a little more resistance than just one. It feels nice, a constant push and pull while he keeps working his tongue over me like he wants to swallow me whole. I'm already starting to get close, but the pressure is still a promising tingle, not an overwhelming buzz.

Tex bumps against the back of my throat, making my whole body contract in surprise.

"Fuck," Ghost curses. "That's a squeeze I wanna feel around my cock and not just my fingers."

But Tex pulls back. "You okay?"

I nod, as much as I can with my mouth full of cock. I was mostly caught off guard.

He thrusts again, keeping himself right at my limit. My nostrils flare as I draw breath around him. It's a little scary, but at the same time, that rush of adrenaline adds to the mix. It feels dangerous, even if I know it's not. I never knew it could be like this. And the steady circles Ghost is drawing with his tongue are really ramping up the feeling.

A finger slides over my butt. I squeak in surprise. It feels... interesting. I know people do stuff back there, but I never thought it was supposed to feel good. "Tap three times if you want me to stop," says

Ghost, sliding a finger covered in spit and my own juices around the naughtiest of places.

Should I?

It's a little weird, but I can't say I definitely don't like it. Not even when he starts pushing a little and his fingertip slips in. I let out a soft moan around Tex, and I think he likes the vibrations, because he moans, too. And the whole time, Ghost never stops licking while he explores this new territory. New for me, anyway. I'm still getting used to the idea, but it's definitely kinda hot.

"Tex, you got lube?"

"Bedside… fuck, bedside drawer." Tex loses his train of thought when I add a little suction. There's an amazing feeling of power from making him come undone. My experience might still be limited, but I'm very much enjoying the practice. "So fucking good, honey."

Ghost is gone for a moment, and then back again. There's a click of plastic and then something wet and cool nudging against me, but this time it's not just a finger. "Told you we'd teach you something new. I'm gonna go real slow, okay? Just try to relax and let me in."

Oh God, that's his cock. I draw a slow breath through my nostrils, then nod. He pours a little more lube over us as he begins.

He's thick, but he's true to his promise. He goes slow, letting me adjust to it, little by little. I groan around Tex, and then draw a sudden sharp breath as the head slips in. This is unlike anything I ever imagined. Ghost stretches me open, not too differently than the first time, but much more gently. Every so often, he pours more lube on, until we're both complete slippery messes.

By the time the fronts of his thighs touch the back of mine, I feel stuffed absolutely full. Every single inch, and it's... *hot*. Nerves I didn't know could feel sexual are all jumbled up down there.

"Good girl," he moans, then resumes the push and pull. His thrusts get longer and smoother as I adjust to him in me. God, I never imagined something like that would make me come, but it's building, and I can feel it, between my legs, in my chest, tingling in my toes and fingertips. It's going to be a big one.

A buzzing sound starts, and I wish I could see exactly what's going on down there, right up until something bumps against my clit, rubbery and vibrating like crazy. Oh my God. I groan deep in my throat as my hips push up against him out of pure instinct.

He laughs. "Brought a little surprise for you in case we had time to kill." He touches me with it again.

It must be a vibrator. I've never had one, obviously, but I'm starting to understand the appeal. The vibration directly over my clit, combined with Ghost's cock in back and Tex in my mouth is all the stimulation I can handle. My whole body clenches tight as I moan and dig my fingernails into Tex's ass, coming like a freight train. I explode around them, losing myself in my own moans and then pulsing waves of heat that thrum through all of me.

"Holy fuck, I can't—" Ghost starts, and then he buries himself to the hilt and stops moving.

I'm so tight around him, I can feel his cock pulse over and over as he empties himself inside me. Bare, I realize. No getting knocked up this way. His strong fingers hold me firmly in place, while his other hand keeps the vibrator steady on my clit. It's almost too much, but while I'm still coming, it's just exactly enough.

Tex groans, low and deep in his chest. His cock swells between my lips and thick, slippery cum slides into my mouth and down my throat as I swallow fast, loving the feel of making him lose control. He fills my mouth in pulse after pulse. We're all coming together, in one big messy finish, and it's amazing.

Tex is the first to pull away, dropping into the couch next to me with a pleased grin on his face. "Fuck, I don't think I want to let you go, Jessica."

His tone is light. It's not a declaration of undying love, but there's honesty in his words, and Ghost grunts in agreement as he gently pulls out, his hands stroking me through the little aftershock shivers.

"I guess staying wouldn't be that bad," I admit. "You guys are kinda spoiling me for all other men."

Ghost gives me a light slap on the ass. "No talking about other men when I can still see our cum all over you."

"Or ever," Tex adds, eyes closed.

29

JESSICA

The city is eerily quiet at night. Even after we've gotten off the bikes and walked into the little plaza in front of the store, I swear I can still hear the faint echoes of the motorcycle engines bouncing off the buildings. But there's no one in sight, only us. Ghost, Riot and Tex surround me, on high alert in case Victor or his men are here to spring a trap on us.

We aren't alone, though. Hellfire sent Skyhigh and Poe over earlier to get into position early and monitor the area. I keep my eyes focused on the ground, not wanting to look around and give them away. There are other members around, waiting nearby, but I still feel very exposed, walking right into the spot we were told to go. We're as safe as we can be.

But tell that to my anxiety.

Riot scans the area. "Nothing's gonna happen to you. We're gonna make sure of it."

I pull my jacket close. The January chill cuts straight through my clothes, but part of it is just being scared. What if there's a bomb? Or Victor's men are hiding somewhere we don't know about? He doesn't seem to want to kill me, so hopefully there isn't a rocket launcher about to fire from a nearby building, but he's capable of it. Not knowing is the scariest part.

But if it isn't a trap, then who would want to lure us out of the compound?

Despite it being night and empty in this part of the city, it's not dark. Sparkie's Megastore has huge display windows full of giant TVs showing endless commercials. There are bars in front of the windows and doors, but we can still see inside and read about their post-holiday clearance sale. Christmas lights and garland still decorate the streetlamps, but I'm not feeling much holiday cheer.

Ghost checks his watch, a plain black piece with physical dials and clock hands. No fancy computer chip for him. "One fifty-five," he says calmly.

This is the Ghost I first met. I'm not scared of him anymore, but I can tell that he's fallen back into a place where he can do his job without worry or emotions. I wish I didn't understand why he does it, but I do. I had to learn a similar lesson while working for Victor. There were a lot of times that I had to lock myself away and cry when it was safe.

I bet it's not quite the same for Ghost. I can't see him going back to his room and bawling his eyes out like I used to, but the same idea.

Five minutes seems like forever when you're waiting, but at exactly two, all the screens in the windows light up, turning completely white. They shine like daylight out the front of the store, illuminating the whole area like floodlights. I squeak in surprise, jumping backwards right into Tex. He puts one arm around me, and his other is hanging loose at his side, a gun at the ready in his hand. "What the fuck?"

The screens dim a little, and then big black letters

appear on them, the same message on every TV facing out of the store.

Look at the front door, Jessica.

God, this is freaky.

Riot steps in front of me, shielding me from an unknown enemy and obviously frustrated there's no one there to stab or shoot. "What in the sci-fi hells is this bullshit?"

Ghost huffs, amused. "Don't like this." He repositions slowly, never stopping his slow scan of the area. Tex does the same from my other side.

The TVs flash bright white again, then settle back on the same text. Well, the message is clear. "I think I have to do what they say."

"I've got your back," says Tex. "This still feels like a trap, but we haven't found out how."

I'm terrified, but I need to know, and in my gut I don't think it's Victor's style. That doesn't mean he hasn't put someone else in charge, but he likes to do things himself.

They stay in a tight triangle around me as I step towards the door.

"Anything feels off, anything at all, and you get the fuck out of the way. We don't want you hurt," Riot says.

I nod and take a step closer. There's a security camera just inside the door, and as I approach, it shifts slightly and focuses on me. Oh God, please don't be a trap. I stop, and do a little wave at the lens.

A new message pops up on all the screens.

Good. Face the camera's when you speak, I don't have audio control.

"Why should we trust you?" Ghost asks, steel in his voice. He moves from my side, to my front, blocking the camera's view.

I still feel exposed. With all the screens typing the messages, it's like having an alien supercomputer focused on us. Tex is right at my back, and Riot is right beside me.

Do you have a choice?

"We could walk away right now," Tex says. "Sounds smarter than standing around talking to a clearance sale."

Fine. Let's make this fast. Victor has recalled one of his commando teams from South America. They are in the air right now, and have his full arsenal at their disposal. If nothing is done to stop them, they will target your compound tomorrow. Once the girls are secured, he intends to do enough damage to destroy the whole compound, and likely the surrounding area.

"Okay, let's say that's the truth," Riot snaps. "What the fuck are we supposed to do? Who are you and why are you bothering to warn us?"

There's a pause, the screens fill with vertical lines, jittering across the surface for a moment before they refresh with a new note.

I don't care about you or your club. I'm risking myself because I don't believe innocents should suffer for the crimes of others. Jessica needs to be safe and I believe you're her best chance of staying free from Kane's reach. The threat is real, and I have given you actionable intel.

Ghost nods. "We'll take precautions. I think we're a harder target than he realizes. Kane isn't the only one with experience and resources. Doesn't mean I trust you."

As you shouldn't. Trust no one.

I cling to Riot's arm while my mind whirs, then push ahead stomping right up to the camera while I yell at it in frustration. "Well I don't believe you! If I'm so important, why did nobody care that I was innocent when I was eleven and locked in a cell every night until I could control myself? Or for the ten years I've been with him punished for every screw up? Oh boo hoo, so noble that you care about me now. I don't buy it."

I can't stay and explain. They're already tracing me. Watch out tomorrow.

The screens go dark, one by one.

Seriously? This is a load of bad spy movie bullshit. I feel like I was just so close, but behind every secret is just another secret. "Who are you?" I scream at the camera.

There's no answer. I watch until the very last screen is about to die, right in front of us under the security camera.

Never doubt that I love you, my little baby owl.

The screen shuts off before I have time to process what it said, let alone figure out a response. There's no way. Absolutely no way.

"Mom?"

30

JESSICA

"You're going to be fine," I whisper to Anne.

She sobs into my shoulder. "I'm soooorrry. I was mad but I love you. I don't want to be sent away. Don't let them send me away."

"I love you, too, but you know why we're doing this, and Bonnie is going with you."

Of course she's scared, I am, too. If we're to believe the strange informant—I'm still having a hard time accepting the final message—then she can't stay in the compound. Hellfire and his men have decided that it's too much of a risk to have us both in the same place. They are sending Anne away to a safe house for her own good.

We have a warning, which means the Outlaw Sons have the advantage. Or at least that's what I'm telling myself so I don't go completely out of my mind.

"Why can't you come with us?" Anne's grip around my waist tightens as she presses her face against my chest.

"You know why I have to stay, and you'll have Savage and Crank with you. They'll make sure you guys are protected. I'm sure everything will be over in a couple days, so pack some books and get ready to watch lots of TV and eat junk food with Bonnie, okay? It'll be super boring and then we'll be together again."

Please don't let that be a lie.

Behind her, waiting in front of the van that's going to take her to a safe house somewhere outside the city is Bonnie. She nods at me, and smiles. I don't know what I would have done without her. Probably not gotten close to Riot, Tex and Ghost, because there's no way I would have let Anne stay with a random biker, no matter how trustworthy they seemed.

"But you're going to do something dangerous. What

if something happens to you?" She pulls back to look up at me with tear-stained cheeks.

"I have Ghost, Tex, Riot and all the other Outlaw Sons protecting me. I'll be safe too. I promise." I do my best to keep the nervous quaver out of my voice, but I'm not sure I quite succeed.

I haven't said anything to Anne about the messages from my maybe mother, or what exactly our plan is, but it's pretty clear that something big is going on even without the details. I want to protect her, but I guess sometimes it's safer to know the reality than to live in a fake bubble.

"Everyone's going to be fine," Bonnie chimes in, repeating it again for Anne's benefit. She holds out her hand for Anne to take. "The safe house walls are armored, the windows are barred, and there's even a secret escape tunnel underneath it. No one's going to find us." She nods her head at the box Savage loads into the back of the van. "And we're bringing the games. The TV there is huge, and the boys will have nothing to do but wait on us hand and foot. We'll make this fun until it's safe for us to come back, okay?"

Both Savage and Crank give her skeptical looks, but they keep their mouths shut. I've seen how all the guys here seem to respect Bonnie. She's a tough chick.

Anne still looks unsure, but she nods and takes Bonnie's hand, letting Bonnie help her into the van. I wave at the door before they shut it. "You're smart, tough and resourceful. You'll be fine. Be good to Bonnie, okay?"

"I promise. Just... just come back to me." Anne takes a deep breath and her expression turns serious. "I know Dad's not a good person. The way he treated you, even Marissa. Or me." She pinches her lips a moment. "I... I think I could handle losing him. I..." She swallows. "I know I probably will. There's a lot of people after him. But I can't lose you."

"You won't."

Savage shuts the door. He bangs the side of the van a couple of times with the flat of his hand, then gives us a thumbs up as he climbs in. Crank takes the passenger seat.

I let my hand drop, knowing they can't see me anymore, and a tear runs down my cheek. She's tougher than she thinks. So I have to be, too.

"They're gonna be fine," Tex says as he puts a hand on my shoulder and pulls me against him. I let him, taking comfort in his sturdy presence. "Savage and Crank are a pair of mean motherfuckers, but they'd walk through lava for Bonnie. General was the beating heart of this club for a long time, but Bonnie was the soul. It's why not a single man here complains about Hellfire letting her stay on. She might not be a member, but she's earned her place. The girls'll be safe."

We sit on the church steps and watch the van drive away. "God, I don't know what to believe."

Riot sits down next to us, sandwiching me in. "It's a lot to take in," he agrees.

"Do you really think it's my mother? If she's alive, why haven't I heard from her until now? I *saw* the boat explode. I went through a phase where I pretended they were going to come and get me and he... he showed me the autopsy reports." And they gave me nightmares for years.

I kick a stone that's found its way onto the steps down, watching it bounce a couple of times before sliding off the side.

"Who else would know she called you her little owl?" Tex asks.

"Um, Dad would, obviously. I suppose I might have more family somewhere. He was in the military so we moved every couple of years and I don't have any real memories of relatives. I remember a funeral I went to for a grandmother when I was little. I don't even remember if it was Mom's mom or Dad's."

Ghost comes over and joins us, standing a couple steps down with his back to the railing and his strong arms crossed over his chest. "You said she worked with computers, right? That would be a point on the side of it being her. Is this the sort of thing she could do?"

"How am I supposed to know? I was eleven when they died. I know she had security clearance because her office had to be off limits. That's it. I might as well be Amish when it comes to technology. I knew Victor's number in case of emergencies, but I've never been allowed my own phone, and the only time I've used computers was when I was doing online schooling. They monitored *everything.* Most of what I know is from watching TV with Anne."

"Alright." Riot blows out a puff of air that turns to smoke. It's chilly today. "So it's at least potentially plausible. But if she's so goddamn good that she's transmitting messages to us and to some random store, I agree that it seems odd that she wouldn't have tried until now. Unless..." His eyebrows knot as he focuses far away. "Maybe."

"What?" Tex pulls me a little closer, nice and warm.

"Her being dead wouldn't be that hard for Kane to fake. Jessica was eleven and probably too scared to really understand what was going on. If he took her, he could have taken someone else, too. The autopsy reports could be for anyone."

"No! I—" I stop, thinking back. The memory of the photos still hangs with me, but they were burned beyond recognition. Would he really be so cruel? Stupid question. Of course he would.

"Think. If he wanted your mother's cooperation, what better way to get it than to dangle her daughter's safety right in front of her? It's a long shot, but it would explain why he's so hell-bent on getting you back. Without you, he can't control her. Boom. Hacker gone rogue."

Ghost nods. "It's not a bad plan. I don't know if it's true, but it would fit."

"But... really? It sounds too wild to be true. This doesn't happen in real life." I shake my head, but part of me wants to believe it. That my mother is alive. That the reason she hasn't contacted me, hasn't rescued me from Victor, is due to circumstances out of her control. So completely out of her control that I can't even blame her for not trying. Maybe she has been trying.

"We should run it by Hellfire." Tex says. "But either way, we verified that a private jet came in from Colombia and landed this morning, and Kane trades in the kind of equipment that could decimate this whole side of town. We deal in small arms compared to him. Biggest thing we ever had was the tank behind the church, and that's not even good for anything anymore. Kane, though, he could have fucking space lasers for all I know. Dictators fucking love him. So when someone says he might have a crack black ops team headed our way, we can't assume it's a lie."

Just the idea sends a shudder through me. The guys like to sound confident, but if all that is true about

Kane, then who knows what he's going to throw at us? "Hold me," I whisper.

Tex tightens his arm around me and Riot squeezes in closer, putting me in a warm, comforting biker sandwich.

But it's when Ghost tells me, "We're gonna make fucking sure nothing happens to you, baby," in a tight, deadly voice that I finally believe it. Because he's going to be between me and anyone coming at me, and that scary tone makes it very clear that anyone who tries isn't going to live to see morning.

31

JESSICA

I know I'm not really a hostage—not really—but being in a cell sure feels like it. But for the plan to work, it has to seem authentic, and like Ghost said, this is probably the safest place for me to be anyway. It still gives me chills.

"How long do you think we have to wait?" I ask.

Ghost is the only one in here with me. Riot and Tex are nearby, but everyone agreed that if there's going to be one guard to make me seem more vulnerable, Ghost was the best choice. "We'd just get in his way," Tex said with a laugh and Riot agreed. So now it's just the two of us, me inside one of six cells in the basement under the barracks for the Outlaw Sons, and him in the room outside, looking bored.

There are no windows. The only light comes from a bare bulb behind a steel cage in the ceiling. A thick steel door separates me from Ghost, but he's left the slot in it open so I can see out and we can talk. I can't wait until this night is over.

"Your mother only told us tonight. We've done everything but draw them a treasure map to where you are, so if they come for you, we'll fuck them up." He's sitting on an office chair next to a table in the corner. A small knife spins between his fingers and I know he has a gun tucked into his belt out of sight.

"I'm nervous. Talk to me." I press my face to the slot in the door, so he can see me too. "I'd rather have you in here, holding me."

His mask falls briefly, showing just a hint of a smile when he looks my way. He gets up and walks over. "I'd fucking love to, but this is business, not pleasure. You could always give me a show."

I blink at him. "Really? Now?"

His smile widens a little. It's nice. "I mean, I wouldn't argue, but no. If you want to play prison guard and sexy inmate another time, I'm more than up for it, but right now any distraction could mean someone dies. After, though?" His laugh is soft. "When the adrenaline is still pumping and the danger is over, it's fucking magical."

"Really? Can I be the prison guard?" Flirting is a lot better than waiting.

He freezes. "I don't think that would be a good idea."

"Why?"

Ghost turns and walks away, heading back to his post.

"Talk to me. I know I touched on something bad. I was just trying to tease you."

He shakes his head. "Forget about it. I'm on edge tonight."

"Does it have to do with why you don't want to sleep with me around? Why you left us the other night? I trust you. Tex, Riot… and you. You make me feel safe. I don't mind if you have secrets, but don't leave me in the dark if I might do or say something that hurts you."

"It's past and gone," he says with a shake of his head.

"Apparently not."

He lets out a little huff. "I enlisted right out of school. Home was shit, just run of the mill stuff, nothing that would make the paper, so the day I could, I was out."

"Okay, a lot of people have been in the military. Like my dad." I'm trying to imagine something that will make me think less of him, of the man he is now, the man that's willing to put his life on the line to protect mine, and I'm coming up empty

"Honey, trust me, I'm nothing like your father." He sighs. "I did my four years, but I didn't fit in well there either. I was good at it, but shit at following the chain of command. Too many forms and regulations. I got out, but civilian life wasn't any better than I remembered it. That's when one of my old officers got in touch. You know what's funny? To this day I don't know if the group that recruited me was government sanctioned or not. They certainly implied that we were, but at the end of the day, I might've been no better than the people Kane is sending our way right now."

"Wh—what did they recruit you to do?" I put a hand on the door, wanting to touch him and remind him that we aren't there anymore.

"I was part of a squad of killers. We sometimes worked in teams, mostly solo. Easier to get one man in and out than two or three. I've taken more lives than I'd care to fucking admit, all for the greater good, or so I believed, but that shit eats at you, little by little, until it's fucking gone. I was already on the edge when an op went bad and I ended up in a cell. You'll excuse me if I spare you the details, but getting out killed what was left of my humanity."

I don't know what to say to that. Not because it makes me care about him any less, but it's heartbreaking to see how broken he feels. "But you did get out. And now you're using those skills to keep me safe. To keep me from getting hurt."

His laugh is completely devoid of humor. "Not meaning to downplay your life, 'cause I'm gonna make sure no one comes close enough to threaten it, but I don't know that saving one life is gonna make up for all the ones I took."

"It's not a scorecard, and I think you're amazing."

"You wouldn't if you—"

"Shut up. I've been a prisoner for ten years. Look at me. I'm not a trained killer. I'm just a girl who some sicko decided to mess with. Do you think that if someone had given me the training and the chance to get out, I wouldn't have taken it? Do you want to know the names of people Kane employs that I would have stabbed in a second if I knew I could get free? I didn't need to count sheep to sleep, I could just list them in order from most to least guilty until I fell asleep." I stand up straight, holding my head high. "So no, I don't think you're a monster. I think you became the man you had to be in order to survive."

"Jessica…"

"I don't care what you had to do to get out of that cell. It brought you here. To the Outlaw Sons, to Tex, to Riot. To me."

"I'm broken goods, Jessica. I don't want to worry every night about if you're gonna roll over in your sleep and then I wake up with your blood on my hands."

"Then we get two beds."

He snorts, but he also puts his hand through the door and I take it, squeezing tight. "You're a lot tougher than you look. I saw it in you the first night we met. You looked like a scared little kitten, but you weren't afraid to hiss. Look, I can't promise you anything, but maybe when this is all over, we'll see how things go. I… Fuck. I'll stay open to the idea, but I can't do it alone. We'll talk. You, me, Tex and Riot. I —" He stops, then lets go of my hand as he cocks his head, listening to the little earpiece he's wearing. He's gotten a message from the others. "Shh. Go sit down, look fucking dejected or whatever. Somethings happening."

Oh God. Someone's coming.

32

JESSICA

Ghost slips away from the door, and immediately my heart starts racing. He puts himself behind a corner right by the table, leaning against the wall like he's not paying attention. If someone's coming, I don't hear them yet, but I trust him. I just need him to be okay, and I'm not going to let him pull back again. I'm not going to pretend I can fix all the pain that he's gone through or the guilt he has to be carrying, but it makes me want to do my best to make it as easy on him as I can. Because I care about him, just like Tex and Riot.

He glances my way and frowns. With a quick hand motion, he gestures for me to move back. I do, but not so far that I can't keep watching out the little viewing window. Maybe it's for my own safety, or maybe he just doesn't want me to see what he can do, but I don't want to go blind into whatever is about to happen. I shake my head, and the frustration is clear in the set of his jaw, but now's not the time for arguments.

Then I hear it. The footsteps are light and quiet, but definitely there. Ghost's waiting quietly, his gun in one hand, and a vicious looking knife in the other. I couldn't look away if I tried.

It's not long before shapes dressed in mottled dark clothing from head to toe appear at the end of the hallway. From inside the cell, my view isn't great, but enough to make them out. They have helmets, dark face masks, scary looking guns, and from what I can tell, every possible advantage on Ghost. Why are there so many of them? And why is anyone expecting him to handle this alone? Ghost might be skilled, but he's only one man.

How did these guys get this far in the first place? My blood chills. Did something go wrong outside? But no, they warned Ghost, right? So they have a reason.

The crack of a gunshot goes off upstairs. One of the soldiers glances over his shoulder, but seems unconcerned. Is it part of their plan? Does this mean they've taken control of the compound? God, I wish I knew more about what's happening.

The front one holds up his hand and makes some kind of signal. The other three spread out and start to move into the room, gliding like shadows. These guys are professionals, but then Victor already lost a man. He wouldn't risk looking weak by sending anything less than the best this time.

Even with Ghost there, my blood is ice. What if they're too much for him? The soldiers don't seem to have noticed me yet, but there's no way out of this room, so they have to know I'm in one of the cells. I'm surprised they can't tell where I am just from the sound of my beating heart.

Ghost explodes. One moment, he's still, a statue in the shadows, the next one of their soldiers drops to the floor like someone hit the off switch. Their leader freezes. By the time Ghost is past him and on to the next, the leader drops to the floor with a knife still sticking out of his masked face and thick, red blood spurting out around it. He never even got to scream.

The next guy does though. Ghost takes the man's arm and wrenches it around to his back with a sickening crunch, then uses him as a screaming shield while Ghost levels his gun and puts a big, bloody hole between the eyes of a fourth one. The massive boom inside the little room has me clutching my ears, but I can't look away from the carnage. Not until I know Ghost is safe.

The one Ghost shot tumbles backwards until he slams against the wall and sags down it. The bullet must've gone all the way through, since he leaves a red streak behind him as he slides.

Ghost never stops moving, spinning and dragging his human shield. There's a second crack, another bone broken, and the guy screams louder. The last one tries to level his machine gun, but Ghost throws the man he's holding at him. Even as the two black-clad soldiers collide, Ghost is right there. I have no idea where he got the second knife from, but he buries it deep in the last guy's neck.

Still not stopping, he kicks the guy with the broken bones over so that the helmet isn't in the way, aims the pistol at the man's face, and executes him. This time I look away, suddenly glad I skipped lunch.

Riot was brutal with Troy, playing with him before

putting an end to it. Making sure Troy felt the pain Riot thought he deserved for messing with me.

This was nothing like that. This was pure efficiency. I'm pretty sure Ghost had all five men down in just as many heartbeats, and he's already got the last knife back and is aiming his gun down the hallway in case there are more. I knew he was cool under pressure, but this was almost machine like. Somehow I'm falling for a man that can do… that.

I should probably be running the other way as fast as I can, but I haven't lived the kind of life that has let me pretend bad things don't happen. I already knew he was dangerous, and I'd rather have him at my side than anywhere else.

But man, it's chilling to see him in action.

I hold my breath while I wait. Ghost is absolutely still again, his gun hand unwavering. Is he getting new intel through his earpiece? Is everyone okay up there? Or are there more coming? Someone must've heard the gunshots.

I don't let my breath out until Ghost's shoulders relax and he sticks his gun into his belt. He gets up, collects his other knife, then wipes both of them off on the pants of one of the soldiers. The knives disappear wherever he keeps them hidden on himself, and then he finally looks at me. There's pain in his eyes. Regret? Not over killing them, but that I had to see it.

"Are you okay?" I whisper, knowing they didn't have a chance to physically hurt him. But that's not what I'm worried about.

He lets out a slow breath, then nods. "Fine. You?"

"Been better, but I didn't throw up this time."

"Shit, I'm not sure if I'm proud of you for being so practical or pissed that I'm even thinking that."

I give him a shaky grin. I might be a little green around the edges but we're alive. "Go with proud, because the other ship has already sailed. What about the others? How did they get all the way down here? Are Tex and Riot…?"

"They're fine." He taps the earpiece as he comes closer. Just the briefest of pauses as he looks at me, and then he unlocks the door to let me out.

I throw myself around him, not caring that there's blood on his jacket and a little on his cheek. I need to hold him, touch him, know that he's whole… and to let him know that he hasn't scared me away. I accept the darkness in him, even if he doesn't. A short sob escapes me, and then his arms are around me too, pulling me in close. When we come upstairs, there's a line of bodies. They're all dressed in black and masked. With the Outlaw Sons knowing they were coming, they didn't stand a chance.

"Jessica!" Riot pushes through to us. Ghost still has his arms around me, but Riot grabs my head and kisses me like he thought he'd never see me again. I'm so shocked, it takes me a second to start kissing him back. He's okay. And then Tex is there too, jumping in as soon as Riot backs up, and I get another kiss. It's nice. It's life, celebrating that we pulled through without getting hurt.

Hellfire comes over, followed by a couple of grizzly looking bikers I don't know yet. "Nice work," Hellfire says. "Barely a scratch, and twelve bogeys down. Any trouble downstairs?"

Ghost shakes his head. "None. Not convinced that Kane got his money's worth with these guys."

Or maybe they didn't count on there being a freaking ninja biker waiting for them down there.

"Hey, Boss. Kept one alive for ya." Between Poe and Sinner, there's a guy in black with his helmet and mask removed. They're as much keeping him up as they are making sure he doesn't get away. His hair is buzzed short, but the little he has is soaked with drying blood from an oozing wound on his scalp. His eyes look a little unfocused and his face is heavily bruised.

It's hard not to feel sympathy, even knowing that he and the others were coming in here to steal me and Anne away. On the other hand, I doubt he would have had any compunctions about blowing away Riot, Tex or Ghost. That thought hardens my heart pretty darn quick.

Poe holds out a little electronic device that looks kind of like a phone. "He had this. He was hanging back a little, and we figured he was the contact man. Either that, or so chickenshit that he hid in the bushes as soon as he got here. If we hadn't been waiting for them, we'd probably never spotted this fucker."

They shove the man forward, and he drops to his knees in front of us, catching himself against the pavement with his hands.

Hellfire takes the device and looks at it. Up close, it seems more like a pager, but who has those anymore?

Skyhigh takes a look. "Narrow band comms unit. Good for communicating if you don't want anyone intercepting. I was taking them apart and putting them back together back in my deployment days." Ghost nods like he recognizes it. With his background, he's probably used them before.

"How's it work?" Hellfire asks, his growl threatening. I wonder if the guy on the ground is with it enough to understand he's a dead man.

"This one looks text based. Probably encodes it on the way. Silent and more accurate than voice. Might require a code, though." Skyhigh takes the unit from Hellfire and examines it closer. He nudges a button, and a screen comes on, so low contrast it's almost invisible, even in the darkness.

Ghost kneels in front of the last of the attackers and grabs his chin to force him to look up. "You've got two options, friend. Quick and painless, or real long, real slow and the worst fucking agony you've felt in your whole damn life. How much loyalty is that money worth when you know you'll never see any of it?" The ice in his voice doesn't just give me chills. Even a couple of the Outlaw Sons look a little uncomfortable with how easily he makes the threat. Killing in the heat of battle is very different from the promise of torture.

The man's eyes clear up, like his body just channeled every drop of adrenaline in his body towards this new threat. I don't know how much he understood but definitely enough that his face contorts in terror. "What do you want from me?"

"Give me the code word."

The man looks around at the glowering Outlaw Sons surrounding him, his expression resigned. There's no mercy to be found here. "Quick?"

"You won't feel a fucking thing."

He nods. I don't see how he can meet his obvious fate that calmly, but I guess you have to be a certain type of person to get into this kind of business at all. "Spoiled brat. Two words," he says.

"You gotta be fucking kidding me," growls Riot. Tex just chuckles.

Ghost nabs the comms unit from Skyhigh, and types on the little screen. I peek over his arm to read.

Target acquired and removed from premises. Mission successful. Spoiled brat.

"Let's see what they say." The screen remains black long enough that Ghost turns his attention back to the man. "If you fucked this up, it's gonna take fucking days."

The man shakes his head. "No, I swear. It's legit."

A faint dark red glow lights up on the comms unit, barely visible and pulsing slowly. Ghost taps the button. There's a new message there.

Good work. Confirm when your team has cleared the blast zone. You've got three hours.

Tex is looking over Ghost's shoulder on the other side from me. "Cleared the fucking what?"

33

JESSICA

"We need to get everyone the hell outta here," Hellfire's voice is low, meant only for the immediate circle around him. There's something else there too. Sadness? The Outlaw Sons are proud of their clubhouse, and now it sounds like it's going to get blown up, and us with it, if we don't get out of here.

Tex pulls me close. "If there's anything you need out of Bonnie's, better be quick." I rack my brain trying to think if there's even anything here I'd even care about. Maybe some changes of clothes, but I'm mostly considering how many of the pictures of General I should grab. Definitely her old 'property' patch.

Hellfire's phone rings. "Hidden number," he grumbles, but he takes it. "Hellfire. This better be fucking important."

The sudden crack of a gunshot cuts through the air. I start to turn, but Tex urges me forwards. "Nothing to look at. We gotta get you outta here." I guess Ghost made good on his promise of making it quick. I've seen more than enough death for one day.

"Tex! Jessica! Back here! Ghost and Riot too," Hellfire calls out, still holding his phone.

We gather around and he puts his phone on speaker. "They're here. Repeat what you said."

The moment I hear the voice that comes through the speaker, a core memory is triggered way back in my mind. It's a voice my body formed a primal connection to from even before I was born. Any doubts about our informant are brushed away with the speed and ease Ghost cleared out the attackers. "Mom," I whisper. Tex pulls me closer. So many emotions run through me that I don't even know where to start picking them apart.

She speaks in a clipped tone with no time to waste. "I have to keep this quick. I was as good as exposed as soon as I tapped into the phone lines, but this is too important. Kane has a missile aimed at the compound. His yacht is somewhere offshore. I'm not exactly sure where and I don't have time to track it. It's more than powerful enough to clear not just the compound, but the whole neighborhood around it. He's already got someone ready to spin it as a chain gas explosion."

Oh my God. My stomach drops, knotting into a lump of tension. I knew Victor hated losing, but something like this? I'm just glad Anne and Bonnie aren't here to worry about. They'll be okay. I grip Tex's arm tightly, taking all the comfort I can from having him next to me.

"Jesus fuck," he rumbles.

"Is there any way to stop it?" Hellfire growls.

"Yes. It's why I'm risking a call, but you'll have to act fast. And it means breaking into Kane's estate before he realizes what you're up to."

Ghost snorts. "Assaulting what's basically a goddamn fortress doesn't seem realistic in so little time. There's a reason we attacked him at his beach house."

"I know. And Jessica knows."

I'm so distracted by the sound of her voice that I'm caught off guard when she mentions me. "Me?" While everyone else is suddenly looking at me, I stare at the phone in confusion.

"There's no time to explain all of it, but I designed and coded the guidance system for that missile. It's why Kane came for me. But I put a backdoor in that missile control code. If someone gets close enough to send the right signal, it won't just abort the launch, but the missile will blow up. I was hoping for an opportunity to take out Kane with it. I have a remote in the lab keyed to the right sequence, but without a way to get out of here to get to the yacht, there's nothing I can do."

Mom's smart, I knew that, but this makes it sound like she's some kind of super hacker. No wonder Victor wanted her on his team. I guess it's too much to wish that Dad survived too.

"The lab's at the estate?" Riot asks.

"Kane likes to keep development close. Look, I have to go before they pinpoint my signal."

"We got no time to lose," Hellfire says. "Can you help us get in?"

"I can take out the alarm systems if you make a hole or two in the walls."

Skyhigh grins when she mentions that, like a kid given free reign at a self-serve ice cream shop. "Holes are my specialty. Be right back. Sinner, come help me carry!"

Mom continues, "I hate to say it, but the easiest way into the mansion itself is with Jessica. Her fingerprints should still be good for the scanners, and I can't access the system that controls that. The lab is in the locked down east wing of the mansion. You'll have to find your own way in there, where the remote is. And I am."

"In, out and done in a couple hours? Easy fucking peasy," Riot says dryly. "Fuck."

"I didn't say it would be easy. I'll keep a presence on the security cameras. I should see you coming if I still have access. The faster you come, the more likely that is." Mom draws her breath as if to say more, then pauses. Then, "I have to go before they finish their traces. I'll hold out as long as I can. Jessica?"

"Mom?" My voice cracks.

"I love you. If I don't make it out of here, I'm sorry."

Oh God. I was tense before, but now my chest goes painfully tight and the corners of my eyes are starting to burn. "Mom…"

The line goes dead as Skyhigh and Sinner return, carrying a couple of backpacks. Skyhigh hefts his happily. He might be the only one looking forward to this.

"Alright, no time to fucking lose!" Hellfire yells while I'm still staring at his phone. "We need volunteers to stick around, pass the word. If they are watching the compound we want it to look like we've just barely survived an attack. Ghost, pick your team for the assault on Kane. Everyone else, we want to tiptoe out of here like little church mice before we split up. Ghost's team storms the estate, and the rest come with me to try and track down the yacht. I don't know what we can do against a fucking missile, but it's better than sitting around and waiting to roast marshmallows on what's left of our side of the city. If we can rescue Cooper and Rebecca, fucking awesome, but the main priority is stopping Kane. Everything else is secondary. Are we clear?"

Ghost nods. "Skyhigh, round up three more guys. You're with me." Then he turns to us. "I don't wanna bring Jessica. It goes against every fiber of my fucking body."

"What?" I shake my head. "No, no, no! You heard her. You'll need my fingers for the scanners."

"Technically I only need a finger. I'd rather have you ninety-eight percent safe than risk all of you," he growls back.

"Wha—wait. What are you suggesting?" I clench my hands into fists out of pure instinct.

Tex holds a hand up, stopping both of us. "Don't be a smartass. Nobody's cutting off fingers. We're bringing Jessica. It's not like she's safe here, if the whole neighborhood is going to be blown to hell."

"Definitely," Riot growls. "She's not gonna be any safer anywhere else than she is with us."

Ghost pauses just long enough to give it a quick consideration, then nods. "Alright. Then let's roll out. We're burning time here."

There's a group of about a dozen bikers around Hellfire. The ones volunteering to stay behind. The only one I know the name of is Sinner. They all look nervous but determined.

"Sinner, man, you're just a prospect," growls Hellfire. "No one expects you to play target for the club. Leave the theatrics to the fucking veterans."

Sinner shakes his head. "Nah, I spent way too fucking long in prison, paying for shit I didn't do. I'd started to think my life had no purpose. I'm too new to be useful in the other missions, but stand here and look busy? That I can do. I trust you guys to save the clubhouse." He crosses his arms over his chest. He's either super brave or super stupid, or maybe both. "I'll stay."

Hellfire nods in respect. "Won't forget it, and I'll consider it a little extra personal incentive. If you die, Eagle-eye isn't going to forget it either, and I already owe that old bastard enough."

With everything else decided, there's no wasting time. The club evacuates slowly, one by one, two by two, grouping up and reforming elsewhere to not draw too much attention to a mass exodus. Hopefully Kane isn't watching at all, but if he is, he'll think the attack squad got in and out and the club is struggling to recover.

"Here, I got space," says Riot and pats behind him on his bike. I'm actually getting pretty good at getting on and off a bike now, and even though we have a lot ahead of us, it still feels good to snuggle right up against his back and enjoy the feel of his strong body between my legs. It makes me feel alive.

Ghost rides at the head of our group, with Riot and me on one side, and Tex on the other. Slowly a group forms behind us, turning into a small army. I don't only have my boys keeping me safe, the whole club is shielding me now. I squeeze Riot harder, drawing on his courage. Ghost puts a hand up, swipes it forwards in the air, and then we're off, winding down the streets like a deadly snake made of leather and chrome.

Hold on, Mom. We're coming.

34

TEX

Victor Kane's primary estate sprawls over a large chunk of the Cornwall district of the city. It's where all the rich fucks have their homes, paid for by money earned off the backs of others, like they always do, and in his case death. We still have a ways to go before we're there, but the floodlights, tall walls and monstrous mansion behind them are impossible to miss.

This is the kind of neighborhood that isn't really a neighborhood. It's a street with private roads, not driveways. Lights come on in guard houses as we rumble by in the darkness. There's only eight of us, but that's plenty more noise than this area's used to. This place is quiet. Civilized. Fucking bullshit.

What are they gonna do? Call the homeowners association?

Jesus, what would I do with the kinda money it takes to live here? Spend it somewhere else, probably. You couldn't fucking pay me to live in a place where the neighbors are looking into buying their fifth Porsche. I bet their only excitement is whether they'll survive tonight's overdose or not. Fuck that. I'll stick to my quarters, surrounded by people who would put their lives on the line for me.

Jessica clings to Riot like she was born to ride the back of a bike. Compared to her first night, she's come a long way. I laugh into the harsh wind. She was so fucking naive and innocent when we met her. Now it's hard to remember what it was like to not have her around. I always worried that eventually we would start settling down, and it would pull us apart, but sharing Jessica has brought the three of us together even tighter than before. The idea of sharing her permanently—if she'll have us—is warming on me.

I'm already looking forward to the celebration back in my quarters after this.

We just have to make sure we actually get through it first so I have quarters to go home to.

Ghost doesn't lead us to the front entrance. Instead we follow the outer walls of Kane's sprawling estate. The street wraps around it, like is typical this close to the city. I try to imagine that the cameras lining the top of the wall aren't following us. If Jessica's mother is on top of things, she should be in control of those. It's what we gotta bank on.

On a stretch between two larger properties, Ghost pulls over, and the rest of us follow suit. It's gonna be pretty fucking obvious we're here with all the bikes lined up, but then we don't have time for subtlety either. Skyhigh's already off his bike, carrying one of his backpacks, eager to punch a big fucking hole in the wall. While he's getting set, I go to Riot and Jessica.

"You okay?" I ask her.

Jessica nods. She looks so fucking small and it makes me wanna sweep her up and keep her safe, if I could. But her pretty features are a mask of determination and she deserves to be here. Fuck, I'd be determined too if my mom was on the other side, and I haven't spoken to her since I was a kid. Guess that's another thing we have in common, even if our stories are different.

"Good. Shit's about to get dirty. Stay close to us, whatever happens. If we get separated, it's gonna be hard for us to protect you. And now that we've got you, I'd hate to fucking lose you."

I get a little smile at that. Fuck, I love seeing her smile.

"Get ready," says Ghost as he comes our way. "There's about to be a big noise, and after that, everyone's gonna know where we are."

"Do you think Mom's okay?" Jessica's voice is thick with worry.

Riot nods, looking surer than I feel. "If she wasn't controlling the cameras, we woulda been shot at already. She's fine."

"Come here." I help her off the bike and into my arms, then Riot dismounts and draws iron.

Skyhigh raises a hand, like him running our way isn't warning enough. He's wild-eyed and grinning.

"Duck," I say and pull Jessica's head against my chest, angling her away from the explosion. A moment later, the ground shakes and a blast of air and debris showers the area. A big chunk of the wall around the estate ceases to be. Shit, the neighbors are definitely going to have something to say about the giant concrete block in the street. Skyhigh's nothing if not thorough.

My ears are ringing, but hearing's coming back. Enough that I hear the chorus of car alarms going off nearby. It's time to fuck shit up.

Ghost is the first one through, followed by Skyhigh, Poe and Junker. Me and Riot keep Jessica between us as we follow, and then Shiv brings up the rear.

We make it most of the way across the massive lawn, keeping low. Something moves in the darkness, followed by the crack and flash of a gunshot. Ghost and Poe fire at the same time and the guy drops outta sight. Dunno about Poe, but if he didn't get him, I'm positive Ghost did.

Jessica stumbles, but me and Riot react at the same time, getting an arm each, keeping her on her feet. "Thanks," she hisses. I know she doesn't wanna feel like a burden, but we're gonna be watching out for her, whether she wants to or not.

We come up on a low wall that separates the lawn from a fancy Japanese style garden, with one of those artsy sandboxes, and a pond with the faint shadows of the biggest fucking koi fish I ever saw in my life moving in the water around a fountain. It's low, but it's granite or marble and gives us cover from the inside. I grab Jessica's hand, feeling her shiver in my grip. She's nervous, and with good fucking reason.

"On my mark, run," whispers Ghost. "Go!"

Still gotta be about a hundred yards to the mansion. This looks like it's a guest house or something like that, and if that's already this fancy, I can only imagine what it's like up there.

Shiv and Poe take the lead, their guns ready. Someone must be visible through the windows, because they fire at once, followed by a crash and a scream inside. Lights blink on around the property, spotlights making it impossible to sneak up on the building, but we can still stay on the outside of the cones until we get around to the back. When no one's shooting back, we run together.

Just as we're having to jump out into the light, the spotlights flicker and shut off.

"Mom," Jessica whispers with awe.

"She's right," grinds Riot, sounding even more gravelly than usual. "Let's not waste it."

We charge down a marble walkway that takes us past a gigantic, L-shaped swimming pool, and then we're right up against the house.

"This way," Jessica says, some of the tremor in her voice is gone. Now that we're on her home turf, I think it gives her a little confidence. Makes me grin, despite everything. It's sexy.

She takes us to a solid looking door with a little window at about head height. There's a panel next to it, and when she touches it and punches her code, the door unlocks with a click. Riot hauls it open and aims his gun down the hallway behind it, but there's no one. Guards are probably still trying to figure out what's up with the lights and checking the main entrance.

"This is going better than expected," I say quietly, our progress bringing a smile to my face.

"Shut the fuck up," hisses Ghost. "Don't say shit like that."

Is the mighty Ghost superstitious? Fuck, I learn something new every day. I keep my chuckle quiet as we close the door behind us and advance into the mansion.

We pass a changing room, a sauna and a smaller indoor pool, only lit by a few maintenance lights while not in use. Enough to see the bar, the glass ceiling and the big, comfortable looking sitting area. Looks nice. Maybe we'll have a pool party after we've iced Kane. Fuck, Anne would inherit this shit, right? I'm sure she'll let us use it.

Then again, maybe not if we've killed her father.

"There!" someone yells.

The first guard drops with Ghost's bullet between his eyes. Riot gets his fists on the other one, spinning him around and slamming him into the wall head first so hard I can hear the crack from here. I wince. Pretty sure the crack wasn't the wall.

And then all hell breaks loose, with more guards running our way. "Which way is the research area, Jessica?" Ghost snaps as he guns down a square-built guy in a suit. The guy runs backwards with the momentum of the bullets until he slams into the wall and collapses.

"This way!" She takes us up a flight of stairs, and I rush ahead so she's not the first one up. Ghost and Riot are right behind, but Poe, Shiv, Junker and Skyhigh get caught at the bottom, holding back the guards as they come.

Shiv yells up, "Go! We'll keep 'em busy!"

I pretend to tip my hat at him, and then we keep on Jessica's heels.

A guard rounds the corner but obviously didn't expect us. He stops dead. "Rat girl?"

"What the fuck?" I growl and drive my fist into his face. It's satisfying to feel the bone crack. Blood spurts from his nose and his eyes roll back in his head. "Have a little respect for my woman, shithead." Not that he's listening anymore.

On the main floor of the house, I'm struck by how fucking clinical everything looks. Like one of those Scandinavian decorating magazines, where everything's white, light gray, slightly darker gray and maybe little brown for flavor. Everything looks deliberate, placed by an interior designer who doesn't have to actually live there. If I ever wondered if Kane was short of a soul, this pretty much fucking confirms it.

"Anne's suite is that way," Jessica notes as we jog past. The door looks as clean and generic as every other door in this place. She should have fucking drawings on the door, or like a big, "Stay out! Anne's room!" sign or some shit like that. Fuck, even I had that, and I hated my home enough that I fucking ran away.

"Where was your suite?" Riot asks with a grin. "In case we wanna take you there to celebrate afterwards."

"I didn't have one. Just a bedroom off her area, and if it's alright with you, I'd rather not. If you want to burn it down, then we can talk."

"Feisty," I note with a small laugh. "But honey, you're never gonna sleep here again, I promise." Not if I've got anything to say about it.

The gunshots fade as we go up another flight of stairs. I'm glad we've got Jessica. This whole place is a maze. We'd be fucking lost the moment we came in without her.

"Here." We round a corner, go down a hallway, through a door that clicks shut behind us and end up in a near circular room. A spiraling staircase follows the outer wall from the first floor, and across from us, there's a steel door. Just like the outside doors, it's got a keypad and scanner. Away from the staircase, deeper into the mansion runs another corridor. Jessica points at it. "Victor's offices are down that way, and meeting rooms and stuff like that. And that door has to be to the research wing. I've never been in there. It's off limits."

"You're sure you can't open it?" I ask.

"I'll try, but I doubt it. I was a nanny, not his assistant, remember." She touches the scanner and tries her code. Instead of the click of the door unlocking that we're hoping for, a blaring alarm goes off. "Nope."

Guess I shoulda kept my damn mouth shut.

35

JESSICA

Alarm? I've never had an alarm go off when I tried a door I wasn't coded to. But it's been a while. I learned pretty quickly not to let my curiosity overwhelm my self-preservation. I hold my hands over my ears to block out the insistent ringing. How can we turn it off?

"Someone's coming. Jessica, stay back," Ghost snaps, as stomping echoes up the stairway, clear even through the horrible ringing.

Was all this a trap after all? No, I can't believe that.

Tex puts himself close to the wall by the door, using the protruding frame to shield himself while aiming his gun. Ghost moves to the top of the stairs, taking cover behind the big balustrade with a gun in one hand and a vicious blade in the other. And Riot pushes me towards the corridor to Victor's offices, putting himself between me and where the shooting is going to be.

"Go!" he orders. "Get behind something so we don't have to worry about covering you at the same time. We'll fucking handle this."

The first couple of gunshots tear chunks out of the ceiling. Even knowing that they were going to shoot, I jump when it happens, then obey Riot, trusting him to watch my back as I run as fast as I can into the reception area for the office wing. I hide behind the corner so I can peek without exposing too much of myself.

Shouldn't Skyhigh and the others have caught up by now? I'm starting to get a really bad feeling about this.

A bullet shreds the wall right above my head, making me draw back with a scream.

"Jessica!" roars Tex.

"I'm fine! I'm fine!" I yell back. If they get hurt because I distract them, I'll never forgive myself. It feels like my fault that we're stuck here to begin with.

Someone screams, but it doesn't sound like anyone I know.

I look around the reception area. It's probably only the second or third time I've been here ever. Most of my time was spent with Anne, either in her rooms or in the recreational areas. I never questioned why, but if he had Mom locked away in his research area, maybe he wanted to make sure we never crossed paths.

I wonder if she ever saw me on the cameras over the years. If she watched me grow up from a distance.

There's not much to hide behind, other than the receptionist's desk and a couple of deep leather chairs for clients to wait in, after they've come up the fancy spiral stair from the front of the office wing. I doubt they're bulletproof. But maybe I can make myself useful. Victor's office is right down the hall. If he has anything that gives access to the lab, it'd be in there. He had me bring him things a couple of times, and at least then, my code worked on his office door.

Worth a shot. The worst that happens is the alarm keeps going off.

So while there's a full war out in front of the lab, I inch down the hall towards Victor's office. I try peeking in through the big windows first, but they're so darkly tinted I can't tell. They're electronic, so he can change the tint when he wants to, but they're set to max darkness now. That's normal when he's not in there, but it means I can't tell if the office is empty. Then again, with all the shooting and yelling going on, I can't imagine Victor just sitting in there without doing anything.

I try using my finger on the door lock, followed by my code.

The door clicks, unlocking.

Yes! Feeling way too pleased with myself, I nudge it open. The lights are off, and with the tint all the way up, the room is almost pitch black. Where's the light switch? I close the door behind me first, and it clicks as the lock engages again.

Fumbling along the door frame, I find a switch and flip it. I'm rewarded with bright light flooding the large room. Victor's massive oak desk dominates one side of the room, the back of his tall leather office chair facing me. The floor's polished wood and partially covered by a thick, tightly woven Persian rug. There are stands with sculptures on them, along with three very comfortable-looking chairs. On the wall opposite the desk, there's a floor-to-ceiling bookshelf, packed with old-looking books. I have never seen Victor read anything, so I have no idea if he has or not, but this room is built to impress, so I bet they're mainly decoration. A couple of doors in the wall across from me are closed. I've never been beyond this room so I have no idea what's in there. On the wall behind the desk hangs a saber and a tomahawk crossed over a shield, like he's some kind of warrior or great hunter. I roll my eyes.

But this is the center of his operations when he's at the estate. So maybe there's something in his desk we can use.

And that's when the chair spins, revealing Victor, dressed in his usual designer suit. "Jessica. You've come home." He's got a gun in one hand and a cigar in the other. "This is just perfect. You came straight to me."

No, no, no. Was he waiting for us this whole time? I need to get out of here. I grab the door handle and shake it, but while it rattles, it doesn't budge.

"It's locked, Jessica. Steel door, bulletproof glass. I was watching you on my screen. You didn't really think I would've let you have access to my private office, did you? Even if your bikers somehow survive out there, they'll never get through." He eases back in his chair, putting the gun on his desk and taking a drag from the cigar. "We have a little catching up to do, don't we?"

I give the door another panicked rattle, hoping that by some magic it's suddenly going to open, but it's useless. "Do we?"

I had hoped that if I ever ran into Victor again, it'd be to see him pushed off a cliff or something. But now he's got me trapped again, and all of this feels like it was just a trap.

Was it really him playing us all along? Was it a computer faking Mom's voice?

"I'm glad you came back. I was worried I might have to find other ways to convince Rebecca to keep working. I can guarantee you that they wouldn't be nearly as pleasant." Victor lights the cigar and puffs a couple of times to get it started. "This is going to make it all much easier now that you know. I can get her off my network again."

I must react, since he laughs.

"What? You think I didn't know? Your mother is a royal pain in my ass, and she's good at what she does—damn good—but she couldn't resist contacting you a bit too much once she got started. She knew it was a risk, but she did it anyway." He shakes his head. "I'll never understand people who get dragged down by their family. No. She's watching now, though. I made sure she has access to watch this office. To see that I've got you again. That she's never fucking getting away from me. Wave to your mommy, Jessica." He glances up at the security camera over his desk, then yells, "Got that, Rebecca? Never."

Is there something I can do? The gun's on his desk, but can I use it? I don't have any problem with shooting him, but I've never held a gun in my life. I'm as likely to hurt myself as him. On the other hand, what other chance do I have? I'll take a failed attempt over not even trying.

"Don't even think about it," Victor says with a chuckle as he follows my eyes. "You couldn't even lift this thing, never mind shoot me with it." Then he comes around his desk towards me, his eyes dark with evil. "You've cost me a lot of time and money,

Jessica. I'm not happy about it. I used to go easy on you. Every few days I'd pass an image to Rebecca to show her that you were alright. But that all changed, didn't it? She knows about you. You know about her. So inconvenient, but it does simplify life a bit. As long as I don't fucking kill you, Rebecca's going to do everything I tell her to. But I think it's important that she understands exactly what I'm willing to do." As he comes closer, he peels off his fancy suit jacket, straightens it, then tosses it over one of the chairs before he removes his diamond cufflinks and rolls up the sleeves to right below his elbows. "I've been looking forward to this, you little bitch."

"Leave me alone!" I back up away from him, right up until I bump up against the bookcase.

"Oh, come on, Jessica. Enough trouble." He smirks cruelly. "Besides, weren't we right in the middle of something when they came and stole you away from me?" He makes a fist with his right hand and swings.

36

RIOT

"Jessica!" I yell. There's been no sign of her during the fight. I know I told her to run back and hide, but she wasn't supposed to fucking wander off. Now I'm getting worried. "Jessica, this isn't funny. Get your pretty ass out here!"

Not that I'm not a little busy. I grunt as a huge fucking guard slams me into the wall, then kick off and propel myself right back into him. Throwing my arms out, I go low and grapple him around the waist. When I straighten, I lift him right off the ground and I run him right into the wall opposite. He grunts, and something in his torso cracks. About fucking time.

I wrestle him down, get my arm around his neck, my other around his head and twist. A snap, and then he goes limp. I jump to my feet to help the others.

Tex fires his gun, and a guard drops. Then again, and another, who was trying to run down the hallway I sent Jessica. He throws his arms out dramatically and does a face plant on the floor. Did I fuck up sending her back there? I thought she'd be safer outta the way.

If anyone's hurt her, I'm gonna break every bone in their body before I kill them.

There's no reply yet, which worries me. A guard makes it past Ghost, but he doesn't make it past me. Compared to the last guy, this fucker's dainty. I yank him off his feet with one hand and slam him head first into the wall. He drops like a fucking sack of potatoes. "Jessica!"

Pretty sure none have made it by us. Ghost's leaving a pile of bodies around the staircase, like the killing machine that he is, but when they slip past and sensibly enough stay away from him, Tex and I clean house.

But now that I've taken down the big fucker, there's

a gap, and the worry's eating at me. "I'm gonna check on Jessica. She's not answering."

"You both go," yells Ghost as he buries his knife in the throat of one of the guards and pushes the body back down the stairs. "I got this."

"You sure?" asks Tex, trying to aim past Ghost, but not taking the risk that he'll miss. "We can—"

"Go! I'll be fine. Find her!"

Fuck, I don't like leaving him alone. He can take care of himself but he isn't invulnerable. "Be back ASAP."

"Just make sure she's safe!" Ghost's gun thunders.

"C'mon." I wave for Tex to follow as we race into the reception area... which is fucking empty. Goddamn it. "Where did she go?"

Past the reception, there's a hallway filled with large, dark windows interspersed with office-ey doors. Bigger than I expected. Fuck, was someone here? Did they get her? Or did she try to do something on her own? Just like her, trying to help somehow.

If she's gotten herself in trouble, I'm gonna be fucking pissed before we make up with a good post battle fuck.

We move down the hallway, guns drawn. The windows into these rooms are so fucking tinted, I can't see through them. Dark, all of them. I try the first door. It opens, but the room's empty. Someone's office, but we're not here to look for tax evasion. Where the fuck is Jessica?

Tex tries the next door. It's locked. I try the one after. Locked too. "This is bullshit."

"We break 'em all down?" He gets his gun out again, aiming it at the lock.

"Fuck, no, there's gotta be a better way. If she's in trouble, we're wasting time breaking into every single office here. What if she's not even here, and Ghost's still out there, murdering people? Even he gets tired."

"Get back!" The yell is muted, but it's definitely female and I'm willing to bet top fucking dollar that it's Jessica.

"Where was that?"

Tex points. "This way. Come on."

"I'm not your fucking punching bag anymore!" Definitely Jessica, and definitely behind that next door.

It's fancier than the rest, and the gold name plate on it with the silver filigree reads, "Victor Kane". Fuck.

I rattle the door handle, but of course it's fucking locked. I hammer the door with my fist. "I dunno what the fuck's going on in there, but if you don't fucking open up, we're gonna bust the door down, and it'll go a hell of a lot worse for you if you do."

"Riot!" Jessica yells. "It's Victor!"

Fuck.

"Step aside," Tex says and I move. A moment later, his gun goes off twice, right into the lock. Both bullets bury themselves in the wall only inches from my fucking head. Jesus, what's that shit made of?

"Stop shooting before you kill both of us. It's bulletproof."

"The window?"

"No way. He wouldn't be sitting pretty in there if he wasn't safe." The question's just how the fuck we get him to open up.

Ideally, before Jessica's hurt.

37

JESSICA

Riot's outside, but how can I help him in?

"It's hard to get peace and quiet in here, isn't it?" Victor looks completely unbothered. "That's fine. I don't give a fuck. They can't get through, no matter how hard they try. Still…" He returns to his desk to push a button. It starts blinking red. "Just so my men know where to find them. I'm tempted to deal with you here while they can listen on the other side of the door, but I'm learning they can be much more annoying than anticipated." He opens one of the doors that lead deeper into his office suite. "Now come on."

"No." I cross my arms over my chest and glare at him. The farther away from the guys he manages to get me, the harder it's going to be for them to find me. I need to stay here for as long as I can while they figure out a way through.

"No?" He laughs cruelly. "Those bastards really have brainwashed you into thinking that you've got any kind of standing in this whatsoever. You're a tool Jessica. Rat girl. I know what my men call you, hiding in the shadows and eating my scraps. You're just a tool, and I'm not going to be talked back to by one. Now come here."

"Make me." And I give him the finger.

Maybe it's stupid. Probably it's just going to get me into even more trouble, but it feels good, especially when his eyebrows twitch. I love that I'm getting to him.

"I always knew you were stupid, but never how much." He sticks his gun in his pocket, stalking closer.

"Riot!" I scream.

The door thunders as someone hammers on it, trying to break through, but it doesn't budge. Maybe there's something they can do if I just manage to delay Victor long enough.

I pay for getting distracted. His open hand connects with my face, the strike so fast I barely saw it coming at all. My cheek lights up in pain as the force of it throws me sideways into the bookshelf. I grab at it, trying to steady myself, but I just get a couple of books with me, and hit the floor hard. My head bonks on the hardwood, making my teeth rattle.

"You little bitch," Victor growls, and for the first time in my life I see him lose his temper completely. It's terrifying. "I'm gonna tear you apart while your mother watches. Break your arms and legs, over and fucking over until they're useless and unfixable. I'm gonna knock out all your teeth so that you'll be drinking your food for the rest of your miserable life. And then I'm going to keep you alive for as long as I can, just to make you suffer. Don't you backtalk me, make gestures at me, or disobey me, ever—and I mean ever—again." He kicks me, the sharp toe of his boot digging into my side and launching me back into the wall, which I hit with a grunt. I draw ragged gasps, trying to get my breath back. Did he break my ribs? It hurts so much.

"Riot! Tex! Ghost!" I cry out with what breath I've got left, and swing one of the books right at him.

He dodges backwards. I throw it at his head, but my aim sucks and the book goes wide.

Something thuds against the bulletproof glass, accompanied by a roar that sounds more bestial than human.

"What the fuck?" Victor turns towards it.

Again, and the window rattles, like whatever's holding it in place is giving.

"You have got to be fucking kidding me," Victor swears, but for the first time, I sense a hint of fear in his voice. I want to do something, find some way to distract him, but I hurt so much I can barely stand. I push myself up on my hands and knees and suck in the urge to puke on his rug.

"Motherfucker!" Riot roars, the thick window unable to muffle his voice much, and he slams into it again. This time, there's definitely something that cracks. A couple of screws pop loose and bounce off the hardwood. I crawl towards Victor's desk while he stares at the loosening window in disbelief.

Riot roars, charges and this time he busts right through, the whole window coming off as a sheet that Victor only barely jumps out of the way of. I launch myself to my feet, running for the weapons hanging behind the desk. Maybe I can't get my hands on his gun, but I can swing that axe at him and at least keep him off balance. At least that's my theory. I'm so sick and tired of not being able to do anything.

I wince at the pain in my side as I reach for it and yank it off the wall before facing Victor. He turns to grab me just as I swing at him, gripping my weapon with both hands.

"Fuck!" I tear a good shred out of his shirt, but he jumps out of the way just in time, leaving just a thin trickle of blood where I got him over his stomach. "Drop it." He draws his gun.

"You drop it," comes Tex's ice cold voice from outside the broken window as Riot's picking himself up. If I didn't recognize the soft drawl in it, I could've imagined it was Ghost's, that's how icy it is. "You touch Jessica, and I'll put another air hole in that thick skull of yours."

I hold the tomahawk in front of me threateningly. "You better listen to them, Victor," I snarl at him, almost laughing in delight at getting to sound like a tough girl for a change.

A gun cracks. "Fuck!" Tex yells, diving in through the hole in the wall. Oh right, Victor called for more guards. On the desk, the red light still pulses slowly. While Tex is distracted, Victor raises his gun hand to shoot Tex from behind.

"No!" I scream and swing the axe as hard as I can towards his hand.

No one's more surprised than me when I connect and the blade digs deep.

Oh God, did I just see his thumb go flying?

Victor screams in a mix of pain and fury, but he drops the gun. Then he kicks me hard, knocking me back into the desk. I roll over the edge, dropping the axe with a rattle as I fall down on the other side, my breath knocked out of me. There's a thunk right next to my head, and when I roll my eyes up to look, the axe is stuck in the floor, barely an inch in front of my face.

Holy crap.

"This is ridiculous," Victor says through clenched teeth, his wounded hand dripping blood everywhere. He pushes the door open behind him and slips through, slamming it shut behind him. The lock engages long before I can even think about throwing myself at it. Then Riot and Tex are behind the desk with me, taking cover while the return fire at the guards that responded to Victor's alarm.

"You okay?" asks Tex, gripping my hand and squeezing it while he fires with the other.

"Bruised, but I will be. Victor's getting away!"

"Can't be helped. We got other shit to worry about. How many fucking men does Kane have?" Riot's drawn his gun and fires back. Someone out there screams. Since I can't help, I'm making myself as small as possible and praying his desk is bulletproof.

Suddenly, there's panicked screaming from outside the room, and the bullets stop burying themselves into the wall behind us. I risk peeking.

A body dressed in leather runs past the broken window so fast I barely believe I saw him. Someone else screams, and then he passes by again. A bunch of guns go off at once, followed by grunts and pained yells. Thumps of bodies dropping on the floor. The light catches Ghost's muscled shape holding a knife covered in dark red blood, and then there's one more strangled cry before everything turns quiet.

Ghost glares through the hole in the wall, his sharp eyes looking for us. He's bleeding from multiple cuts and something has torn a stripe out of his jacket, but he doesn't look seriously hurt. We stand up together.

"Good timing," says Riot.

"Jessica," Ghost says hoarsely. Despite being as hard and gray as slate, his eyes soften with worry. "You're okay?"

"Yeah. But Victor got away."

"Doesn't fucking matter. Anything in here that can open that door? We can get Kane later, but if that missile gets launched, the club and the neighborhood around it is rubble."

He's right. I pull open drawers in Victor's desk, looking for a key card or a code or something. Anything that might help or be an override or something. Tex opens the laptop on the desk, but it's stuck on the lock screen. "I'm no hacker," he declares.

Something catches my eye on the floor. It's bloody and gross, but it might be exactly what we're looking for. I pick it up with just my fingertips and grimace as I hold it out for them to see. "Think this will help?"

Riot chuckles. "That breaks our no cutting off fingers plan, but technically you started it. Ghost's wearing off on you, but it might work." He takes Victor's chopped-off thumb from me and wipes it off on the expensive suit jacket still flung over the chair. "We still need a code, though."

The laptop screen flickers, and the lock screen is replaced with six digits, black on white, just like on the screens down at Sparkie's Megastore. Smiling with all this carnage feels a little unhinged, to be honest, but I do anyway. I look up at the security camera.

"Thanks, Mom!"

God, it feels good to say that.

38

JESSICA

THE DOOR OPENS WITH THE FINGER AND THE CODE. It's gross and messy, but when the lock disengages, I couldn't care less. Only Ghost holding me back keeps me from rushing inside to find Mom. And to get away from all the bodies left behind in the stairwell. I'm so, *so* glad that Ghost's on my side.

"Easy. Don't wanna go through all that only to have you get hurt on the fucking finish line. We go first."

"Okay." Even so, I keep trying to look past them to spot her.

God, I don't even know what she looks like. My memory is of a woman with long hair like mine, but more honey blonde instead of mousey brown. She was beautiful, my mind tells me, but that's probably just because she's my mother. Every kid thinks that, right? Still, everything is fuzzy. I'm positive I'll recognize her if I see her, but if I were to draw her from memory, I couldn't do it. I hate that, and I hate Victor for having taken me away from her for so long.

I'd expected that we'd find a lab like in a movie, with big data screens all over the place, halogen lights in the ceilings, large dashboards with dials, knobs and blinking lights, but if there is such a place in here, it's not where we first come out. Just more doors and a hallway. I'm so sick of hallways.

There are a couple of guards, but apparently they weren't expecting anyone to manage to sneak past the security. The guys make quick work of them. It should probably worry me how desensitized I'm getting to it, and I suspect I'm going to have a major breakdown later, but right now, there's just no time. We have a mother to rescue and a city to save.

Riot and Tex try doors while Ghost stays close to me. His face is stone, but he's got an arm around my waist, holding me so hard it makes my bruises ache, like he's afraid I'll run off if he doesn't. I don't complain. My track record isn't super great. The feeling of him at my side is worth the ache, so I just ignore my bruises and put my arm around his waist, hoping he won't have to use the gun in his free hand.

"In here!" Tex calls, waving for us to follow.

By the time Ghost and I come in, he's sliding open the windows in the steel doors and peeking inside. I get chills when I'm reminded of the attack on the clubhouse earlier. God, was that really still today? It feels like a million years ago.

"It's Cooper." Riot's opening one of the doors. "He's still alive."

I recognize him when he stumbles out, looking like he's had a rough time. His clothes sit a little loosely and he looks like he hasn't seen the inside of a shower in a week. His gray hair is slicked back and greasy, thick stubble covers his face and his eyes are wild. But when he understands who we are, he lights up. "Jesus H. Christ, I thought I'd never make it out of here alive. God, I messed up." He pauses. "This is a rescue, isn't it? Not an execution squad because I jeopardized the mission or anything?"

Riot bumps his head with the flat of his hand. "Don't be an idiot. We're getting you outta here once we get what we came for."

"Kane? Is he—"

"Running for his life," Ghost says coolly. "We'll worry about him later. First we need to get everyone out alive and stop that damn missile."

"Missile?" Cooper stares wild-eyed like he's waiting for the punchline.

"Come on," says Tex, already back out in the corridor. "We'll catch you up while we look for Rebecca."

"Rebecca?" Cooper's eyes bulge out in shock.

"There's a lot to get caught up on and not much time," I say. "But until we find Mom, we're not getting out of here."

Cooper finally stares at me, suddenly realizing I'm here. "Holy shit," he whispers. "You look just like her. Jessica?"

I nod.

"Jesus Christ," he mutters.

"Down here!" Tex yells.

We follow down the hall and Kane's finger gets another use. The door slides open to reveal a room that's a lot more like I expected a lab to look like.

Not quite like the movies, but there are several computers, a worktable with wires and circuit boards, and a big wall screen with all kinds of data on it, next to a whiteboard that's been scribbled all over—diagrams, notes, a table of numbers, all sorts of stuff that I wouldn't know where to start with.

However, what steals my attention immediately is the woman who's standing there, holding her arms out, her blonde hair still long, her face a little thinner than I remember, but with a smile that's so familiar I can't believe I ever thought I couldn't remember what it looked like.

I see it every day. It looks like me.

This time, Ghost can't hold me back. Or he's decided he doesn't want to. I rush forward and throw myself in her arms.

"Mom!"

When she pulls me close, it feels like I just came home.

I squeeze her like I might never see her again, even though I just found her again. My face hurts, I want to cry so bad and lose myself in her arms, but there's no time. Not yet. But I don't let go, and neither does she. "Jessica. You don't know how hard it's been, knowing you were right out there, and not being able to get out. God knows I tried."

"I know, Mom. I know."

She chuckles softly. "I can't believe you're taller than me now. Some things aren't obvious through the security cameras."

Tex clears his throat. "I fucking hate being the asshole who's interrupting this, but you said you have something that can stop the missile?"

"Oh! Yes. Over there." She gently pulls away so she can grab a small device that resembles a remote control for a TV, though there's exposed circuitry and a wire hanging off it. Definitely a work in progress. "We have to get much closer, though."

Ghost pulls out his phone. "Hellfire. We got 'em. Got anything for me?"

"Rebecca," Cooper says almost reverently while Ghost and Hellfire update each other. "I can't believe you're alive."

"Terrence? You've looked better." She softens it with a little laugh, like something old friends might say.

He chuckles too, sounding a little raw. "I've had better weeks, to be brutally honest. But seeing both of you alive... I don't have words. You don't suppose Chester..." He trails off, like he doesn't dare even finish the question.

Mom shakes her head, her expression drawn. "I'm sorry, no. I wish I could say otherwise, but no. Victor needed me for my skills and Jessica to keep me obedient, but... Chester was a potential liability. I wish it were otherwise, but no."

He nods like he didn't expect anything else.

"We're on our way," Ghost says and hangs up. "Hellfire and the boys have the yacht in sight. A helicopter just passed over and landed there. Guessing that's Mr. One-thumb."

Tex takes the moment to give Victor's finger one last disapproving look before tossing it on the floor and kicking it under a cabinet. "Hopefully it'll take them a while to figure out where the smell's coming from."

"Let's get outta here. Skyhigh and his boys are meeting us up front. There'll be time for reunions and catching up later. We gotta stop this motherfucker."

Mom's face takes on an expression of grim determination and she clutches the remote tightly. "Right."

Two minutes later, we're racing to the harbor, me clutching Ghost tightly, Mom riding behind Riot, and Cooper seated behind Tex. Mom looks comfortable enough back there that I wonder if she hasn't ridden on the back of a motorcycle before. God, there's so much that I don't know about her and never have had the opportunity to ask. But now I'm finally going to get the chance. It's a dream come true, at least if we manage to stop Victor's missile.

We rumble onto the dock to find Hellfire and the rest of the club waiting for us.

39

GHOST

"I CALLED BACK TO HAVE THE CREW CLEAR OUT OF THE clubhouse and start doing what they can to evacuate the neighbors," Savage reports to Hellfire as we approach.

Behind him, floating well out of shooting range is Kane's luxury yacht. It's sleek, gray, and gotta be over a hundred feet long, easy. The kinda boat that you don't just take the family out on the weekend in without a full crew. There's a helipad near the back with a familiar chopper on it, the same one that Kane took off with when this whole shitshow started. Unfortunately, we can't ride our fucking bikes out there and show him what's up, so now it just sits there, taunting us, so damn close but still way the fuck out of our reach.

"Good." Hellfire turns to me. "You got something that'll get us outta this mess?"

I nod. "Thanks to Jessica and her mom. Shit show as usual, but we got it."

"I need to get closer." Rebecca jogs our way, trailed by Jessica.

When they get close, I pull Jessica against me, needing to feel that she's fucking okay. I'm not gonna pretend it's any kinda redemption for anything I've ever done, but I've never been so goddamn worried about anyone in my whole life.

"You're hurt," she says quietly, running a finger gently over my skin where my jacket ripped, next to the grazing wound left by one of the guards' bullets.

"It looks worse than it is. Just bloody." Honestly, it hurts like a sonofabitch, but it's not going to kill me so we've got more important shit to worry about. If she wants to play nurse later, I'll be happy to let her. "I'm fine."

"Rebecca, you can't do that!" Cooper exclaims heatedly, and I realize I just missed something important. "Out of the question! I didn't go through all of this just to have you sacrifice yourself."

"What's going on? What's he talking about?"

Rebecca's face is grim, but she's not backing down on whatever it is. "The range of the remote is only about thirty feet. The launcher is near the back of the yacht. Do any of your boys know how to hotwire one of the little boats here? I'm good at code, but not so great at grand theft naval. I suspect you might be more experienced here than I am."

"What she's not telling you is that she intends on getting there and doing it herself even if there's no guarantee that she'll make it away in time," Cooper snaps. "Don't you fucking dare!"

"Don't you swear at me, Terrence."

If I ever had any doubts about where Jessica got her backbone from, that voice kills them dead. I'd laugh if this wasn't fucking serious shit. "What the fuck are you talking about?"

Cooper looks as angry as I've ever seen him, even more than when he was heading in to make an ass of himself with Kane at the beach estate. "The range of that damn remote is shorter than the blast radius of that missile. If she takes a boat up there to blow up the missile, she's not coming back, and I'm not allowing her to do it."

Jessica stiffens in my arm, and I squeeze her closer, part to comfort her and part to keep her from doing something stupid like charging out there and stealing one of the boats on her own. "Mom?" she asks, her disbelief thick in that single word. Fuck, losing her mom this soon after finding her would fucking kill her.

"It's the only way," Rebecca says, clutching the remote. "And it's not a guarantee. Someone has to do it, and I'm the obvious choice. I'm the one who designed and programmed the launcher system on that missile, along with a lot of other horrible tools that I don't even want to think about. If anything goes wrong, I'm the one with the best chance of fixing it."

"That's the dumbest thing I've ever heard," snaps Cooper. "It's got one button. Are you really going to do this to your daughter?"

Rebecca hesitates. "I… I feel so useless. I wasn't expecting to make it out and now I don't know what I'm supposed to do."

Shit, I know that feeling. "What do you mean?"

She looks down at her nails, fidgeting. "I've spent ten years being very careful. Taking tiny, microscopic risks because I wanted to be able to help one day if Jessica had a chance at getting free. When this started, I was terrified because she was out of Victor's hands, but someone else's prisoner. Still, I thought that if I could keep her away from Victor for good, it was worth getting caught. I knew the first time I sent a message that they would track me down eventually. I covered my tracks well, but my resources were limited. We don't know how long we have." She points at the helicopter on the yacht's helipad. "He could be pushing the button to launch right now."

As if on cue, one of the motorboats tied up to the dock rumbles to life. "Got it," Poe yells.

"I'll do it," I say and hold my hand out. "It's our club that's under threat. Show me how to use the remote."

"What? No!" Jessica clings to my arm like she's gonna fucking tear it off. "What are you doing?"

"Not letting your mother go out there and fucking blow herself up just to save our goddamn club. What does it look like?" I shake my arm free, but she jumps right back on it.

"But... you can't! None of you. Riot, Tex, you're all... No! You're mine! You don't get to go!" She clings harder, like I won't be able to get out there with her attached to my arm.

"Something's happening on the yacht," Crank yells, pointing. A high pitched whirring sound carries over the water as a dome on the deck pulls back, revealing a launch tube. We're running outta time.

The stupid bitch runs. Motherfucker. I know she's Jessica's mom, but fuck.

I charge after her, but Cooper's there first, crashing into her and knocking her right out into the fucking water. Rebecca screams, followed by a splash. Jesus fucking Christ, does everyone here have a death wish?

"Mom!" Jessica runs to the edge of the dock to look for Rebecca. Tex gets there ahead of her, throwing his jacket aside and jumping in, not caring that it's fucking January.

"I got her!" he yells a moment later. He's got her up over the surface while she's coughing up harbor water. Lovely, I'm fucking sure.

The outboard engine on the little boat Poe started revs like one of our motorcycles and peels away from the dock like it's late for a date.

"Who's in that?" Hellfire snaps.

The boat's racing away fast enough that it's already hard to make out details, but there was only man here not wearing biker leather. "Fucking Cooper."

Riot calls to Tex, "Ladder over there."

"On it." Tex drags Rebecca with him.

"What?" Jessica runs to the end of the dock so fast I dart after her to make sure she doesn't follow her mother into the ocean. "But…"

"He took the remote when he pushed me," says a dripping wet Rebecca. Savage is coming with a blanket for her that he got out of the saddlebag on his bike.

"Does he know how it works?" Tex asks as he comes up after her, dripping wet.

She sighs. "It's not complicated. Fuck!"

We all look at her, including Jessica.

She almost looks embarrassed. "Terrence was always unpredictable and impulsive. Apparently there's no fool like an old fool. I should've seen it coming." She pulls the blanket close around her when Savage drapes it over her shoulders. "Thank you."

Jessica wraps her arms around her mother, squeezing her close and not caring that she's soaked. We're gonna have to get both of them somewhere warm in a minute. Question's just if we're gonna have somewhere to bring them.

"Stupid men and their main character complexes," Rebecca whispers.

On the yacht, the launch tube rotates and extends, getting into position. Nothing more we can do now. Either Cooper gets there in time, or the clubhouse and everything around it is about to become one big fucking crater. I hope those who stayed behind got the fuck out in time.

Someone on board has spotted the boat. Cooper zigs and zags while pot shots are taken from the deck. His shape jerks suddenly and collapses over the steering wheel, setting the boat on a straight course for the yacht.

"No," whispers Jessica.

Not looking good. I brace myself for the roar of a rocket and having to watch it streak by, knowing where it's heading. Fuck, the club was just starting to feel together again too. What the fuck are we gonna do now?

Dark gray smoke billows out of the tube. "It's gonna launch," Riot says, his voice flat and unreadable.

There's a thunk as Cooper's boat hits the yacht, not hard enough to break, but the engine's pushing it against the hull, slowly turning the back of the boat against the side. He struggles up into a sitting position and weakly waves.

Oh fuck.

The explosion starts inside the tube, fire and smoke shooting out like a fucking firecracker. A moment later, it's too much for the tube to hold, and the whole thing shatters in a massive ball of fire that engulfs the entire back of the ship, launching big chunks into the sky. Barely a second later, the sound wave hits us, a thunder crash so powerful it nearly knocks us off our feet. Jessica takes a step back, and I catch her against my front, wrapping my arms around her.

Oily, black smoke billows out, chased by deep red flames like Hell itself opened its maw to swallow Kane whole. The power of the explosion sets a tall wave racing away from the ship in all directions, including ours.

"Back," I yell, pulling Jessica with me. Riot grabs Rebecca, and we all race to get the hell away from the dock and up on higher ground. We just barely get high enough before the wave spills over it, clearing anything loose right off the dock and throwing the boats against it.

I turn in time to see the yacht crack in two, the bow and stern coming up in opposite directions. The whole fucking thing is going down. A couple of crew jump over the side and start swimming, but unless they're fast, the drag from the ship's gonna pull them in anyway. Jesus.

"Alright, let's get some boats together and look for survivors," Hellfire orders. "If we're lucky, Cooper got himself away, and the ship's cook doesn't deserve to drown just because his boss was a fucking asshole. Poe, get some more of those boats going. See what you can do, but boys, no risks. Enough people have died today. And be quick about it. Cops are gonna be here real soon asking questions I don't want to answer."

40

JESSICA

I wake up feeling like yesterday was a dream.

They found Cooper's body. I wish I'd had the chance to thank him for everything. He might not have known his need for revenge would end up saving both me and Mom, but it did, and it's given me so much more, too. We'll never forget what he did for us, even unintentionally, and in the end, he sacrificed everything to save a lot of people.

Mom and I talked late into the night at Bonnie's. She and Anne won't be back until later today, so we could have time by ourselves.

It was emotional, wonderful... strange.

We love each other, but we're strangers now. Bonded by our relationship and our shared, but different, trauma. Mom wanted me to stay with her last night, but I couldn't. I was exhausted, and all I wanted to do was be with Ghost, Tex and Riot. We crashed in Tex's room. At some point during the night, Ghost moved to the couch.

I hate that he doesn't trust himself, but some things don't get solved overnight. It's a work in progress.

It must be early, because even Riot is asleep. I look over and see him on his stomach, facing away from me with one arm under his pillow and one leg bent with the other stretched out. His butt looks so good that I want to tug his briefs down and give it a pinch.

Tex is on my other side, dead asleep with one hand resting on the top of my thigh. His skin is warm against mine, and even though he's not awake, something farther down definitely is. The tip of his cock is juuuuust peeking out of the top of his boxers. I giggle under my breath, reaching out to give it a tiny poke. He grunts, shifting in his sleep. It looked at me first, right?

He's definitely the one that's the most out and ready, so I start there. Rolling over slowly and carefully so I don't wake anyone yet, I slide down the bed until I'm face to face with his morning erect cock. Carefully hooking my fingers in his briefs, I tug them down a little more, just to get more of him out. Freed from the pressure of the waistband, his full length springs up and almost bops me on the nose. Hey!

Then I lean in and give it a soft kiss. It twitches and Tex mumbles something sleepily, but doesn't wake up. I lick softly. It's kinda fun to play without any performance anxiety.

"Hm?" He shifts, starting to wake up.

I wrap my fingers around his thickness, at least as far as they'll go, and start teasing the thick ridge around the head with the tip of my tongue while I stroke slowly. I still feel so new at this, but they're good teachers, and if I don't practice, how am I going to learn, right?

"Oh, fuck," he groans.

I take the whole head into my mouth, tasting the salty drop that just formed at the tip. I keep looking up at him, waiting for the moment he opens his eyes and sees me. It's totally worth it.

"Good morning to you, too." He laughs softly and smiles, brushing the hair out of my face so he can see better. "You can fucking wake me up like this anytime you want."

I start to bob, eager for more. He moans, his strong fingers sliding into my hair until he's guiding my head up and down. He's so thick between my lips, his pulse thrumming through his whole length. He's even harder now that he's awake, gone from casual morning wood to horny steel.

Riot rolls over, grinning when he sees what we're up to. He strips out of his underwear, revealing a cock that's rapidly waking up to join the fun. "This a private party?" He gives himself a couple of strokes, helping the process along.

I shake my head, never letting Tex out of my mouth. The next thing I know, Riot's shifting down to caress my butt. He places a kiss on one cheek as he slides a hand between my legs. He finds me so excited and slick that his finger slides right in. I moan around Tex, which gets another moan in response. There's no way Ghost is going to stay asleep much longer. I'm surprised he's not awake already, or maybe he is, enjoying the show before he decides to join in.

Riot gives my butt a little swat. "Up. All fours. Knees spread," he orders like a drill sergeant. I obey immediately. It gives me a better angle anyway.

He slides in underneath me, on his back, so that when his huge hands settle on my ass cheeks, he can pull my pussy right down to his mouth. With his beard brushing against the insides of my thighs, his tongue delves deep, making me squirm on his face as he drives me wild.

We form a pleasure chain, Riot plowing his tongue through my folds, before dipping inside me or flicking over my clit. At the same time, I do my best to bring Tex over the edge, to give him the best wake-up call of his life. He lets go of my hair and reaches down to palm my breast, then captures my nipple between his fingers and starts rolling it. Pleasure shoots through me in a steady stream, washing down my body in a hot wave of lust. I moan and flutter my tongue along the thick vein up the underside of Tex's length. I roll my hips, pressing myself harder against Riot.

A hand wraps itself in my hair again. My first thought is Tex, but the angle is wrong. I glance to the side and find that Ghost has joined us. He's watching me with lust-darkened eyes. The corner of his mouth quirks up. "Room for one more?"

"Mmmhmmm," I hum around Tex's cock.

Ghost uses his grip to guide my head down on Tex, controlling my speed for a few strokes before letting go so he can get naked and join the action. He must've been watching for a bit, because he's already fiercely hard. I love it when they take control, and straight up show me how to please them.

Riot tongues me harder. Faster, like he's trying to distract me while I'm busy with Tex and Ghost. It works. Each swipe feeds the tingles and drives the wave of my approaching climax higher. The only question is, can I get Tex there before Riot takes me over the edge?

Tex moans harder and louder, his hips rolling gently, going deeper with each thrust. He's getting close, but so am I. I close my eyes and let the sensations flood me, push me higher, bring me closer. God, how are they so good at this? I'm losing the race, I think, but I'm winning anyway.

I explode from the depths of my core, the shock wave spreading through me and raising goosebumps the whole way. My body goes tight and Tex's cock springs from my mouth as I lose control and cry out. The orgasm tears through me, driving me completely over the edge. I dig my fingers into the bed sheets, hanging on for dear life while my body quivers and my ability to reason scatters to the winds. When I finally come back down to earth, I roll to the side, flopping to the bed with Ghost on one side, and Tex and Riot on the other.

Ghost shifts, lifting and moving my legs so he can get between them and line himself up. His cock, already wrapped, presses at the opening of my sex. "Ready for me?" He teases, using his thick head to massage me everywhere except inside where I want him. I groan and wiggle my hips. If he doesn't hurry up, I might just murder him.

But when he slides inside, all's forgiven. I was definitely ready for him. So ready that I take all that thickness with nothing but pleasure and a soft moan. He doesn't go fast, doesn't rush. He just drives into me, long, slow and powerful, and when he bottoms out, I can't hold back my cry of ecstasy.

I'm still twitching with pleasure and he's just started, grinding deep and hard with every stroke. "Please... don't... stop..." I manage to gasp.

Tex and Riot claim spots on opposite sides of me. There are hands everywhere, and I don't even know whose are whose anymore. Along my hip, across my throat, digging into my hair. Riot tilts my head and guides me to a hard cock that I open my mouth to accept. These men have made me feel more pleasure in one morning than in the lifetime that came before.

My senses are overwhelmed with the taste of Riot, the rocking of Ghost thrusting into me, and the two men working their agile fingers over my breasts in perfect rhythm. My legs and stomach tighten as a second wave builds. This time, I'm not the only one. Riot groans and his hips flex as he holds the back of my neck, his other hand caressing my breast while I suck him.

"Fuck!" Ghost snaps, pulling out suddenly. "Tex, take over. Not ready to be done yet."

The next thing I know, Tex is between my thighs, his thick shaft pushing into my pussy. He groans as he slides deep, making take all of him. God, that's good.

"Lube, top drawer," he growls. "You feeling daring, honey? Time to teach you something new."

God yes. I nod. Riot slips out of my mouth. I'm breathless, I can't talk, but I want it so badly I'm shaking with need.

Tex grabs the bottle when Ghost tosses it over, pouring a generous amount into his hand. His cock slides out, leaving me empty and aching for more, but I trust it'll be worth it. He spreads the slick liquid over my pussy and lets it trickle between my cheeks. By the time he's done, I'm slippery everywhere.

He angles my hips a little higher, and his hazel eyes bore into mine as his cock nudges my ass. I take a deep breath. I've done this before. I know how good it can feel, and I trust them to take care of me.

"Just relax, honey. I'll go real easy."

He pushes, and the pressure is enormous, but not painful. Just so full. A breath hisses between my teeth and he freezes.

"No, no," I gasp. "Keep going."

Riot takes one of my breasts in his mouth while Ghost does the same on my other side. I gasp at the sudden pleasure as Tex eases his thick length in little by little until I feel his balls resting against me. He gives me a second, letting me adjust to being filled up, before he withdraws, until the tip is barely inside me.

"You're so fucking sexy," he says, his voice rough as gravel as he thrusts back into me. "Stay with me," he warns, right before carefully rolling us over until he's under me and I'm lying with my back against his chest. "Lift your legs, honey. Let Riot in."

Oh. Yeah, okay, this will be new.

I'm so nervous, and yet I want it more than anything. I lift my legs and Riot slips in between my thighs. It's so slick between us. "Oh my God," I whisper at the thought of what's to come. They're both really big, but having both of them in me at once...

"Ready?" asks Riot.

I nod. Pretty sure I am, at least.

He smiles, and slowly pushes himself in. The pressure is unbelievable, but there's no pain. He's barely an inch or two inside me when my legs start trembling.

"Go slow. Please," I pant.

Tex stays completely still as Riot slowly fills me, easing me onto them.

Riot growls. "Fuck, that's tight. So fucking good."

They move slowly at first, but soon they find a rhythm. Ghost watches, condom discarded. He strokes himself until my breath evens out and I start moving. Then he comes closer and points his cock toward my face.

"Open."

I don't even hesitate. His cock slides in, thick and hard. They work together, constantly pushing me to take more, but never all three at the same time. Tex and Riot go slow as Ghost takes my head firmly in his hands and fucks my mouth. And when Tex and Riot start to move, Ghost backs off so I don't get overwhelmed.

We become four parts of a greater whole, with me at the center. It's not just that my pussy and ass are being stuffed at the same time, or that Ghost's thick head keeps hitting the back of my throat. It's the power they have over me and the pleasure they give. It's obscene, but also beautiful.

I want it to last forever, but finally I can't hold back anymore. My back arches, pressing my shoulder blades into Tex's broad chest. My legs wrap tight around Riot's narrow hips, and my nails dig gouges into someone's skin as I unravel between the three of them.

I can barely breathe. My body tenses. My pussy and ass both clamp down as I unravel between them. Riot curses as he buries his face between my breasts and groans. He bites me lightly, and that extra bit of stimulation is like an electric current straight to my core, adding to the intensity of my release. Then his thrusts lose rhythm, his hips jerking and grinding into me.

Ghost comes next, flooding my tongue with his thick cum, so much that I can't swallow it all. Some runs over my lips and slides slickly down my chin while he pulses over and over again, like there's no end to it. I tease him, sucking hard until he has to pull away with a shiver.

"Jesus," he sighs as he sags back to sit on the bed.

Tex holds back, last man standing, until he pushes all the way and releases with a groan so deep I can feel his chest rumble against my back. He holds me tight as his cock throbs inside me. When he finally relaxes, he rolls me sideways off him, settling me back onto the mattress between the three of them.

I'm surrounded by killers, and never felt so safe and protected in my life.

Content.

That's a concept I couldn't even imagine a couple of weeks ago, but here I am. My future is still very much undecided, but it doesn't feel insurmountable anymore. With the guys at my side, there's nothing I can't do, or overcome.

"Promise you'll never leave me," I murmur. "I don't know if I could ever deal with being without you."

Riot pushes himself up on one elbow and looks at me like I'm crazy. "Why would we leave you?"

Tex trails a finger over my hip and up my side. "You're stuck with us, Jess. You gotta know that."

I look over at Ghost, half expecting him to pull back, but he nods.

"I'm broken as fuck, no point in hiding it. Probably always will be, but you and me? If you're willing to deal with the sharp edges, I'm too selfish to say no."

"If you're broken, so am I." I laugh softly. "We can help each other glue ourselves back together. I just need to know that you guys aren't going to trade me in for the next crazy girl that comes along."

"The fuck?" Tex rears up, and I think that's the first time I've seen his anger pointed at me. "You really think this is normal for us? That we sit around talking about our fucking feelings all the time? Sex is sex, but love is a whole different thing."

"No." I shake my head. "I just... Love?"

"Well, I don't know what else to call it," says Riot. "We're not fucking poets, Jess. If you need fancy words all the time, you're in for disappointment, but words are cheap. We'll fucking show up for you. Every day. Don't doubt it."

Ghost's eyes are gray steel under knit brows. "Our life ain't easy, baby. You've seen Bonnie. Do you think it's worth it to hitch yourself to men like us? I can't promise that shit won't get tough again, but I can promise you that I'll bleed myself dry to keep you safe, and so long as there's breath left in my body, I'll do what it takes to come home to you. Can you take that risk? Can you accept us for who we are?"

Tears spring to my eyes, and there's nothing I can do to stop them. He's right. I've seen how devastated

Bonnie is after losing General, and I know he gave his life for the club. One day that could be me.

But I've also seen the look on her face when she's looking at their pictures. When she talks about their life together, and when her fingers trace her patch on the wall. I know that if someone asked Bonnie if it was worth it, she would say exactly what I'm about to.

"Yes. A thousand times, yes."

41

GHOST

I let Tex and Riot through the door first, then shut it tightly behind me. What's about to happen isn't suitable for anyone else to see. It's too fucking personal.

The cell is bare, the same one that Jessica hid in when Kane sent his troops here. It feels like poetic justice. Something the man curled up on the floor opposite from us, his legs and arms still tied together, will never appreciate.

It doesn't fucking matter, and I don't fucking care.

Riot kneels next to him, makes a fist in his hair and forces him to look up at us.

Victor Kane has seen better days.

"How you feeling?" Tex asks with deceptive light-heartedness. "We picked you up outta the water just in time, I think. Close call. You mighta missed out on this little reunion if we hadn't."

We let him mellow for a couple days, let him think real hard on what might be waiting for him while we made sure Jessica was good. She's never ever gonna hear about this. Doesn't feel real good to hide it from her, but we don't want her having to think about this shitheel again, if we can fucking help it. And what's gonna happen next would only upset her.

But Kane has earned himself a real dose of the kind of justice only three angry members can show him. Just drowning out there was too good for him after what he did.

He looks between the three of us, a little wild-eyed. Fearful. And I fucking love that. The monster that hurt Jessica for so long, I'm almost surprised he remembers what it means to be scared.

But he chooses bravado. "What are you animals planning? Extortion? Ransom? I'll give you money."

I shake my head. "Don't need money."

"Weapons? I can get my hands on anything you could possibly want. Tanks. Bombs. A fucking fighter jet if you want it."

"Nah. I think we're good."

Realization is starting to come to him. I can see. Eyes widening just a little, pupils widening a little more. The tic of the artery in his neck as his heart speeds up. The nervous wetting of his lips as it sinks in that we didn't bring him in here because we wanted anything from him.

Other than blood.

Riot draws Kane's attention back to him. "So... unfortunately, none of this is going to undo ten years of using Jessica as your personal punching bag, but I have to admit, I'm looking forward to this anyway. If you can't fix it, at least fuck shit up, right?"

Tex leans in and smirks cruelly. "In case you didn't figure it out, you're the shit."

"Don't be stupid. There has to be something I can give you to make this go away. I'm filthy rich. I can give you just about anything." Desperation now that he fully understands. "Please, we don't have to do this."

Grabbing his collar with his huge fist, Riot hauls him up to his feet. I pull out one of my knives, and Kane finally fully panics.

"No! Please, no!"

"Relax. I'm just cutting you loose." Riot spins him around and presses his face against the wall so I can get at his wrists. His hand is bandaged where his thumb used to be. Woulda hated to have him bleed out early. Then I slice through the rope, barely even nicking him. Maybe a little. I crouch, and cut his legs free, too, then put the knife away. "See? If you can get out of this room, you're free to go. How's that? I promise. And unlike you, I keep every single promise I make. Think you can do it?"

Kane eyes the door, briefly, but his gaze keeps flitting between the three of us, trying to watch us all at once. We all know he doesn't have a chance.

I'll give him this. He tries. Not very well, but he tries.

He pretends to lunge towards Tex, then jumps the other way, trying to dash past us to the door, his only chance of getting out.

Riot's fist in his gut stops him dead. Kane collapses, trying to catch the breath that's been knocked out of him. We give him time. We're not in a hurry. He abused Jessica for ten fucking years.

He tries again, even knowing that he doesn't have a chance. I punch him right in that fucking face of his, knocking him right off his feet and flat onto his back. He screams in pain as his head bounces off the hard floor. He tries to roll over, but he's dizzy already.

He tries to get up on all fours, but Tex kicks him hard in the side, dropping him right back to the floor.

"See, normally I'm not a fan of unfair fights," I say, happy to watch him squirm on the floor. "But then again, most people don't murder a girl's parents before keeping her around to beat on. She didn't have a fucking chance. You never gave her a fucking chance. So this feels appropriate. Right, you know?"

He grunts and spits out a mouthful of blood.

"So I'm gonna make you a second promise. You're not gonna leave this room alive."

He doesn't last nearly as long as he deserves, but when we haul his corpse out to the pier, tie a hunk of concrete around its neck and toss it into the water, it's still a sense of fucking closure. And now when she wakes up in the middle of the night because of a nightmare he gave her, we can honestly tell Jessica that he's never gonna fucking bother her again.

42

JESSICA

It's not often that women and outsiders are welcome at Church, but this is a special occasion. I don't think this is the wedding that Mom ever envisioned for me, or that I ever did, for that matter, and I guess technically it's not even really a wedding, but Ghost, Riot and Tex are claiming me as their old lady, and that's good enough for me.

At least I'm wearing a dress today. Most days it's tight jeans and T-shirts, and after a decade in an ugly nanny uniform, I've grabbed the opportunity to find a new me with both hands. But today's special. Besides, the guys expressed a preference for me wearing a dress with nothing underneath so there was less to get in the way of the celebration afterwards.

I *am* wearing something under, but I don't think they'll mind when they see.

My dress starts out white on top with a tight, strapless corset. From the waist down, it spreads out in a wide, flowing, layered skirt of tulle that grows darker the lower and deeper you get, creating a color transition from pure white to almost pure black that stops right around my knees. Instead of dainty pumps, I'm wearing leather boots that lace all the way up to mid-calf, and over my shoulders, I have a sheer black embroidered shawl that's light over my shoulders, accented to match the darker shades further down. My hair's up, a silver tiara perched on top. I feel like a biker princess. It's awesome.

"You look so beautiful!" Anne beams at me, standing close to Bonnie.

With Victor gone, it turned out that Anne really wasn't in any official system. She'd been tutored at home, kept out of the public eye, and I doubt Victor filed a single official government form in his life. That left her adrift when Victor disappeared, and it was probably a sign of how absent of a father he'd been that she handled his death so easily. Not that she wasn't sad, but it's more aspects of her old life she misses rather than Victor. And she's still got me.

But more importantly, she's got Bonnie, who—once we realized Anne didn't have any near relatives and was basically adrift—was quick to take her in, and now Anne's getting the closest thing to a normal life she's ever had. She smiles up at Bonnie and takes a step closer for another hug. Is Bonnie perfect? No. Does Anne probably get a little too much coffee for her age? Yes. Is she learning way too many bad words way too early? Almost definitely. But Bonnie's been adrift too, after losing General, and with all the love she's got to give, I think Anne moving in was the perfect solution. More importantly, I think both of them do, too.

I've learned that Church is a pretty common term for meetings in MCs, but I love that the Outlaw Sons can have theirs in an actual church. It adds a whole new level of gravity to it. And it makes what we're about to do seem a little more... real, a little more legitimate, in a way. Not that it truly matters. I would do this with the guys anywhere, and it would be just as real. But I like it. It makes me feel good.

"Here, you can hide in this," says Bonnie and hands me a long black cloak. "So you can see the rest of it, but the guys don't get to see how gorgeous you look for them before it's their turn. Good to keep an element of suspense, right?"

She grins as I take it from her and wrap it around myself. It's just a little bit longer than my dress. Perfect.

I feel a smile spreading on my face. The boys had better have a good reaction in store for me when I reveal my look, or they're not getting any afterwards.

Oh, who am I kidding? I wouldn't deprive myself like that.

There's someone here today that I'm actually curious to meet. Over on one side, watching the altar platform while sipping a bottle of water, is a woman with honey blonde hair almost all the way down to her waist. She's got a baby bump well on the way, and she's watched over by three big bikers from the Screaming Eagles MC. Tex pointed them out to me earlier, since apparently several guys taking a single old lady together has become a thing over there, and she's one of them. Mila, I think they told me. And her brother's getting blooded in the Outlaw Sons today.

I'll have to try and talk to her later, though, because Hellfire strides up to the front and takes the steps up to stand next to the altar. "We got a new member to bring on board today. He's shown bravery, skill and concern for his brothers in ways most prospects never manage. Fuck, some of you boys could do with some pointers. Sinner, come up here."

Sinner approaches the altar, and now I see the resemblance between him and Mila. Knowing how close MC members are, not to mention forward, I can understand why he might not want to be at the same club where his sister was getting frisky with three of the guys.

Hellfire, his long hair loose and every inch the president, nods at Sinner. He holds up a sharp-looking knife. "You started life as Danny. But you've chosen and earned the name Sinner. Are you free of all other loyalties and ready to take up your role in our brotherhood?"

"I am," Sinner says without hesitation.

"We have expectations and you know 'em. You ride when we say ride. You fight when we say fight, and you always put the club ahead of everything else. You listen to your seniors. You never betray a brother. Within the club, you will always show integrity. Your soul is ours, but we're gonna protect it. You're not just joining a club, you're becoming a brother amongst brothers. If you have any fucking doubts whatsoever, now's the time to take your leave. It's a hard life, and no one's gonna think less of you."

"I'm not going anywhere."

"Then merge your blood with ours." Hellfire hands him the knife and puts a large steel chalice on the altar.

Sinner takes the knife in his right hand and puts his left forearm above the chalice. Then, in a move that makes me wince, he makes a cut about halfway up to his elbow. He makes a fist, making a thick line of blood well out and drips into the silver container below.

"Welcome to the Outlaw Sons. You're now one of us," Hellfire declares.

Sinner turns around and holds up the bloodied knife. Now I know why they're referred to as blooded members. And here I thought it was just an expression.

The whole club cheers for Sinner, so loud that it rattles the stained glass windows. Hellfire holds out something to him while taking the knife back. "Here's your patches. They better fucking be on your jacket and cut next time I see you." Then he pats Sinner on the arm. "Sit down and have a beer. We got one more thing to take care of today. Ghost, Riot and Tex, get your asses up here."

Oh God. It's us. It's our turn, and suddenly after wanting to get it over with all day, I'm nervous. Not cold feet anything, but it's insane that this is even happening. A weird moment of what the hell am I doing, getting hooked up with not just one, but three dangerous bikers.

Mom's sitting right up front after she gave me a good luck hug and the oh so encouraging, "I think you're insane jumping into something like this, but I see that they make you happy. Just make sure they know that if they hurt you, I'll come hunting them. And now that Victor is gone, they'll never see it coming."

I completely believe her. We're still getting to know each other again after all the time apart, and honestly? I think being locked up for ten years doing nothing but designing weapon systems makes a person a little strange. But she could say almost the same thing about me. I love her, and she loves me. Her smile is honest, even if she doesn't understand me.

"I gotta be straight with you all. I'm not sure where to start with this." This has to be the first time I've seen Hellfire uncertain, and from the surprised looks on the guys' faces, it might be for them too. "The Outlaw Sons has always been a dangerous club to belong to. More than many clubs, violence or preventing violence is what we deal in. Old ladies have been few and far between. There's Bonnie, the Boss Bitch herself, of course." He gestures at Bonnie and she nods graciously. "A few others, but the Sons have a nasty habit of expiring before anything permanent happens. You fuckers—all of you—are the survivors. The men that I would fucking trust my own life to, and you trust me the same way every day you let me be your president. So what I'm saying is that this is new to me, and three members with a single chick? Even newer."

He looks my way, and the guys follow his gaze to me, to where I'm standing at the end of the church aisle, still covered in my cloak. Whether Hellfire is still uncertain or not, they definitely aren't. The way all three of them watch me like a pack of predators hunting a baby bunny… Well let's just say that saying they look hungry doesn't cover half of it. And those nerves I felt earlier? Replaced by a swirling heat that starts at my core and goes all the way up.

I drop my cloak dramatically, and start my walk up to them.

I swear their jaws drop to the floor and their eyes get twice as big. When they get past the initial shock, Tex's mouth quirks into a disbelieving grin. He's wearing his Stetson hat, which gives him an extra dose of dashing for the big day. Riot struggles to drop his expression of surprise, his eyes wide and his mouth open. Ghost's expression has turned calculating, like he's already planning exactly how he's going to peel this dress off me before having his way with me. Or maybe how to leave it on. I was feeling hot at their hunger before, but the way he's watching me now has it going nuclear. And we're not even through whatever ceremony Hellfire has in mind.

It's exactly the kind of reaction I was hoping for, so luckily, I don't have to pretend that we're not going to fuck like rabbits after this.

There's a murmur through the crowd as I walk up, but all I've got eyes for are Tex, Ghost and Riot. Tex hops down to take my hand at the bottom of the altar and lead me up the stairs to stand with him and the others. "You look fucking beautiful," he says loud enough for everyone to hear. Ghost nods slowly, his slate gray eyes never letting up a moment. Riot's still shocked.

When I get close enough, I whisper to Riot, "You're going to catch flies like that."

He laughs and puts his big hand on my hip. I feel a little bit claimed already.

"Well, boys, you went and did it," Hellfire grumbles. "Somehow you convinced her to put up with all three of you. For good. You must be fucking amazing lays, that's all I can imagine, and I don't want to imagine that hard. You don't see a lot of ladies interested long term in the Sons. They love coming here for danger and fun for a while, but they never stick around. I know you know what you're getting into, Jessica. More than most, but it gets rough around here. Just ask Bonnie."

I glance her way, and find her looking grim. She nods briefly. But I can't back out now. I don't want to. "I know," I say, barely loud enough to be heard. The idea that I might someday lose them terrifies me, but not as much as trying to live without them. It just feels so right. So louder, I add, "But I'm not going anywhere."

Hellfire nods as Tex grabs my hand and squeezes it. He turns and grabs a leathery bundle off the altar that he holds. "Good. You guys are lucky to have found someone who's willing to put up with your shit. If I ever, and I mean fucking ever, hear that you boys mistreat something that fucking precious, I'll come right on over and tear those damn patches off you myself, before I kick your asses out of the club. At the very fucking least. Clear?"

"Clear," Ghost says for all of them. Tex and Riot nod.

Hellfire hands the leathery bundle over to Ghost. "By wearing this, Jessica, you are carrying the name of the Outlaw Sons and are expected to show loyalty to both the club and your men, just as by claiming you, they will be responsible for you so long as you bear their patches. Do you understand?"

I nod. "Yes."

Ghost smiles, like an actual big, real smile, and it only makes it even more obvious how amazingly handsome he is. Him and Riot and Tex. Then he holds up the bundle and lets it unfold. It's a leather jacket, shiny and black. He turns it so I can see the back.

In the middle is the Outlaw Sons logo. Over the top, it says "Property of" and around the bottom, it says "Ghost, Tex and Riot." Then he turns it again and holds it so I can put it on.

I pull my shawl off so it doesn't get bunched up under it and hand it to Tex. Then I slip my arms into the smooth leather until I'm all the way in. When Ghost lets go, it settles on my shoulders. "It fits perfectly."

Riot grins. "Got a little help from Bonnie."

I turn around to the crowd just as Hellfire declares, "Make a little noise for Jessica, the first old lady to claim three Outlaw Sons at one time. Welcome to the club."

And everyone cheers. The members, Mom, Bonnie, Anne, whose high pitched voice cuts through all the men's rumbling, even the Screaming Eagles and Mila. And I feel so loved, in a way I never thought I could. That I never thought I would. I'm the most protected girl in the whole city, and I'll sic my bikers on anyone who tries to tell me otherwise.

43

JESSICA

I used to hate the holidays.

It's been a year since I stood in Victor's beach estate, not daring to hope for freedom, but just hoping to live to the next year. And the universe answered. Ghost, Tex and Riot charged into my life, guns blazing and shattered my entire world. Who'd have thought they'd be the ones to help me put it back together, better than I could ever have hoped for?

We're gathered at Bonnie's, with a real Christmas tree, complete with presents, eggnog, decorations, so many blinky lights I almost want to switch my regular glasses out for sunglasses. And I'm part of it. I can barely believe it myself. This isn't a life I ever would have imagined. It's so much better. I'm surrounded by people who actually care about me. I know how much work the boys and Bonnie put into making this right, and I love them so much for it.

Even Anne is smiling, rearranging the ornaments that she made so they show better on the tree.

My arm aches a little. One of the gifts from the guys was taking me to get my first tattoo. A sunrise on my right arm, so I'll always remember where my life really started. It hurt less than I thought it would, but then, maybe I've just known what being hurt really feels like, and a few needle pokes didn't seem so bad. Like Ghost told me, we're always going to be a little bit broken. But that doesn't mean we have to let it rule us.

And they got some, too. One each. My name right near their hearts.

My only complaint is that it isn't snowing, but that would be exceptional around here. Still, it's been cold this year, more than last year, so I've been hoping.

"Jess! Look!" Anne holds up something for me to look at, so close that I have to take a step back to see what it is.

I read the cover of the plastic case. "Mayhem City Six?"

"It just came out! Now me and Bonnie can start the campaign from scratch, and they've added building your own homes and designing them, and a whole new fight mode where you can pick up almost anything around you to use it as a weapon, and there's a ladder now and a battle pass with all these cool cosmetics, and—"

I hold up my hand, laughing. "You lost me like five steps ago, but I'm glad you're happy." Bonnie's grinning almost as widely as Anne, so much that I suspect it to be something that's just as much for her as for her overly energetic adoptive daughter. It wouldn't be my first choice, but so long as it makes them happy.

Tex swings up behind, wrapping his arm around my waist and pulling me close. "Everything good?" He kisses the top of my head.

"Everything's amazing." I reach behind me to give his hard ass a squeeze. "Just perfect."

Riot toasts me with his beer from the couch. "We did our best. Everyone deserves a little Christmas, right?"

Oh God, that almost has me tearing up. I never thought I'd be here, and it's so much better than I imagined.

Mom smiles as she comes out of the kitchen and stops next to me, sipping on eggnog taken from the grown-ups bowl, the one with the rum in it. "Well, I have to admit I was a little skeptical at first, but I'm really proud of you, you know? This isn't the life I would have chosen for you, but they love you so much. Your dad and I had that once, and it's worth grabbing and holding on tight when you find it, no matter where that may be."

"Oh come on, I'm going to get weepy soon." Never mind that I'm basically there already.

"Then I won't drag it out." She finishes her mug, before giving me a warm hug. "It's getting late, and I'm getting back to my place. The taxi is here already. These old bones could do with their own bed tonight." Once she managed to prove that she was in fact still alive, it turned out that she had considerable assets to draw on. Now she's got a nice little house, just big enough for her and a big orange tabby named Cooper.

"Jeez, you're still in your forties. Don't you old bones me."

She smiles and pulls me in for another hug. "Fine, but I'm tired. I can tell that Anne and Bonnie are itching to get that game up and running, and I'm sure you and your boys have celebration plans of your own." She winks, and I don't know whether to blush or just be scandalized that the suggestion is coming from my own mother.

"Honestly, you're welcome for as long as you like."

"We'll meet for lunch tomorrow, okay? I'll call you. There's a new place down the street from me that has an amazing soup and sandwich combo."

I nod, amazed again that this is my life now.

Mom was right, of course. Anne and Bonnie lose themselves in the game almost immediately, and after humoring them for a bit, but mostly just smiling and nodding at each other every time Bonnie and Anne achieved something new, we decide to take off, too. Riot and Tex still have their old rooms in the school, but they use them more as hangout space than for living these days. We rearranged Ghost's place and got a bigger bed. It's not going to work long term, and the club is eyeing a row of run down houses on the other side of the wall, but for now we're happy.

As we cross the compound, a tiny flake of white lands on my nose. "Snow? Seriously?" We all look up. It's not much, just a very light dusting, but for a part of the country that rarely gets any at all, it's like a sign. Like I made the right choice. My perfect Christmas, with my... well honestly imperfect guys, but they're perfect for me.

But it's cold too, so we hurry back inside where we can rely on shared body heat. As soon as we're in, the guys are more than ready to throw me on the bed, but I hold up a hand. "Stop! Wait!"

Ghost frowns. "Something wrong?"

That makes me smile. "No! Everything's perfect. But I have presents for you guys."

"You didn't have to," says Tex, getting behind me so he can kiss me on the head. "You're gift enough for us."

"But I wanted to. And... well, I'm pretty sure you'll like them."

"Well, now I'm curious." Riot grins widely as he leans

his butt against the top of the backrest of one of the chairs.

Out of a bag that I sneakily hid behind the leather couch, I pull out three boxes, rectangular, a little bigger than a regular piece of paper and a lot thicker. "One for each of you."

After a couple of curious glances, the three of them tear their gifts open. A sudden flash of nervousness hits me. They're pretty personal, and now I'm wondering if this was a good idea after all, but I'm already committed.

Riot's the first one to get his out. "It's a... calendar?" He's confused for almost a full second before he flips it open to January and grins. "Holy fuck, this is perfect."

Tex gets a glance of it, and then shreds the wrapper on his so he can get it open. Riot's already flipping through the months like a horny teenager who just discovered centerfolds. Because that's basically what they are.

Of me.

"I used my phone camera, so they're not really professional, but I got that little tripod and just...

you know, tried. I printed everything out myself since I didn't dare send it anywhere. And I found some ribbon to tie the pages together. They're all different, one for each of you." I'm rambling because I'm so nervous. "So they're real basic, but—"

"Fuck, it's perfect. This is giving me some ideas." Riot has stopped on one page and he's rotating it in front of himself like it'll get him a better angle. "Some serious, fucking ideas. Or some serious fucking, ideas."

Ghost looks up over his, and I have no idea which month he stopped on, but his eyes are smoldering so hard they're almost on fire. Maybe I didn't do so bad after all. "Bed. Now."

Merry Christmas to me, because I think I'm about to get exactly what I hoped for: three big, strong, dangerous, naked bikers who'd do anything for me.

And hopefully, *to* me.

his butt against the top of the backrest of one of the chairs.

Out of a bag that I sneakily hid behind the leather couch, I pull out three boxes, rectangular, a little bigger than a regular piece of paper and a lot thicker. "One for each of you."

After a couple of curious glances, the three of them tear their gifts open. A sudden flash of nervousness hits me. They're pretty personal, and now I'm wondering if this was a good idea after all, but I'm already committed.

Riot's the first one to get his out. "It's a... calendar?" He's confused for almost a full second before he flips it open to January and grins. "Holy fuck, this is perfect."

Tex gets a glance of it, and then shreds the wrapper on his so he can get it open. Riot's already flipping through the months like a horny teenager who just discovered centerfolds. Because that's basically what they are.

Of me.

"I used my phone camera, so they're not really professional, but I got that little tripod and just...

you know, tried. I printed everything out myself since I didn't dare send it anywhere. And I found some ribbon to tie the pages together. They're all different, one for each of you." I'm rambling because I'm so nervous. "So they're real basic, but—"

"Fuck, it's perfect. This is giving me some ideas." Riot has stopped on one page and he's rotating it in front of himself like it'll get him a better angle. "Some serious, fucking ideas. Or some serious fucking, ideas."

Ghost looks up over his, and I have no idea which month he stopped on, but his eyes are smoldering so hard they're almost on fire. Maybe I didn't do so bad after all. "Bed. Now."

Merry Christmas to me, because I think I'm about to get exactly what I hoped for: three big, strong, dangerous, naked bikers who'd do anything for me.

And hopefully, *to* me.

ABOUT THE AUTHOR

International bestselling author Stephanie Brother writes high heat love stories with a hint of the forbidden. Since 2015, she's been bringing to life handsome, flawed heroes who know how to treat their women. If you enjoy stories involving multiple lovers, including twins, triplets, stepbrothers and their friends, you're in the right place. When it comes to books and men, Stephanie truly believes it's the more, the merrier.

She spends most of her day typing, drinking coffee, and interacting with readers.

Her books have been translated into German, French, and Spanish, and she has hit the Amazon bestseller list in seven countries.

Printed in Great Britain
by Amazon